The Last Layer

Lawrence Perlman

iUniverse, Inc.
New York Bloomington

Author photograph by Sara Rubinstein

iUniverse books may be ordered through booksellers or by contacting:

iUniverse
1663 Liberty Drive
Bloomington, IN 47403
www.iuniverse.com
1-800-Authors (1-800-288-4677)

Because of the dynamic nature of the Internet, any Web addresses or links contained in this book may have changed since publication and may no longer be valid. The views expressed in this work are solely those of the author and do not necessarily reflect the views of the publisher, and the publisher hereby disclaims any responsibility for them.

ISBN: 978-1-4502-1621-0 (sc)
ISBN: 978-1-4502-1619-7 (dj)
ISBN: 978-1-4502-1620-3 (ebook)

Printed in the United States of America

iUniverse rev. date: 04/22/2010

CHAPTER ONE
Paris

THE TALL MAN DRESSED entirely in black parked his car at the edge of the Bois de Boulogne and walked quickly into the nearby elegant neighborhood. He blended into the Paris darkness, almost invisible to someone who might be taking an evening stroll along the tree-lined streets. Pausing, he stared intently at a large darkened house protected by tall ivy-covered brick walls.

He crossed the street to the front of the house and reached behind his back to take out a coil of nylon rope attached to a grappling hook. Without breaking his stride, he tossed the hook over the wall and pulled it firmly against the top of the wall. He quickly pulled himself up, the soles of his rock climber's shoes pressing the ivy into the brick. As he reached the top, he reversed the hook and let himself down into the garden, leaving the hook and rope in place.

He ran across the lawn and the gravel driveway and, with a climber's grace, scaled the facing of the house, his gloved fingers grasping the uneven brick surfaces as his shoes again provided traction. On a second-floor balcony, he removed a small diamond drill from his waist pack and placed a suction cup on the window next to the handle of the French door. He then drilled a small circle in the glass, which he silently removed with the suction cup. Putting his hand through the hole, he turned the handle, opened the door, and then repeated the process on the inside door.

Moving softly over thick Persian carpets, his flashlight beam soon found the closet door of the book-lined study. He pulled the closet paneling back, exposing a safe. Removing a stethoscope and a compact headlamp

1

from his pack, he placed the stethoscope next to the safe's dial and rotated it patiently until he heard the telltale clicks. He then opened the safe, feeling that moment of satisfaction that comes to all professionals when they accomplish a task for which they have trained well. He removed precious stones from their velvet sacks and bracelets, necklaces and rings from their boxes, and transferred each object into his waist pack before closing the door of the safe, now only protecting empty bags and boxes.

Retracing his steps, the black-clad figure and his new possessions disappeared into the starless Paris night.

At least, Gerard thought, *it could have happened that way.* Gerard could see the torn ivy at the top of the wall where the thief had shifted his weight on his climbs. The detective also noticed the scraping of the brick where the thief climbed to the second floor of the house.

Senior Inspector Gerard de Rochenoir of the elite French National Police had been solving difficult cases for a long time. Now, sitting in his black BMW M6 across the street from the villa where the robbery occurred and reflecting on his recent inspections of the crime scene, he thought that he had seldom seen a crime so surgically executed. He wondered if there was a connection to the robbery of the jewelry store on the Place Vendôme, which had occurred several weeks before this burglary. That crime too, he thought, was characterized by a precision that Gerard, a patron of the Parisian dance scene, thought of as almost choreographed.

Gerard finished his observation of the crime scene and drove along the Seine to the Île Saint-Louis, where he kept his BMW. His apartment on the old island in the center of Paris overlooked the river and the right bank of the city. His office was in a large building on the Île de la Cité, a short walk from his apartment.

After handing his car off to the garage attendant, Gerard crossed the Pont Saint-Louis, a walking bridge linking the Île Saint-Louis with the Île de la Cité. Gerard never tired of the view from the bridge: the east end of Notre Dame and its magnificent fourteenth-century flying buttresses. His destination was a restaurant on the Place Dauphine and lunch with his longtime assistant, Pierre Abou. The small V-shaped park was on the west end of the island, and on this day, it was crowded with office workers from the government buildings on the island enjoying the bright noon sun of a Paris spring, along with boulé players rolling their metal balls along the bowling ground.

As he approached the restaurant, Gerard reflected on how much he enjoyed his lunches with Pierre Abou. While in some ways they were the odd couple of the department, the differences in their backgrounds, he thought, added to their effectiveness as investigators. Gerard was tall and elegantly tailored. Pierre was stocky and probably owned only four suits and two jackets. Pierre didn't trust dry cleaners and tended to clean his clothes by applying saliva and then rubbing the spot with his fingernails. Gerard, part of an old and wealthy Parisian family, was a product of the elite École Nationale d'Administration. Pierre's father was a fisherman in Marseilles, and after a brief period of working with him, Pierre had enlisted in the French Navy.

Pierre was recruited into the National Police from the Marseilles police force, and most of his law enforcement training was on the ships of the French Navy and the docks and back alleys of Marseilles. But he was driven by a desire for self-improvement that manifested itself in studying English, in part by reading as many English and American crime novels as he could.

Parisians look down on anyone who does not speak French with what they consider the appropriate accent, including other Parisians. They view the accent of the Marseillanese the way a Bostonian views the accent of someone from the Gulf Coast of Alabama. So Pierre's accent meant that he received the kind of tough ribbing from his fellow Paris detectives typically found among athletes, police, and soldiers. Gerard was above the locker-room world of the French cops and didn't care that he was sometimes referred to as the count. He was broadly respected as a detective, and Pierre, with his quick, wise-guy wit, infectious sailor's grin, and Popeye-like forearms, didn't need Gerard's help.

They were an effective team, Gerard with a knowledge of finance and the life of the wealthy, as well as much-admired patience and intuition that had solved many complex cases; Pierre's street smarts and sailor's attention to detail backed up Gerard effectively.

Gerard entered the restaurant, stepping down into its plain but bustling interior. Pierre was sitting at their customary table. They could survey the whole restaurant from their table, although the only criminal activity they had witnessed in several years of delicious lunches was an attempted theft of an American tourist's carelessly slung purse. Pierre had thwarted the thief by tripping him as he tried to run out of the restaurant. Neither of the two detectives regularly carried handcuffs, let alone a gun, so they had to bind the perpetrator's hands with Pierre's stained tie until a uniformed police officer could march him away. Then, since Pierre had to return to the office after lunch, Gerard gave him his Charvet tie, which Pierre subsequently wore only to church. Gerard walked across the river to the Place Vendôme to replace his tie and bought a cashmere sweater as well. It was a beautiful shade of blue.

The American tourist, an attractive brunette in her midforties, was very thankful that her purse was saved. That night, Gerard took her to dinner at Lassere, where she was impressed by the ceiling that opened to the sky. She was so impressed that Gerard almost invited her back to his apartment to see its view of Paris, but she was leaving for home early the next morning. She called him from Chicago, but he never returned the call.

"Did you solve the great jewel robbery?" asked Pierre as Gerard sat down. "A mysterious, very rich guy from Mexico who sure didn't make his money developing a new strain of wheat to feed the world's poor gets ripped off—is that a reason to take up the time of Paris' greatest crime solvers?"

"We have eight open investigations, two of them very big jewel heists. We had better solve something, or you will be back chasing smugglers through the alleys of Marseilles," said Gerard.

"At least when I caught one, I could beat him up," replied Pierre. "Since I started working with you, it's bank robbers, financial manipulation, counterfeiters, terrorists, political corruption—I haven't muscled anyone in five years. The only time we shoot our guns is in target practice, and as I recall, the last time you carried your Beretta, it was on a date."

"She was a model," said Gerard. "I needed to protect her against the paparazzi."

"She needed protection, all right, particularly when you took her to St. Moritz for a skiing weekend. I don't think the paparazzi were the problem there."

"Let's order," said Gerard. "The usual?" The usual was oysters in season. One of the only foods both Gerard and Pierre enjoyed were oysters, a food that transcended classes. Gerard ordered a dozen of the creamy Belon oysters and a dozen of the briny Portugaises, along with a small carafe of the restaurant's house Puligny-Montrachet.

The waiter went off to place the oyster order, and Gerard asked Pierre, "What will you have as a main course?"

"Today, maybe I will try your veal," Pierre said, surprising Gerard. The specialty of the restaurant was veal *en papillote*, and Gerard often ordered it with the wonderful fried potatoes that were a favorite of the restaurant.

Pierre always viewed Gerard's interest in Parisian haute cuisine with suspicion, partly because he thought any meal that cost more than he made in a week was a betrayal of his parents' struggle to raise him and his four brothers. Gerard considered dinner with a close friend or an interesting woman at one of the Parisian temples of gastronomy or small bistros as natural and as pleasurable an act as lingering over a cappuccino on a sunny Saturday morning at a small café.

Gerard gestured to the waiter and ordered two veal *en papillote* and a carafe of Bordeaux wine. Gerard always ordered a wine from Bordeaux to accompany his veal, and Pierre preferred the reds of the Rhone grown closer to his native Marseilles. But Gerard knew his wines, and the family wine cellar below the banks of the Seine in the subbasement of Gerard's apartment building contained more than fifteen hundred bottles, some dating from before the Second World War. Gerard's mother had protected the cellar from the Nazis, who were particularly suspicious of the de Rochenoirs because of Gerard's father, who had spent the war in England with de Gaulle's Free French forces. When Gerard was born, after the war, his father taught him not only about wines, but also the English language.

The oysters arrived. Sprinkling a bit of mignonette sauce on them, they each expertly sucked them from their shells. They talked about the parallels between the Place Vendôme jewelry store robbery and the Bois de Boulogne crime.

"What do you see as the similarities?" asked Gerard.

"They remind me a bit of Sherlock Holmes's story called *The House of Fear*, in that, for each there are no clues." Pierre was reading Arthur Conan Doyle as part of his English studies, and he loved to look learned, cup his chin, and quote Sherlock Holmes. The problem was, as a result of his imperfect English and crash-course approach to reading Doyle, he often remembered the stories incorrectly.

"Pierre, in *Sherlock Holmes and the House of Fear*, Holmes was suspicious not because there were too few clues but because there were too many."

"Okay, okay, but there is one striking similarity in both these robberies."

"What's that?" asked Gerard.

"Let's go over what happened. In both of our cases, and in the robbery a few months ago of the guy from Naples, most of the jewels stolen were pieces that had been acquired in the last five years, were not well-known and were quite rare. The guy in Naples didn't exactly inherit his money from a wealthy grandmother in Florence."

"How do you know they were acquired in the last five years?"

"I went through the insurance records, and I talked to the detective in Rome working the Italian case," Pierre said.

"That's very interesting, Abou. You do have a flair for detail. It's too bad you don't apply it to your table manners."

Pierre, suspicious of any food that came wrapped in paper other than the fish his father had sold off the boat in Marseilles, had attacked his veal *en papillote* as if it was some kind of crockery. When his knife and fork pierced the firm covering, a mixture of sauce and diced veal spurted out, covering a portion of his lapel and pants leg. Thinking that at least the stain was brown, the color of Pierre's suit, and marveling at Pierre's obliviousness to the mess, Gerard handed him his napkin, signaled for a replacement and, without breaking stride, asked Pierre how he accounted for the detailed appraisals of each piece of jewelry that supported the insurance valuations.

"I don't know much about expensive jewelry. That's your department. But the stolen pieces were each appraised by firms that I have heard have impeccable credentials. Sometimes there were even two appraisals."

"Two appraisals strike me as unusual," observed Gerard. "In our family there are paintings and jewelry, and the insurance company seems satisfied with just one appraisal—maybe two for some of the paintings, but that is the exception."

"The only thing I own that is insured is my flat, and the mortgage company handles the insurance. I just pay for it," observed Pierre. "But I saw something interesting this morning in the Italian police report of the Naples robbery, which, incidentally, took a week to get translated by our staff."

"A little charm, Pierre, would work wonders on Isabella." Isabella was one of the department's Italian translators.

"She just likes you because you wear Italian suits," Pierre retorted. He went on to describe the Italian police report between bites of veal and large portions of fried potatoes. "The robbery in Italy had a pattern similar to the two Paris robberies. A cat burglar striking without witnesses, opening a safe and making off with millions of euros-worth of loose stones and jewelry, all fully insured, without leaving a clue."

Pierre stopped his report to comment on how good the fried potatoes were. "What do you think their secret is?"

"I think it is both careful preparation and the addition of a bit of beef suet to the olive oil before they heat the oil. They let the cooked potatoes sit and drain and then, just before serving, they reheat the oil, quickly fry the potatoes and add sea salt while the potatoes are still hot."

"It sounds like it takes a lot of time, but they do taste good. But you don't cook. How do you know so much about the recipe for these potatoes?"

"To appreciate the finer things in life, Pierre, one should know how they are made, but you don't have to make them. I couldn't make a fine suit of clothes, but I know how one is made. I think well-prepared fried potatoes are one of life's small pleasures. Unfortunately, originally created in Paris—some say five minutes from here, near the Pont Neuf—they have become an international dish, and certainly as an ubiquitous fast food they are a long way from these delights. But enough food philosophy. Keep talking about the case."

After another forkful of potatoes, Pierre continued, "The list of what was stolen in the Italian job is now in our files as well. The type of stones, such as rare-colored diamonds, large emeralds, one-of-a-kind necklaces, a sapphire bracelet comprised of perfectly matched stones, supposedly seventy years old, are very similar to the other robberies."

"Now, Pierre, when rich people buy jewelry, they buy unusual stones, bracelets, earrings and rings. Men buy jewelry for women, and that's what women want. So, what is unusual about these collections?"

"You would know about women, but do rich people buy most of their jewelry from the same two jewelers?"

"What do you mean?"

"The appraisals note the place of purchase of each piece, and many of the pieces that were stolen were bought at a shop on St. Barth or from a jeweler in Rome. And if the appraisals were made when the stuff was bought, every piece was bought within the last five years."

"Interesting," said Gerard, suddenly alert and less interested in studying the color of his glass of Château L'Évangile.

"There is more. My new Italian cop friend said that the Rome operation is a workshop and retail store and is owned by a French corporation headquartered on St. Martin. When I tried to find out who owned that company, the trail led through several corporations and ended in the stonewall of a Swiss corporation. Why so many levels of ownership of a jewelry store? And—it gets even more interesting—some of the Naples stuff was sold to the St. Martin company by the St. Barth operation."

"Who owns the St. Barth store?"

"I don't know yet, but I have a call in to the chief of police in St. Barth."

"Abou, you are a great detective because you are suspicious of everyone. I have to go to an antiterrorism briefing this afternoon at the Quai d'Orsay. I will see you at the office tomorrow morning, and we can continue this discussion. And if you get more reports from Italy that you need translated, I will give them to Isabella—you will have them back the next day."

The two detectives finished their coffees and left the restaurant. Twenty minutes later, after a brisk walk along the Seine, Gerard was sitting in a small auditorium on the Rue de l'Université with various French security officers, listening to a senior Foreign Ministry official drone on about the latest intelligence on terrorist cells. Pierre, back at the office, read a fax from the chief of police of St. Barth. He then offered to get a coffee for Isabella, who was startled by this sudden solicitousness from the gruff Marseilles cop.

That evening, Gerard dressed carefully. He chose a powder blue Brioni suit, which he matched with a white shirt from Charvet and an intricately woven tie of blues, yellows and violets. He was off to a reception at the Canadian embassy, which he did not look forward to. Not only would the English-speaking Canadians speak French with an attitude, as if a burden had been thrust upon them, but the Canadians always served Canadian wine, which Gerard didn't consider a strong point of their cuisine. However, he was planning to take an attractive official in the embassy to dinner after the reception, and at least at dinner he would be able to order the wines.

He changed his tie to one he had bought at Hermès, with more daring dominant colors of orange and purple that seemed fitting for a dinner date with the embassy official, a former Olympic skier.

The evening was less than satisfactory. Gerard's date never mentioned his tie. And she asked him if he had grandchildren. The *magret de canard* was overcooked, and the salt cod in a Florentine sauce was served too cold. The restaurant near the Canadian embassy was removed that night from Gerard's list of Parisian restaurants. Not only was the food poorly prepared but the white wine overly chilled. He decided the Canadian skier was a bit overly chilled as well, and she too came off another of Gerard's lists.

The next morning began as it usually did for Gerard, with a half-hour workout in the basement gym of his apartment building. As he exercised, he thought about his lunch the day before with Pierre. The conversation convinced him that his interview shortly after the robbery with Valerie Pickett, the owner of the jewelry store on the Place Vendôme that had been robbed, had been too perfunctory. He said to himself, *When one has been a cop as long as I have, the danger is that having seen or heard everything, cynicism blocks the very intuitive sensors that come only from that long experience. Pierre's information raises the possibility of a connection between the robbery of Pickett's store and the Bois de Boulogne burglary. I should change my approach to Pickett.*

When Gerard got to his office, he called Valerie Pickett and in effect ordered him to come to his office later that morning. After Gerard had reviewed the file and his notes on the jewelry store burglary, Pickett arrived at Gerard's office. Gerard kept Pickett waiting long enough to make him nervous and then had him ushered into his office.

Gerard's office in the cavernous police headquarters building was reached by walking down a drab hallway, escorted by an unsmiling woman who seemed to view every visitor as a potential felon. On entering the office, one first noticed a big desk, obviously Gerard's personal possession. It was a semicircle of beautiful walnut. The carpet was an old Persian in warm shades of gold, gray and deep red, and on the walls hung several prints by well-known French artists and an old map of Paris. The only signs that this was the office of a policeman were the police publications in French and English, neatly shelved in a wooden bookcase, and a collection of handcuffs, mounted on a display board and hanging on a wall in direct view of the chairs facing Gerard's desk.

Looking up from his desk as Pickett entered the room, Gerard motioned him to a chair with the view of the handcuffs and began the interview with only a perfunctory greeting.

Pickett was a short overweight man in his late fifties. He had a fringe of graying hair, and he seemed perpetually out of breath and red in the face. He wore an expensive light gray double-breasted suit that Gerard thought was not a very flattering cut for him. The only signs that Pickett was the proprietor of an exclusive jewelry store were a gold ring, set with a large diamond, and an Audemars Piaget wristwatch with a prominent diamond bezel. Gerard wondered if Pickett's obvious nervousness was the predictable reaction to a visit to a police office or something else. In their first meeting at the jewelry store, Pickett was matter-of-fact and a bit dismissive of Gerard. This morning, he was perspiring and fidgety. Gerard also remembered that Pickett was reluctant to have a second meeting, saying that he had nothing to add to the first interview and complaining of how busy he was. Pickett was silent on the phone when Gerard told him that the meeting was to be at his office and not the store. The unanticipated change of venue took some of the hauteur out of Pickett. A visit to the police station generally has that effect, observed Gerard.

Gerard decided to begin the questioning with the St. Barth and St. Martin connections. "How often have you been to St. Barth, Monsieur Pickett?"

Pickett was obviously rattled by the shift in attitude from their first meeting, where Gerard had been supportive and conversational in his approach, an attitude reinforced by Pickett's perception of him as wealthy and aristocratic—perhaps even a potential customer. Pickett blurted out, "A few times. On holiday."

"Did you buy gemstones or other items of jewelry on your visits?"

"Not that I can remember."

"What about St. Martin—how many times have you visited?"

"I don't remember."

"Did you buy jewelry on any of your trips there?" Gerard asked.

"I might have—I don't know. Why do you ask?"

"Do you go to Rome often?"

"I have been there."

"Do you do business in Rome?"

"I am confused by your questions," Pickett said. "I do business all over the world."

"You don't remember if you have sold jewelry to customers in Rome or bought items there?"

Sweating profusely, Pickett looked at one of the office windows, wishing Gerard would open it. Gerard ignored his imploring look.

"I would have to check my records," Pickett said.

"Do you have records on every piece you have bought?"

"Well, yes."

"Do those records show the dates of purchase, the seller and the price?"

"I think so."

"Monsieur Pickett—either the records contain such information or they don't. Which is it?"

"They probably contain such information."

"What about descriptions of the pieces?"

"Probably."

"Photographs?" Gerard asked.

"Sometimes."

"And do you keep records on sales?"

"Some of the time."

"Ah, but if your records are not complete, how can you accurately account to the taxing authorities?" Gerard then reached for a fountain pen and began to make a note.

Pickett, wiping the sweat from his forehead with a pocket handkerchief, said, "Inspector de Rochenoir, as I think about it, my sale records are complete and in order. ... Inspector, could I have a glass of water?"

"Certainly," said Gerard. He poured a glass of water from a carafe. He filled the glass to the top and handed it to Pickett. Pickett's hands were shaking, and he spilled some water on his suit before he could take a drink. Gerard just looked as Pickett tried to wipe the water off his suit with his pocket handkerchief.

"Let us resume. Back to your records. You now say they are complete. For your sake, I hope they are. So you can account for every piece you have sold, the name of the purchaser, the date of sale and the price?"

"Probably—but why are you asking me all these questions? I have insurance appraisals on all the stolen pieces."

"I am sure you do. How do you select the appraisers?"

"I have worked with many of them over the years."

"Do they always inspect the pieces, or do they depend on your description?" Gerard asked.

"I think they sometimes look at the pieces, sometimes they don't. My assistant usually handles insurance matters."

"So some of the stolen pieces were insured, but the insurance company never visually inspected them?"

"Maybe I would send them pictures of the pieces."

"For someone who deals in very expensive objects, I hear a lot of vagueness about how you do business. Do you know which of the stolen pieces were inspected by the insurance company and which were not?"

"Uh-uh—I don't know."

"Monsieur Pickett, who would know? Your assistant?"

Pickett seemed to shrink before his eyes, Gerard thought, as he mumbled a barely audible, "I don't know."

"Are you the sole owner of your store?" Gerard continued.

"Yes."

"No backers or investors or silent partners?"

"No."

"Do you ever buy a piece in partnership with another?"

"No."

"So every piece that was stolen was completely owned by you?"

"I think so. I don't know for sure."

"How can you not know for sure? You just told me that you are the 100 percent owner of every piece."

"You are asking so many questions I can't keep track," Pickett said. "I need to consider my answers. Maybe my lawyer should be present."

"Would your lawyer know better than you what the ownership of your jewelry was? I don't think he or she could help you. But, Monsieur Pickett, this is just an informal chat. I have no more questions. I am going out of town for a few days, and when I get back, I would like to review the provenance of the stolen pieces and perhaps get a better sense of how you source your pieces. It will aid my investigation. Perhaps you could be so kind as to prepare a history of each stolen piece, and you and I can review it when I get back at the end of next week. I will also want to talk with your insurance company. Incidentally, have they paid your claim?"

"Yes."

"In full?"

"I think so."

"I would think you would know that detail. Thank you for coming in."

And with a wave of his hand, Gerard motioned that the interview was over. He then pressed a button underneath his desk, the office door opened, and Pickett saw his stern escort of a few minutes ago at the door. Gerard did not look up from his desk as Pickett left his office, wiping the sweat from his face as he walked.

Shortly after Pickett left, Pierre Abou walked into Gerard's office. "Well, boss, you scared him good." Pierre had listened to the interrogation over an intercom that connected their two offices.

"That was my intention. Something about this guy doesn't feel right. See what you can find out about him. I need a change of scenery and some sunshine. Paris is gray this April. I think I will spend a few days on St. Barth. Maybe I will even do some jewelry shopping. Please call the St. Barth chief and let him know I am going to visit his island and that I will drop in and introduce myself. Don't tell him why I am coming. If he asks, imply that I am taking a short holiday. Thanks."

Gerard's efficient assistant had made travel arrangements by lunch.

The next morning, Gerard put his black leather valise from B. Goyard, his favorite Parisian leather goods store, above his first-class seat on the Air France flight to St. Martin and signaled the flight attendant for a glass of Pommery Brut Royal.

CHAPTER TWO
New York

GERARD DE ROCHENOIR WAS not the only person thinking about stolen jewels and packing that day for a trip to St. Barth. Across the Atlantic, in a small but elegantly furnished Manhattan apartment in the East Seventies, Catherine York was staring at a pile of clothes and an open suitcase on her bed. Forty years old with thick dark hair and five foot six in height, Catherine was one of those quietly beautiful women who did not immediately turn men's heads but who lingered in their memories. As a principal in the firm of Larsen and McTabbitt, one of the world's preeminent reinsurance companies and one that generally provided the last layer of coverage on the largest of assets, she specialized in the investigation of large claims.

Looking somewhat ruefully at her closet, Catherine realized that she had little in her wardrobe appropriate for an elegant Caribbean island. Her last trip to the Caribbean had been in the early stages of a five-year relationship. Catherine believed that the breakup occurred because her boyfriend had not been able to handle her business success and the accompanying high income it produced, but in the two years since the end of the relationship, she had thrown herself even more than usual into her work.

CHAPTER THREE
St. Barth

CATHERINE'S AMERICAN AIRLINES FLIGHT from New York and Gerard's Air France flight from Paris arrived at the St. Martin airport one-half hour apart. As he waited in line for the fifteen-minute flight from St. Martin to St. Barth, Gerard noticed that one of his fellow passengers was a shapely brunette in large sunglasses, carrying a Louis Vuitton bag and matching purse. Gerard had both a policeman's keen sense of observation and a well-honed appreciation of attractive women.

As the passengers from the St. Martin flight entered passport control, Gerard noticed that the brunette had an American passport. He heard her comment to the officers of passport control that she was still shaken from the landing, which requires a rapid descent over a mountaintop to a short runway ending at the edge of beautiful St. Jean Bay. After Gerard exited passport control, he picked up his rental car and drove the short distance to the Eden Roc. The small hotel sat on a large rock outcropping at the end of a beach and had a spectacular view of St. Jean Bay, its half-moon strand of white sand and the azure Caribbean beyond.

Meanwhile, Catherine, who had been advised against renting a car and braving St. Barth's notoriously narrow and steep roads, met her driver from the Carl Gustaf hotel. He drove her along cliffs with views of the sea and then dropped down to the port of Gustavia. Gripping her seat at one particularly harrowing turn, Catherine thought that she had been wise not to rent a car.

After settling in her room, Catherine called her boss in New York.

"Kate, have you solved the mystery yet?"

"Give me a few hours, Nick. I just got here."

"I don't get it. I'm the executive VP, and I am sitting in my office looking out my window on a rainy New York while you are on a sunny Caribbean island."

"Consider it a bit of compensation."

"For what?"

"For the firm being in business for over one hundred fifty years and my being only the second female officer."

"Ooh. Touchy. Touchy. You earned the trip to St. Barth because you figured out that a lot of the stolen stuff originated there. Just don't talk to the local cops."

"Nick, sometimes you carry your distrust of local police a little too far."

"Not if the local police are French. So what is your next step?"

"I intend to have a luxurious dinner on Larsen and McTabbitt and get a good night's sleep, and tomorrow I will visit the store, Sofia Mostov, to see for myself a place that apparently carries so much expensive jewelry."

"Be careful and don't buy anything expensive."

"But if I am going to learn anything about this store, I have to spend a lot of time there and appear to be a wealthy potential customer. Sometimes the best cover costs a little."

"I can't wait to see your expense report—just before I send it to internal audit. Call me tomorrow."

Downtown Gustavia contains outposts of some of the world's finest retailers with a heavy emphasis on jewelry. It also had many bars and restaurants. Among its well-known is Le Select, the oldest bar on the island. Gerard learned that it had become famous when the American singer, Jimmy Buffet, used it as a setting for his song "Cheeseburger in Paradise." The next morning, Gerard sat at a table in an open air café across the street from Le Select with a clear view of the front entrance to the jewelry store, Sofia Mostov. The store occupied the first floor of a three-story building on the corner of Rue de la France and Rue du Général de Gaulle—a short street lined with expensive shops.

Gerard decided that he would have to partake of one of Le Select's famous cheeseburgers before he left the island. But for now, he was observing the jewelry store as the clerks placed items that had been removed for the night back in their positions in the shop's windows. The window displays were artfully designed to lure buyers for whom sticker shock was not a problem. He noted with interest his attractive American traveling companion of yesterday entering the store shortly after it opened. She stood out from the Bermuda shorts–clad, camera-toting, sunburned tourists in an elegant tan sheath dress with straw and leather sandals.

––––––––––

Upon entering Sofia Mostov's store, Catherine first encountered a large display case consisting of three counters arranged in a U shape. The case contained numerous necklaces, bracelets, brooches and rings, all set with colored diamonds ranging across the spectrum from red to yellow to orange, as well as green and blue. The effect was stunning. Center stage in the front case was a necklace densely set with diamonds of several colors. The pendant at the front of the necklace was made of two stones suspended from the main body, the upper piece a large kite-shaped orange diamond. In a design reminding Catherine of an hourglass, the top diamond was connected to a smaller oval-shaped stone in shades of brown and orange. Catherine thought that the upper piece was almost five carats and the lower more than three. The yellowish orange oval in the main piece of the necklace, from which the two large stones were suspended, appeared to be more than a carat. Next to the necklace was a brooch in the shape of a starfish that looked to be made of yellow diamonds set in platinum. On the other side was a display of stud earrings, in all colors, some of which rivaled or exceeded her own three-carat diamonds.

In the other two cases, at right angles to the center display, there was a similar staging. A stunning matching bracelet and ring were in the center of one display. The bracelet combined pink diamonds with alternating circles of white diamonds. The ring had a five-carat pear-shaped stone. The other case held earrings, each with an intense blue diamond in the center—Catherine guessed each of these rare stones was more than a carat—surrounded by pear-shaped white diamonds, each one-half carat. On each side were more pieces—rings in one case, brooches, necklaces and bracelets in the other—all featuring large and beautifully colored stones.

Arranged on the sides of the store were more cases. There were watches from Jaeger-LeCoultre, Jaquet Droz, Blancpain, Breguet and Patek Philippe in one case, but gems dominated the displays. Deep red rubies set in necklaces with white diamonds, sapphires in bracelets—one Catherine noticed looked like each stone was of equal size and almost identical deep blue color. The sapphire bracelet was next to a necklace and earring set of perfect emeralds, the earrings surrounded by small diamonds.

Except for the light coming in through the front street windows, the store had no natural light. The jewelry was displayed on black felt, and bright lights inside the cases illuminated and enhanced the pieces. The store lighting was indirect and the temperature cool, in contrast with the bustling, hot Caribbean street outside.

As Catherine was adjusting to the light, a clerk approached her and said something in French. Replying in English, Catherine said that she was interested in an unusual and interesting piece—perhaps a necklace. The clerk's English was not good, and as Catherine tried to explain that she was interested in a blue diamond piece, a tall, striking blonde woman walked by her. The woman was coming from the back of the store, escorting a distinguished-looking couple to the door. The blonde spoke with them in what appeared to Catherine's untutored ear as fluent French and shook hands with each of them as they exited the store. As Catherine tried again to communicate with the clerk, she heard a French phrase spoken over her shoulder and the clerk stood aside. The blonde woman said to Catherine, in perfect, unaccented English, "Perhaps I can be of assistance to you. My name is Sofia Mostov."

Catherine turned to her and said, "So this is your store?"

"Yes, it is, and I would be delighted to show you some pieces. What are you interested in?"

"You have some beautiful colored stones here. I was thinking of a necklace, perhaps, and I have always wanted a piece with a blue diamond."

"You have excellent and expensive taste. Where in the States are you from?"

"I live in New York, and this is my first visit to St. Barth. The jewelry stores here are quite exceptional, and your collection is stunning."

"Thank you. What is your name?"

"I am Catherine York." Opening her Louis Vuitton bag, Catherine extracted a business card from a beautiful leather holder and presented it to Sofia.

The card, engraved on expensive stock, simply said, *Catherine York, Partner, Reynolds and Company, Investment Bankers.* The address was the same Park Avenue building where Larsen and McTabbitt had its headquarters, but the floor and phone numbers were different.

Anyone checking it out would find that Reynolds and Company

was a small private boutique investment banking firm known in upper-level New York financial circles and that Catherine York was indeed one of only a handful of partners. In fact, each senior executive of Larsen and McTabbitt was a member of Reynolds and Company, Reynolds and Company being a wholly-owned subsidiary of Larsen and McTabbitt. Not only was such an affiliation an excellent cover for people doing discrete, high-level underwriting and investigative work, Reynolds and Company also provided a second flow of income to Larsen and McTabbitt, since it had a small complement of real bankers who, operating behind the scenes, carried out a successful investment banking business.

The investment firm was named after a Larsen and McTabbitt CEO, who had created it in the early 1960s to provide a greater return for Larsen and McTabbitt. The firm was an early entrant into what is today called "alternative investing," and it engaged in business on behalf of a select group of clients primarily from the insurance world, as well as on behalf of Larsen and McTabbitt. Catherine was kept informed enough about Reynolds' work to speak knowledgeably if pressed. She benefited, as a senior Larsen and McTabbitt executive, directly from its success, since a component of her annual bonus came from Reynolds' profits.

Sofia gently rubbed Catherine's card between her thumb and forefinger, as if she was determining the substance of the firm and Catherine's net worth through tactile transfer.

The momentary pause in Sofia's questions gave Catherine a moment to observe her. She was perhaps four inches taller than Catherine, in her early forties, beautiful with blonde hair and sparkling green eyes. While not slim, she had a graceful figure with full breasts, a slender waist and long legs. Catherine, who tried to work out at least three times a week, noticed Sofia's muscular arms, and, as Sofia turned to give a direction to one of her clerks, her well-shaped strong calves. There was an athletic litheness about her, thought Catherine.

Sofia's jewelry stunned Catherine. On her right hand, she wore a ring set with two green diamonds with orange flashes. Catherine guessed each diamond was almost four carats. Sofia's earrings were also green diamonds, each stud about three carats.

In contrast to the exquisite ring and earrings was Sofia's watch: a man's Jaeger-LeCoultre diver's watch with what appeared to be a titanium band and case and three buttons to set it with. The black face and wide band gave Catherine the impression of no-nonsense toughness, and she felt self-conscious about her gold Piaget, which seemed a bit delicate at that moment.

"Well, Catherine York, it is good to meet you." Sofia extended her hand, which Catherine shook, noting Sofia's strong but restrained grip. "If you are looking for blue diamonds, you must know that they are rare. I have an emerald-cut blue diamond that is beautiful because its color is very intense. I have set it in a platinum band with a trapezoid-shaped white diamond on each side. The stone is 2.2 carats. It is unusual to find a stone of that size with such deep color saturation."

"You said that you set the stone; do you create pieces as well as sell them?"

"I have workshops in Rome and Tel Aviv. Most of my business is custom work. Creating unique pieces from rare stones is my passion. But let me show you the ring."

"I would love to see it, but I have my heart set on a necklace," Catherine said as she followed Sofia to one of the side cases, where Sofia pulled a tray out from beneath the counter.

Catherine realized that the store was on two levels, following the slope of the hill it was built on. In the back, there were three steps that led to a long, narrow room. As Catherine followed Sofia to the stairs and then into the back room, she couldn't help but notice the firmness of Sofia's body as it moved against the thin fabric of her black silk dress. *I don't think she is wearing underwear,* thought Catherine. The image that came into her mind as she continued to follow Sofia was of a jungle cat, relaxed, but ready to spring at any moment. The back room had a large display counter along the right wall and a door just beyond the counter. Then it widened to the right into a room with a table and several large safes.

"I must show you this stone under the scope, and if you are interested, I can show you some other stones and pictures of necklaces that I have done. But first, let me ask you, who is the necklace for and what price range do you have in mind?"

"The necklace is for me. As to price, the firm had a good year last year. My male partners buy Maseratis and Aston Martins with their bonuses; I buy jewelry. So let's say lower six figures."

"Rich men are just boys who can afford expensive toys. They buy things like cars and boats that begin depreciating before the ink on their check has dried. Jewelry, if you buy it from me, will only go up in value because my stones and settings are the best. You are a banker—you understand about investments. I sell an investment that not only will increase in value, but investments that are beautiful, you can admire them every day—not like a stock certificate or a bond. Those you might only see when you buy them or sell them, and today you don't even have the pleasure of holding the certificate; they are only computer printouts. But let me show you the blue diamond in the ring. Would you like a glass of champagne?"

Catherine thought to herself, *I won't find much out unless I can keep her engaged, so a glass of champagne it will be.* "Yes, thank you," she said.

Sofia called to one of her assistants and said something in French. She then led Catherine through a door into a small room which contained a round mahogany table with three leather chairs arranged around it. On the table sat a large white optical device designed to inspect gemstones under lighted magnification. On the wall were enlarged backlit photographs of models wearing some of the most beautiful jewelry pieces Catherine had ever seen. As she settled in one of the chairs, Sofia noted that she had designed each of the pieces in the photographs. An assistant came in with a silver tray and two glasses of champagne. Sofia handed one to Catherine, took the other for herself and clinked glasses with Catherine, saying, "To the pleasure of getting to know you."

After studying the ring under the scope, Sofia escorted Catherine to the room with the safes. Again she gave instructions to her assistants, in French to one and in Spanish to another, a dark-haired girl who Sofia said was from Cuba.

Sitting at the table, Sofia opened three trays that had been in the safe. Each black felt tray contained a number of compartments. Each compartment contained a beautiful colored stone.

"I also have some wonderful white diamonds, although you seem more interested in colored stones," Sofia said. "Your studs, though, are magnificent. May I see them?"

Catherine removed her studs and handed them to Sofia, who looked at them with a jeweler's glass. "Very nice. About three carats each, excellent color and almost flawless. I like your taste."

"Thank you," said Catherine as she reattached her earrings. "I only carry a few things with me when I travel. I am afraid of thieves."

"You have to be careful. Do you have good insurance coverage?"

Catherine covered up a cough as she said, "I think so."

"Everything I sell is accompanied by a certificate from an international gemological association, as well as an appraisal from a well-known appraiser. Sometimes for the more expensive pieces we arrange for two appraisals to facilitate my customers' insurance coverage."

"So you would—uh—find the appraisers?"

"Of course. We have relationships with several."

As they looked at stones, Catherine marveled at the variety and intense colors. She paused at a diamond that had a particularly deep blue color. "This looks like a miniature of the Hope diamond," she said.

"Catherine, you know your stones. It has a very similar color, but it is only 2.4 carats; the Hope is forty-five carats."

"Well, the Hope is priceless. How much is this stone?"

"I would prefer to set it in a ring, but if someone who collected stones—and some of my customers do—wanted it, it would probably be between $2.5 million and $3 million. I have turned down $2 million."

"That is out of my price range. Do you have anything smaller?"

"As I said, blue diamonds are rare, but I have two in another location, and I can show you photographs."

Opening a file cabinet, Sofia pulled out an envelope from which she removed several photographs of blue diamonds. "This is a one-carat stone of particular intensity, and this one is a little more than a carat. Each would be around $1 million unset."

"I am overwhelmed," Catherine said. "I may have to set my sights on something less rare."

"You can see I have many beautiful pieces with a variety of stones in a number of price ranges. And if your heart is set on something I don't have in inventory, I should be able to locate it for you. The pendant in the display is in your price range and has three beautiful diamonds." An assistant, who had been hovering discretely, quickly brought the pendant which had been in the front display case. Sofia held it up for Catherine to see.

"It is beautiful, and I will put it on you," said Sofia. She walked behind Catherine, reached around and unbuttoned the two top buttons of Catherine's dress, exposing the top edges of her bra, and hooked the clasp on the back of the pendant, letting it drop slightly into her cleavage.

Admiring the piece in the mirror, Catherine said, "I would like to think about this piece, but it could work."

"I would be happy to show you some photos of other pieces, but I am expecting a telephone call from a client in Monaco. Perhaps you could come in tomorrow morning. But—I have an idea. Have you been to one of our beautiful beaches?"

"Well, no."

"You can't visit St. Barth without going to the beach. I like to swim each day at lunch. The Eden Roc hotel is at the end of St. Jean beach. It's a wonderful place to swim, and it has a very nice beachside restaurant. Where are you staying?"

"At the Carl Gustaf."

"Good. If you don't have a car, their driver will take you to Eden Roc. I will meet you on the beach side of the restaurant at twelve thirty. We will swim and then have lunch. Don't worry, it is a small beach, you will find me."

"But I don't have a bathing suit."

"No problem. This is a fabulous place to buy one. And you are, what? An American size six? You will have no trouble finding one that fits here. I have more trouble. I am bigger than most of these French girls. Across the street there is a shop with great suits. It's next to the shop that sells cigars and panamas. See you at twelve thirty."

With that, Sofia turned and walked back toward her office. To Catherine, the swim rendezvous was not an invitation but an assumption. Sofia was apparently not in the habit of asking. But, Catherine thought, her jewelry business certainly had possibilities for the investigation, hardly the dead-end predicted by her always skeptical boss.

After a while, the American woman left the store and headed along the Rue du Général de Gaulle away from Gerard. Paying his bill for the juice, coffee and a croissant, which he noticed was in the Paris price range, Gerard straightened his summer-weight Kiton cashmere jacket and walked across the street. He felt a sense of excitement because, as he told himself, this could well be an important piece of the puzzle that he was working on.

Before entering the store, Sofia Mostov, he decided to stroll a bit and observe the other shop windows to get a feel of where it fit into the economic eco-structure of St. Barth. Local and regional stores such as Carat and Assioma matched wares with internationally known names such as Cartier, Chopard, Bulgari and Hermès. There was even a jewelry shop called Goldfinger.

The atmosphere of wealth and luxury was reinforced by large multistory yachts lined up at the pier just a block from the main shopping street and visible to all. Gerard thought some of the yachts were quite sleek and beautiful, while others were essentially steroid-enhanced, manufactured houses that floated. Beyond them were rows of sailboats swinging lazily from buoys in the harbor. The sounds of their rigging softly filled the sea-scented morning air.

As Gerard walked along the Rue du Général de Gaulle, he stopped in an elegantly merchandised shop that sold cigars, panama hats and, he noted, fine fountain pens and single-malt scotches, along with vintage rums. After selecting a few H. Upmann cigars for the stay, he bought a straw panama that he thought would provide protection from the hot Caribbean sun and give him a suave jauntiness that seemed to fit this beautiful island.

Next door to that shop was one that sold women's clothing, including, based on the window displays, some stunning bathing suits. Looking into the window, Gerard's eye was caught by the movement of a curtain at the back of the shop as a saleswoman brought a garment into a dressing room. As the curtain was moved, it partly revealed a nude woman trying on a bathing suit with her back to the street. Startled at this unexpected moment of beauty, Gerard could not help but notice how shapely she was. As she turned slightly to take the suit offered by the saleswoman, he realized that this naked lady was the American from the St. Martin airport who had left Sofia Mostov's a short time before. His moment of recognition was cut short by the saleswoman quickly closing the curtain and angrily shaking her finger at him.

Quickly moving away from the shop window, an embarrassed Gerard could only observe to himself that he was now perceived as a voyeur on an island where every beach was topless and some were totally nude.

———————

As Catherine walked along the Gustavia waterfront on an indirect route that would take her up the steep hill to her hotel, she looked at the sailboats in the harbor, the large yachts at the docks across the water and the waterfront restaurants that blended a Caribbean casualness with the feeling of the outdoor tables of Parisian restaurants. She thought that St. Barth almost overwhelmed the senses with the colors, sea breezes, expensive shops and the feeling of Paris crammed into a small island. Catherine also was processing her visit to Sofia Mostov's jewelry store.

———————

Meanwhile, Gerard, careful to cross the street so as not to walk past the shop window where he had offended the clerk, headed toward the shop of Sofia Mostov. *What kind of a name was Mostov?* he wondered. *It sounded Russian. Curious.*

Gerard knew his jewelry. He had investigated jewel robberies. Over the years, he had purchased jewelry for some of the many women in his life and had supervised the sale of items from his mother's extensive collection after her death. But he was not prepared for the array of pieces of apparent high quality, or for the coolly elegant ambience that he encountered as he entered the store of Sofia Mostov. He was struck by the variety of colored precious stones, as well as by the size and interesting cuts of the white diamonds.

As he was looking around, a clerk approached him, so he asked to see a few items. He commented on the number of pieces with colored stones and asked where they came from.

"Oh, monsieur, Madame Sofia has almost all of these pieces made. They are of unique design."

"Is Madame Sofia the owner of the shop?"

"Yes, monsieur."

"And is she in the store?"

"Yes, but she is on the phone."

"If I want to see pieces that are not out or even unset stones, should I talk to her?"

Noting his expensive clothes and perfect Parisian French, the clerk decided that she was out of her league and told Gerard she would check on how long Madame Sofia would be on the phone. The clerk returned to report that Madame Sofia would be with him shortly.

Soon he noticed a tall blonde woman wearing a black sleeveless dress standing on the second level of the store. He knew she had been observing him. She strode down the stairs and walked quickly through the store. She nodded to an overweight American couple wearing identical shorts and T-shirts and gawking at the jewelry in a display case. She motioned to a clerk to assist them.

She addressed Gerard in excellent French, tinged, to his discriminating ear, by a slight Russian cadence. His friends joked that he could discern minute differences in accents among the arrondissements of Paris. She said that she was Sofia Mostov and offered her hand in a firm grip. She was taller and broader than a typical French woman. Gerard, with a policeman's talent for quick observation, noted her strong build but decidedly feminine beauty, accented by her deep green eyes.

"Welcome to St. Barth," Sofia said. "What brings you to our island?"

Not used to doing undercover work, and not wanting to alert her prematurely, Gerard uncharacteristically mumbled a reply that his name was Gerard and that he had come to St. Barth from Paris for a few days break from an unusually cold and rainy spring.

"Well, Monsieur Gerard, you have come to the right place. The weather here is always beautiful and the jewelry in my store superb. What kind of jewelry are you interested in?"

Gerard replied that he understood that she designed pieces, and he was thinking of acquiring an unusual bracelet as a gift for a lady friend. He was particularly struck by the number of colored stones she had and, he added, turquoise had always fascinated him. Did she have any pieces of turquoise? And what about rubies and sapphires?

"We close for the afternoon shortly, but come with me, and I will show you some pieces," she said as she led him up the stairs to the room where the safes were located.

Removing a tray from a safe, she selected a necklace composed of almost identical pear-shaped turquoise stones set in platinum. "This necklace is made of Iranian turquoise, the finest in the world. Notice how uniform the surface is, like unglazed china—and how rich and sky-blue the color is. Some turquoise is too soft. These pieces are naturally quite hard—another advantage of Iranian turquoise."

"It is indeed beautiful; the platinum work is particularly intricate. What is its origin?"

"The necklace was made in my workshop in Rome; the platinum work was done for me in Tel Aviv."

"Where did you get stones of such beauty? Iran does not export turquoise now, does it?"

"No, it doesn't, but I have sources with families that left Iran at the time the Shah fell. If you want a bracelet, I can make one for you out of comparable stones. For either this necklace or a bracelet, your friend would love matching earrings. How much are you thinking of spending?"

"How much is this necklace?"

"It is one hundred thousand euros. A bracelet would be about eighty thousand euros, depending on its size and the amount of silver work required."

"That is in my price range. I saw once a bracelet of rubies and sapphires that I still remember. Could you make one with those stones?"

"I have access to some of the most beautiful stones in the world, so I am sure we could design a piece that would be unique and would enchant your friend."

They talked for a few more minutes, and Gerard looked at additional pieces. He knew he was in the presence of a great salesperson because she gave the impression that, even if you paid her price, she would be reluctant to see a beloved piece leave her possession.

Sofia ended the session by telling Gerard that she was leaving the store and would not be back until the next morning, but if he was available, she would see him in the store then. They agreed to meet in the morning, and Gerard walked out of the store, his senses jarred by the contrast between the cool dark store, with its brightly colored jewelry, and the bright sunshine, heat and hectic activity of the narrow streets of Gustavia. He reflected on Sofia's directness and strong presence. *This Sofia,* he thought, *is one formidable woman.*

CHAPTER FOUR
St. Barth

J UST BEFORE TWELVE THIRTY in the afternoon, the Carl Gustaf hotel driver deposited Catherine at the entrance to the Eden Roc. The narrow road was only perhaps one thousand yards from the airport. It was crowded with the small Japanese and Korean cars that the St. Barth roads could more or less safely accommodate intermingled with noisy motorbikes weaving in and out of traffic.

In the few steps from the busy road to the hotel property, the atmosphere changed dramatically. Catherine marveled at how quickly one's sense of place shifted on St. Barth. On the left were a shop, the hotel office and a bar that was open on two sides and looked like it had been airlifted, Pernod bottles and all, from Paris. On the right was a small bay. Straight ahead, the hotel appeared to be an outgrowth from the huge rock on which it was built. Stairs led to a restaurant high on the rock, and rooms and balconies jutted out at various angles from the structure. To the left beyond the bar was a wooden terrace with another restaurant. It sat two steps above the small beach with red wooden chairs and tables, contrasting pleasantly with the white canvas beach lounges. And beyond it all lay St. Jean Bay, large and crescent-shaped, with white sand and surf foaming in the ocean. The whole scene was infused with the bright light of the Caribbean and colored by the sea in shades of turquoise fading to the azure of the cloudless sky.

Catherine carried her bathing suit and purse in a straw bag she bought on her walk back to the hotel and wore a white sundress from the Carl Gustaf shop. She walked along the restaurant's wooden platform and located Sofia on the small beach, lying on her stomach on a lounge off the corner of the restaurant, a few yards from the water. Sofia was reading the *New York Times* through large white-framed sunglasses. Her swimsuit bottom was white. She wore no top. Neither did most of the women on the beach.

Sofia gracefully arose from her lounge and said, "Catherine, that is a lovely dress. You look like you belong here. You have a bathing suit?"

Catherine gestured at her straw bag, and Sofia, without looking back, snapped her fingers, and one of the waitresses immediately appeared.

"Show my friend to a changing room," Sofia said. "Catherine, we can swim and then have lunch."

Well aware of her own curves, as Catherine put on her bathing suit, she thought, *I can hold my own with these women, if only my skin wasn't as white as a fish's belly.*

As she walked back to the beach, she saw that Sofia had arranged for a second lounge to be placed next to her own. As Catherine settled in the lounge chair, Sofia gave her an appraising look from behind her sunglasses and complimented her on her choice of swimsuits.

"But dear," she said, "you are so pale. You will burn under this hot sun. Turn over on your stomach, and I will put some lotion on to protect you from burning." As she lay on her stomach, Catherine took in the beautiful bay surrounded by green hills with villas hanging from their sides. The cliffs were assaulted by breaking waves, and the smell of the sea perfumed the air.

Why, she wondered, had she come to the Caribbean so seldom, and how had she missed this island? The rueful answers were, she concluded, hard work and a Manhattan-centric male companion of several years whose idea of travel was going to New Jersey for the day.

She felt a gentle pressure as Sofia rubbed lotion on, first, her ankles, then the back of her thighs, drawing a line with her fingers along the bottom edges of Catherine's suit. Sofia then applied lotion to the small of Catherine's back and, with a quick motion, unsnapped her swimsuit top and rubbed lotion over the rest of her back. It had been a long time since anyone had unhooked Catherine's bra, and it wasn't a woman who had done it. As she gently rubbed lotion on Catherine's neck, Sofia said, "Dear, this is St. Barth. Being topless is part of the experience. Now turn over, and I will do your front."

Not knowing what else to do, Catherine turned over, and Sofia began applying lotion with gentle circular strokes to her shoulders, throat, and then to her breasts. Before Catherine could react, Sofia had coated her breasts, her long fingers gently applying the lotion. Lying on the lounge as Sofia coated her stomach, Catherine could feel her nipples harden. She closed her eyes and felt the sun as Sofia put lotion on her thighs and ankles. Her legs were slightly parted as she lay there, and she concentrated on not opening them more and not prudishly closing them. The sun and Sofia's gentle hands felt warm.

Then Sofia said, "Here's the bottle. Put some on your face, and we can swim to the raft." They swam to a swim raft anchored perhaps thirty yards off the beach, and then Catherine followed Sofia as they swam along the rock, enjoying the sensation of swimming on her back and looking up at the rock and the balconies of the hotel rooms built upon it. The edge of the rock was a steep reef and, diving down only a few feet, Catherine could see a variety of multicolored fish swimming just below the surface.

Returning to the beach, Catherine surprised herself at how unselfconscious she was. The stares from the middle-aged American men amused her, as did the irritated look on their wives' faces. Sofia led her to the changing room, where there were shower stalls—mercifully, thought Catherine, with curtains. Sofia showered quickly, toweled herself off and put her black dress back on. She wore no underwear. Catherine couldn't help but look at Sofia as she dried herself and changed. She had a firm, beautiful body, Catherine acknowledged, and she didn't dye her hair.

Earlier, Gerard had taken his seat at a table on the restaurant terrace when Sofia arrived. Now that his lunch over, he was walking up the stairs from the restaurant to his room as Sofia and Catherine left the changing room and entered the restaurant. As he walked, he was trying to put the events of the morning together. Sofia Mostov clearly had an unusual and significant capacity to source and sell very expensive jewelry. She also apparently had some very wealthy clients around the world. At least three of these clients had been robbed, an unlikely coincidence. But how could the robberies benefit Sofia? She sold jewelry and precious stones. What happened after the sale wasn't her affair. And what about the American woman? A friend? A lover? A business associate? How might she fit in? There clearly was something going on between them. Who was this woman?

During lunch Sofia made suggestions for Catherine's afternoon tour of the island. Catherine subtly steered the conversation to Sofia and her business. Sofia had been born in Cuba. Her father was a Russian stationed there, her mother Cuban. She left Cuba as a young girl and had lived in both France and Russia. She deflected questions of how she got into the jewelry business and who her business associates were, but she talked freely about her workshops in Rome and Tel Aviv, her worldwide network of customers and her inventory of colored diamonds. Catherine commented on how expensive those stones were.

Sofia replied, "My dear, they are expensive because they are so rare. And the more intense the color, the rarer. The more common pink and yellow diamonds are lightly colored. The saturated ones are rarer and the most expensive if they are relatively flawless, and if they are cut properly. Intensely colored red, orange and green diamonds are the most expensive because they are hard to find. And blue, well—the rarest of all. That ring you looked at this morning is a wonderful example of an exceptional blue diamond."

"But how do you get access to such a wide range of precious stones?"

"My dear, that is my competitive advantage, as you Americans would say, and one never should disclose how they achieve an advantage, or it is no longer an advantage. No?"

"I guess so. It is your secret."

"*Oui.*"

Catherine said, "I couldn't help but notice your earrings with the beautiful green diamonds. Could I see them?"

"Of course," said Sofia, and she took them off and handed them to Catherine. "Our soup has not yet arrived. Let's go into the dressing room, and you can see how they look on you."

They walked to the dressing room, and Catherine put on Sofia's earrings. Catherine saw herself in the mirror, and she had to agree that the deep green color set off her complexion and dark hair quite well.

Back at the table, eating a wonderful seafood soup flavored with saffron and bay leaves and enjoying a bottle of Taitinger rosé champagne, Catherine said, "Those earrings are so beautiful. I am surprised you wear them while swimming. What if one came off in the water?"

With a Gallic shrug, Sofia said, "No problem, they are insured."

That reply struck a warning chord with Catherine, but before she could process it, she heard Sofia talking about the difficulty of finding colored diamonds. "In Africa, in Russia, after a lot of money is spent, a mine may produce many white diamonds, but that same mine will produce only a small number of colored diamonds and fewer yet that have the intensity of color that is so desirable."

"Some diamonds, most famously the Hope, have stories, even legends attached to them," said Catherine as she lit into their second course of perfectly ripened avocado topped with sautéed prawns in a tomato and onion sauce. "Are your customers interested in the history of the gems they buy?"

"They are more interested in their beauty," Sofia said.

"How much do you know about your customers?"

"For many people, diamonds and other precious stones are the ultimate currency. Easily transported, hard to trace, susceptible of objective valuation, the owners who sell or trade them value their anonymity in much the same way that the stones are anonymous. My sources can count on my confidentiality just as much as they can rely on a Swiss bank."

"But you must keep records of sales."

Sofia was silent for a moment and looked at Catherine with a slight tilt of her head. "You are curious about my business. That must be a trait of investment bankers.

"If a customer wants to pay with a credit card, we will take it, but transactions of substance are usually made in cash, mostly confidential bank transfers," Sofia continued. "I provide certifications, appraisals, if the customer desires, or the names of appraisers if they want to get their own, and then I say goodbye."

Catherine watched Sofia cut her avocado with a deftness that made her think of a precious stone being shaped. "Okay, I understand why you want to keep your customers confidential, but what about the records you need for the taxing authorities?"

Sofia looked up from her plate and gestured with her empty fork. "Ah, my dear Catherine, you are such an American. You are all so record- and paperwork-obsessed. You make things so easy for your taxing authorities. For the French, the Italians and the Russians, taxes are a sport. Sometimes the tax people win, sometimes we win. But why would you keep records so as to make it easy for them? Do you play tennis? Well, okay. Would you lower the net when your opponent is serving?"

Catherine nodded, and Sofia continued, "When I was growing up in Cuba, in spite of Castro, there was still a strong Catholic presence in the country. I have always admired the Vatican as an institution that has survived and thrived for hundreds of years. Its approach has been to think a lot, say little and write nothing down. I try to follow that approach. And now I have said too much about my business, but tomorrow when you come in I will show you a piece made out of green stones that does have a history."

Sofia paid for lunch, arranged for a taxi for Catherine and bid her goodbye.

CHAPTER FIVE
St. Barth

THAT AFTERNOON, GERARD WENT for a swim and then drove into Gustavia to introduce himself to the St. Barth chief of police.

Jean-Claude Sourel had headed the St. Barth police for almost ten years, moving there from Martinique, where he had been a senior officer. Short, muscular and with a bald head that reminded Gerard of a large artillery shell, Sourel had an excellent reputation, according to what Pierre had reported to Gerard that morning during a phone call. From Sourel's accent, Gerard surmised he was originally from Lyon, in the north of France.

The St. Barth police headquarters were in a stone building on a narrow road just up the hill from the main shopping area. Gerard said to Sourel, "I like the quaintness of this building, and this street seems much older—from another time—than the area closer to the port."

"As you know, this island was once a Swedish possession. This building and some others on this street date from that period. The building offers a little Scandinavian solidity on this hurricane-prone island."

Gerard thought, *I like this guy—a cop with a philosophical view of architecture.*

Sourel had done his homework. "You are a distinguished and busy officer of the National Police," he said to Gerard. "What brings you to our out-of-the-way island, Inspector de Rochenoir?"

"Oh, just a short break from a dreary Paris spring."

"Your stay is certainly short for a vacation. You should stay longer and enjoy our beautiful island. But if I can be of help to you, you just have to ask, although senior inspectors perhaps don't need help from provincial police chiefs."

Sourel, thought Gerard, *was obviously a good cop—both skeptical and cynical.* Skepticism was a cop's habit of thought; cynicism came after about two years on the force. "This is a preliminary visit," Gerard said. "If something comes of it, I will most certainly need and appreciate your assistance. I leave tomorrow afternoon, but you may hear from either me or my associate, Pierre Abou, again. Here are both our cards."

Gerard then asked Sourel about his work and the size of his force. St. Barth was a low-crime place, and Sourel seemed both determined to keep it that way and tough enough to be effective. As they shook hands and Gerard left Sourel's office, Gerard had the feeling that they would meet again.

Catherine's tour of the island left her with even more positive feelings about St. Barth. Inland, away from the glamour and activity of Gustavia and St. Jean, there were tiny villages that seemed timeless. Stone walls enclosed rocky fields where a few sheep or cattle grazed. There were remote and beautiful beaches where the surf crashed with the full power of the Atlantic against rocky shores, and several beautiful hotels sat in picturesque settings overlooking the water. An occasional sign announced an artist's studio or a restaurant. That evening, she walked a short distance down the hill from her hotel to have dinner at a restaurant overlooking Gustavia harbor. As she watched the sunset over her predinner cocktail, she felt quite alone. This island was a place for romance, and romance had been lacking in her life for a long time.

Uncharacteristically for her, she called her mother in Wisconsin.

"Catherine, I got your message that you were going to St. Barth in the Caribbean. Where is St. Barth? Are you okay? Did you finally take a vacation?"

"Mom, I'm fine. No, this isn't a vacation. I am down here working for a few days. It is a small island, not too far from Puerto Rico.

"How are you feeling, honey? You haven't called for a while."

"I know, Mom. I have been really busy at work. Just wanted to catch up. This is a beautiful island. I am sitting on the hotel terrace looking at a beautiful red sunset over the ocean."

"Alone?"

"Yes."

"Honey, you sound a bit sad."

"Oh, I guess I am down a bit," Catherine said.

"No new men in your life?"

"No, Mom. I have been busy."

"You are always busy. Catherine, ever since you were a little girl you were determined to succeed. Studying was more important than your social life. Your father and I have always been proud of you, and I am not one to give out motherly advice, but I will. Loosen up and enjoy life a bit, sweetheart. Let down a bit of that guard and see where it takes you. Okay, that is it for motherly advice."

Catherine could imagine her mother sitting at the kitchen table and taking a deep breath after an uncharacteristically long monologue.

"Mom, I love you. You are right. I have to go to dinner now—yes, alone. I will call you when I get back to New York."

Sofia greeted Catherine at her store the next morning with a firm hug. Catherine noted that Sofia was wearing a light blue dress made of what appeared to be raw shantung silk. The silk set off Sofia's smooth, tanned skin, and the deep V-neck revealed a substantial amount of cleavage, but where one might have expected a necklace, there was only the hint of beauty. Sofia knew, Catherine thought, that a woman who dressed not to show but to suggest understood the essence of seduction. A man who came under Sofia's influence would never know what hit him.

Sofia's bracelet was made of sapphires, each stone of a similar size and in a transparent blue color with an almost silklike appearance. Sofia noticed Catherine staring at the bracelet and said, "These stones are from Sri Lanka. While few people would notice, the silk effect of the sapphires works well with a raw silk dress or pantsuit. Most women understand the relationship of the color of jewelry to the color of what they wear, but few think about matching the texture of their clothes to the patina effect of their jewelry." Catherine felt even more out of her league around Sofia than ever.

"Do you like sapphires?" Sofia asked.

"Of course," said Catherine.

"While I like the silk effect of Sri Lanka stones," Sofia said, "the best sapphires to wear during the day come from Kashmir because their color becomes very deep in daylight. Kashmiri stones have always been rare and are even harder to come by now because of the political troubles there, but I have access to some wonderful Kashmir stones."

As they sat at a table, Catherine looked at several pictures of necklaces and pendants. Sofia gave her several pictures of pieces and agreed to hold a particular pendant in the display case for one week while Catherine considered it.

The conversation turned to rare pieces, and Sofia brought from the safe a black leather case. Before opening it she said, "Yesterday I promised that I would show you a piece with a history. Here it is." With a flourish, she opened the leather box, revealing a pendant with a huge briolette emerald in the center. It was surrounded by a ring of square-cut emeralds with more smaller briolette emeralds hanging off the ring, all fitted in gold framing. Each gem was a clear deep green color. She opened another box, which contained earrings, each with a huge pear-shaped emerald. Catherine guessed the emeralds were sixteen or more carats. They were set in borders of gold which, like the pendant, seemed to reflect the brilliant green of the emeralds. Catherine was having trouble breathing.

Sofia sat back with a smile and said, "The emerald in the center of the pendant is twenty-two carats; the earrings, sixteen and one-half carats each; the square cuts, twenty carats; and the eight stones attached to the ring, eight carats each. Each stone is perfect. They come from Colombia, and stones like this are worth more than almost all comparably sized diamonds."

"And they have a history?"

"Yes, they were intended for a queen."

"A Spanish queen?"

"Yes, indeed. You are one smart Yankee. Early in the eighteenth century, Philip V of Spain married Elizabeth. Portraits don't show her as very attractive, but maybe she was good in bed. You know men, and Phillip was a bit of a nerd. Like many men, he promised her more than he could deliver. He was losing territories, and the flow of gold, silver and jewels from South America that the Spanish crown had depended on during the seventeenth century and even before had all but dried up. Phillip sent a fleet to bring back gold, silver jewels and slaves, and specifically, to bring him emeralds from the famous Chinor and Muzo mines of Colombia. Like turquoise, fine emeralds are identified by the mines they come from. Sailing back to Spain in the summer of 1715, the treasure fleet ran into a hurricane. All the ships were lost off the coast of Florida. The flagship carried the treasure specifically designated for Queen Elizabeth. Behold a queen's treasure! Would you like to try on the earrings?"

Catherine nodded and, removing her studs, put the emerald earrings on. Sofia then motioned to a mirror and dimmed the lights in the windowless room. The emeralds were visible and clear. Sofia commented that these emeralds were exceptional because they held their color in dim light; emeralds of lesser quality would turn dark in low light.

"These are incredible," said Catherine, slowly handing back the earrings with a hollow feeling in her heart. "And the pendant is beyond incredible. Where did you get these?"

Sofia put her forefinger over her lips and said, "Remember the Vatican. But I have access to more emeralds from that shipwreck."

Catherine said that she had to go back to her hotel, pack and leave for the airport. Agreeing to call Sofia from New York the following week, she headed back to her hotel.

Later that morning, Gerard visited Sofia's store. In a silk and cashmere gray plaid Kiton jacket, a white cotton sweater and dark gray slacks, he gave the appearance, accurate in his case, of understated wealth.

In the room where the scope for examining jewels was located, there was a large photograph on the wall of a beautiful dark-skinned model wearing an emerald necklace that glistened against her skin. Someone looking at the photograph would focus on the beauty of the model and the necklace and not notice that it was mounted on a panel. Sofia stood before the photograph and moved the panel, revealing a one-way mirror which provided a view of the whole showroom. She watched Gerard move around the cases, looking intently at the jewelry, almost as if he was memorizing each piece.

Yesterday, she had seen him on the terrace at Eden Roc eating lunch and intently watching Catherine and her. He gave the appearance of someone wealthy and almost effete, but keenly observant as she was, she had noticed his broad shoulders and strong hands. Who was this man? She didn't know, but her instincts told her to be careful, and Sofia had been trained to always trust her instincts.

She walked into the showroom and greeted Gerard with a handshake. They proceeded to the back of the store, and the two of them sat at her table, looking at photographs of bracelets and at a tray of stones. Gerard said that he knew Rome well and asked where her store and workshop were.

Did he want an address? He wasn't going to get one, she thought. She replied that it was near the Ponte Cavour, not even saying which side of the river it was on. When she asked him for his card, he felt the breast pocket of his jacket and said that he must have left his cards in the hotel but that he would send her an e-mail or fax with his address in Paris.

Gerard then asked to look at the sapphire bracelet she was wearing. She removed it. As he looked at it, he asked her if it was for sale.

"Oh, monsieur, it is one of my favorite pieces. It would be hard to part with it."

"Does it have a price?"

"Perhaps, but let me tell you about it and why it is so valuable."

Sofia gave him a short discourse on the bracelet, and they agreed that she would consider whether it was for sale and at what price. He then asked for an envelope and swept the photographs into the envelope by their edges. *Curious,* she thought, *they would get smudged in transit anyway.* As they shook hands, she noticed again the strength of his hands. After he left, Sofia thought to herself, *My antennae are up. I just don't know why yet.*

Gerard finished packing and called Pierre Abou from his hotel room. "Has Pickett provided the details we asked for on the stolen pieces?"

"No," said Pierre.

"I am getting a bad feeling about this guy. Pay him a visit and sweat him a bit. Bring one of our security technicians along. We need a better understanding of how someone could circumvent his security system. And try to see him tomorrow. Don't give him much time to think about your visit."

Both Catherine and Gerard had each planned to spend two days in St. Barth, and their return flights to New York and Paris were leaving only an hour apart. Each found themselves in the departure lounge at the St. Martin airport where, for twenty-five euros, passengers could escape the tumult of the main airport but not the highly perfected indifference to passengers of the airport personnel. If Catherine recognized Gerard from the day before, she didn't show it. But Gerard had noted her Louis Vuitton carry-on rolling bag, and he placed his bag next to hers in the closet. Looking around to see that she was not in the vicinity, he checked her luggage identification tag and wrote down her name and address in New York City.

He was looking forward to getting back to Paris and moving this jewelry theft investigation forward. Sitting in the lounge, he watched Catherine out of the corner of his eye. Her long dark hair was pulled back, and she wore a well-tailored dark green pantsuit and white blouse and read the *Wall Street Journal*. She appeared to be an American businesswoman. Was she, he wondered, in a romantic relationship with Sofia Mostov? He would find out who she was when he got back to Paris. And with Sofia's fingerprints on the jewelry photographs, he might find out more about her as well.

CHAPTER SIX
Paris / St. Barth

PIERRE ABOU WAS NOT one to waste time. He called Pickett right after Gerard's call and was at his store with a National Police security specialist at ten thirty the next morning, about the same time Gerard was emerging from his shower, refreshed after his night flight from St. Martin to Paris.

It was 6:00 AM St. Barth time when the phone rang in Sofia's villa, high on the hills overlooking St. Jean Bay and the Caribbean. Not being an early riser and unaccustomed to calls that time of morning, Sofia somewhat sleepily answered the phone. The sound of Valerie Pickett's voice quickly shook off her torpor. "Pickett," she said angrily, "why are you calling me at this time? I told you not to call me at the villa. We have a business relationship only. All calls should come to the store."

"Madame, I am sorry for the early call, but things are not going well here. I had to talk to you."

Sofia was alarmed at Pickett's tone of voice. She could visualize him sitting in his small office above his store, the sound of traffic on the Place Vendôme coming through the tall windows. She imagined Pickett sweating profusely in spite of the air-conditioning, his pale skin whiter than usual, and his omnipresent and ill-fitting double-breasted suit wrinkled. Involuntarily, she winced at the image.

"What's the problem?" she asked, her tone of voice changing from heat to ice.

"Madame, I waited to call you as long as I could. Last week I was called to police headquarters and questioned by a senior detective." He then went on to summarize his questioning by Gerard.

Sofia said, "You called me at my house at six in the morning to tell me that you were questioned by a detective last week? What is the matter with you?"

"No, no, madame, the police came again today. It was another detective and some kind of technician who came and studied my security system and safe. They asked a lot of questions. This detective was brusque—I would say rude—and the technician—well, he was very skeptical. I overhead him say to the detective that he did not see how someone could bypass the system and open the safe unless they had help. Then he wanted all my security system installation and service records. They want the details on the insurance claim. How can I give them records on my purchases of the stolen pieces and stones without making them more suspicious? They all came through you. And the service records—they will show that the system was checked and was working fine last month."

The more Pickett talked, the more high-pitched and whiny his voice got. Sofia's tone was back to heat. "What do you mean, you idiot, all the stuff came through me. I told you to include some of your other pieces."

"I know, but I didn't." And then he blurted out, "We need to undo the robbery."

"Well, brilliant one, and just how are we going to do that?"

"I don't know. Maybe I will tell them that the stolen pieces were returned to me with a note saying that the thief felt guilty, or I will pay a reward or something."

"*Qué mierda,*" she exploded, reverting to the expletives of her native Cuban Spanish. "And I suppose you also think that the French police believe in the tooth fairy? And how will you repay the insurance company the 60 million euros they so promptly paid to you?"

"I have most of my share. You give me back your 30 million and—I don't know—I will borrow the rest. I can't continue. I would die before I could go to prison."

Sofia was silent for a few moments. Then, sounding suddenly reassuring, she said, "Okay, don't provide the police with anything. Don't meet with them. Stay away from the store. I will leave for Paris this afternoon, and I will meet you tomorrow afternoon. We will talk this through. Everything will be all right. I promise you. You won't go to prison."

Sofia immediately called her assistant, awakening her from a sound sleep, and told her to book a seat from Martinique to Paris on the 5:20 PM Air France flight.

CHAPTER SEVEN
New York

THE MORNING AFTER HER return to New York from St. Barth, Catherine worked out extra vigorously in the gym and, with her dress pumps in her shoulder bag, walked from her east side apartment to her office on Park Avenue, just north of Grand Central. It was a glorious Manhattan morning, and she loved the walk to work.

She first dictated her report on the St. Barth trip, then reviewed her e-mails and the other work that came across her desk. Working through lunch, as was her habit, she then walked into the office of her boss, Executive Vice President Nick Reschio.

One of the many things she liked about her job was working for Reschio. Reschio was in his midfifties and was one of the top five people in Larsen and McTabbitt. At five foot ten, with blond hair turning to gray, Reschio still had the strong shoulders and neck of a former wrestler and linebacker at Williams. Following college, he had spent five years as an officer in the Marine Corps before getting his MBA at Harvard and then joining L & M. He had recruited Catherine from Harvard, where she had gone to business school after several years with a large New York commercial insurer. Early on, her analytical skill and somewhat adventurous spirit had led her into the fraud investigation part of L & M, and she had risen steadily, with Nick as her mentor. Now, at age forty, she was the second-highest-ranking woman in the firm. Only the chief financial officer was a more senior woman than Catherine.

Reschio's office always reminded Catherine of a men's club, with dark wood and leather. Except for a Marine Corps sword in a glass case, the only things on the wall were sailing scenes, even though Reschio's only involvement with water was to drink it, frozen, one ice cube at a time, with single malt scotch. The pictures came from the L & M collection and had been chosen by Nick's assistant. He rarely noticed them.

"Not much of a suntan for the Caribbean," Nick said when Catherine walked in.

"If we figure this case out, at least I now know where to go for a real vacation."

"It's all yours. I don't like islands—all that water."

"You work on an island," Catherine said.

"I know, but there are lots of bridges and tunnels. That Sofia sounds like an interesting woman."

"She sure is, and her store is no ordinary jewelry store. The pieces seem quite carefully crafted. Beyond the rings, necklaces and bracelets, she has an incredible collection of colored stones. The white diamonds are nothing to sneeze at, either."

"You mention in your report rare Iranian turquoise and treasures from sunken Spanish galleons. What the hell is that about?"

"She implied that she had access to rare turquoise and to many other stones that could be made into pieces she would design and then fabricate in her workshops in Italy and Israel. The two old pieces that she said were from the galleons were stunning. I did some quick research, and there was a Spanish treasure fleet that went down off the Florida coast in 1715. She implied that she can get more of the stuff from that wreck."

Nick scratched his cheek. "There can't be many pieces from a wreck like that around. I wonder where she gets them and how she does authentication. You remember the trouble we had a few years ago with that ownership dispute over jewels supposedly recovered from an old Spanish wreck? Our appraiser—as I remember—took one of the pieces apart to look for sulfide residue or something that would be consistent with being in the ocean for a long time. Those treasure hunters are a strange lot. All that time under water." He almost shivered at the thought. "Doesn't Florida make you get a permit to look for sunken treasures and give them a cut if you find anything?"

"That's right. There should be provenance from the state on her jewelry."

"I doubt that everything that comes off those wrecks gets reported."

"Probably, but what I find interesting is her access to stones, including this Spanish treasure. And I have to tell you, these emerald pieces were unbelievable, and so were some of her stones. I couldn't spend a lot of time studying them, but I did look at some pieces under the scope and others through her glass, and they all looked to be of very high quality. She also claimed that she could provide buyers with certifications and appraisals. There are plenty of appraisals for the stolen pieces. And they are all solid—almost too solid."

"That's a hell of a lot of near flawless jewelry. I like a little imperfection in life," said Nick. "What about this Sofia character? Did she look like the type who would be part of an insurance fraud?"

Catherine laughed. "What kind of question is that? You think that anyone who makes a claim on their policy is part of an insurance fraud."

"That is not true. My mother once lost a diamond ring. She got paid by the insurance company, and a year later, she found the ring in her underwear drawer and sent a check to the insurance company for the amount of the claim they had paid."

"Your mother was a saint."

"I know—in a world of sinners," Nick said.

"Sofia is a fascinating woman. She seems to be strong and shrewd, and she wants things her own way."

"Married? Kids?"

"I don't think so."

"Boyfriends? Girlfriends?"

"She didn't talk about it. She is quite beautiful. Sexually, I couldn't tell—well, I think she made a pass at me."

"You think she made a pass at you?! You haven't been on a date for so long you probably don't remember what a pass is like. Let's have some details."

"Forget it, Nick. Let's get back to the case."

"Kate, you are working too damned hard. If you are ever going to find a prince—or princess—I don't give a damn which—you are going to have to start kissing some toads."

"My social life—or lack of it—is none of your damned business!"

"Okay, okay. I got a bit nosy. Sorry. Back to work. I think you found out enough in St. Barth to add Sofia Mostov to our list of highly suspicious folks. She is the only tie to Paris, Naples and the Miami robbery. But what would her angle be? That's what I can't figure out. What do you think?"

Calming down, Catherine replied that she didn't yet have an opinion. But it was probably time to talk with the French and Italian police and step up discussions with the Miami cops, and what about the FBI?

In spite of his reluctance to share information with police, and particularly foreign police, Reschio agreed with Catherine. He said that they needed police cooperation to locate any of the stolen pieces that showed up on the market.

"You get in touch with our Paris office and have them find out what, if anything, the French police are doing," Nick said. "Probably not much. They can also check with the Italians. They are probably doing even less."

"You are certainly a model of transatlantic cooperation."

"I went to France on a vacation once. Do you know what they eat over there?"

"Okay, Mister Meat and Potatoes, I will get on it. Are you going to handle Miami?"

"Oh yeah. It's not the first robbery we have investigated down there. I know some of the guys in the department."

"Guys? As I remember, on the last Miami case, we got a lot of help from a woman detective."

"Yeah, right. I am incorrigible. But I am working on it."

Chapter Eight
Paris

It was ten in the morning Paris time when Sofia got to her hotel. For this trip, she chose a small hotel off the Place des Vosges in the eastern end of Paris, not far from the Place de la Bastille. The hotel was reached through colonnades that led to a cobblestone courtyard with a small garden. The elegant but small and private hotel appealed to her, and she loved the renaissance symmetry of the Place des Vosges, as well as the medieval feeling of the surrounding Marais district.

As always, she had booked a room for the night before her arrival. Sofia was not a patient person, and few things about travel irritated her more than arriving in a city in the early morning, tired from an overnight flight, and having to wait until mid-afternoon to get into her hotel room.

Her first call, made from a phone box outside of the hotel, was to Valerie Pickett. He answered his apartment phone on the first ring and wanted to meet her right away. In a calm voice, she said, "No, Valerie, I am tired from my trip, and I have some business to attend to. Let's take a walk and discuss the situation later this afternoon. I will meet you at four o'clock in the afternoon at the café on the Place du Rond Point des Canaux, at the end of the Parc de la Villette where the canals Saint-Denis and de l'Ourcq cross." Then she hung up. She made one more call from the same coin phone.

After a quick shower, Sofia changed into a pair of black slacks, a gray silk blouse and a black cashmere sweater. A silk scarf covered her hair, and a pair of large dark glasses shielded her eyes from the sun, as well as from passersby. Then, with a black tote bag over her shoulder, she left the hotel and walked up the Rue de Turenne, past the various clothing shops. She glanced left at the renewed neighborhood around the Picasso Museum and stopped for a coffee at a café on the Place de la République.

Leaving the square of the Place de la République, Sofia made her way to the Rue Dieux and stood on a bridge over the nearby canal, peering intently for several minutes at the canal and the bridges and locks that intersected it. After a few minutes, she made her way back through the neighborhood of shops and cafés to the bustling Boulevard de Magenta. She walked until she reached a nondescript apartment building between the Gare de l'Est and the Gare du Nord, just off the Rue La Fayette. In the entryway, she rang the bell opposite the name M. Androff and then climbed to the third floor. She walked into a long dark room full of overstuffed furniture.

"Boris," she said, "every time I come here, I feel that I have to pull the curtains and open the windows. I can almost smell the mothballs. This is spring in Paris, not winter in Moscow."

"Ah, my *plemyanitsa* Sofia, always you try to improve me. But I do not change." And Boris Voroshilov, built like a small bear, engulfed her in an affectionate hug. "When you visit, it brings happiness to your old uncle's heart." He offered her tea from a large samovar.

Turning down the tea, she said, "Is there anything except tea in this kitchen?"

"Of course not, *plemyanitsa*. You know that I cook nothing and eat no meals in this place. This is Paris, the capital of gastronomy. I have no place to spend my money except on eating three meals a day in excellent restaurants, visiting art galleries and museums, and attending the best of opera and ballet. The Moscow Philharmonic comes next week, and I will go to every performance."

Sofia studied Voroshilov. *He really does never change,* she thought. He wore the same outfit as always: dark pants, an open-collar white shirt and a sweater with a shawl collar. Even in Cuba, when he was younger, he dressed the same, just without the sweater. In his early seventies, five foot seven in height, with a gray beard and overweight, but strongly built, he moved surprisingly gracefully as he motioned Sofia to sit down and lowered himself into a large reading chair.

"I haven't seen you since you made your annual winter trip to Havana in January," Sofia said. "How is your health? I worry about you. Have you left Paris?"

"I am fine. You know that we Russians are indestructible. I have left Paris only to go to Zurich to visit my money. I am a man of simple habits."

Habits, yes; simple, no, thought Sofia. She knew that Boris spent his days walking the streets of Paris, browsing jewelry stores with a casual air that covered up an ability to assess jewelry quickly that surpassed the skill of anyone else she had ever met. Once in Cuba, they placed in front of him a group of diamonds identified only by number, and he correctly identified the country of origin of each stone with only the aid of a jeweler's glass. Without the aid of any glass, he could quickly classify diamonds by color, matching the CIBJO, the European classification, perfectly and by grade. He had the same facility with other gems.

When he wasn't studying jewelry or gemological technical publications, or occasionally visiting the French National Library to do what he called "his research," Boris applied his discerning eye to paintings. He regularly went to music and dance performances. In the fall, he went every year to the Strasbourg Music Festival in Austria. He had a lively interest in the European art world, visiting galleries and museums and carefully following the art auctions in Paris, London and New York.

He often sent Sofia ideas for pieces, and during their annual meetings in Havana and St. Barth, they studied gems together. Rarely, he would travel to Rome to visit her workshop and review the quality of the work there. He often said that music, art and trains were his antidote for loneliness. He talked about returning to Moscow, but although he avidly followed Russian happenings, he had returned to the country of his birth only once since leaving Cuba in the mid-1990s. He adored Sofia, and she made sure he had all the money he needed. Without friends or other family, he only had Sofia.

"Why don't you ever go back to Moscow?" she asked.

"I can't stand to visit another failed revolution. You know I was a dedicated communist. We got rid of the czar. There was hope. The people— all that stuff. Then we got Stalin and another repressive tyranny. I went to Cuba. I thought if they got rid of a right-wing dictator, then maybe their revolution would live up to its hope. So, what happened? Hope died. And Cuba's revolution ended up as a repressive tyranny. Then the communists in Russia fell of the weight of their own ineptitude. Gorbachev, then Yeltsin standing on top of a tank staring down the bad guys. Another revolution and maybe a chance. I went back to Moscow. I hoped. Then the slide back to tyranny. The KGB and their friends still running the country. No chance. Now I live in France. The French Revolution. A new future for mankind. *Liberté. Fraternité. Equalité.* Maybe they have gotten one out of three right. Sofia, you know who has gotten revolution right? The Americans."

"The Americans! They are rich, but I don't think of them as revolutionaries."

"That is my point. A conservative revolution. A pragmatic revolution. Freedom. Yes. Freedom to make money. The British king wanted too big a cut. It cost him America. The Americans now have freedom so they can make money. They are the richest, most powerful country in the world. And no tyranny. No police state. Their revolution worked. I have never been to America. If I were younger, I would go there. You could teach me English."

They went to lunch at a small restaurant just across the Boulevard de Magenta from the Gare du Nord. Boris liked the restaurant because it had excellent food cooked in the style of Brittany. As they returned to his apartment, Sofia said that it must be dangerous to walk the streets of Paris as much as he did.

He thought that a curious remark from Sofia and replied, turning the key to his apartment door, "Not very dangerous. The Paris police are okay, oscillating between incompetence and brutality, but they make up in numbers what they lack in law-enforcement skills. Besides, you know I always carry a little protection."

"What are you carrying these days?"

Opening up his sweater, Boris showed Sofia a shoulder holster with a small Beretta Tomcat automatic.

"Pretty small," said Sofia.

"I know you like bigger calibers, my dear Sofia, but this is loaded with .32-caliber 150-grain, hollow-point cartridges. It will do just fine at short range against any street thug I might run into."

"I suppose a girl needs protection, too, when in Paris."

At first surprised by her comment, Boris stood up and said, "I have been a little slow on the uptake, *plemyanitsa*. Let me offer you some of my hospitality." He motioned her to a large dark wood armoire. Taking a key from his chain, he unlocked it and pushed aside the back panel, revealing a safe flush with the wall. When the safe was opened, she saw three shelves, the top two holding several handguns and ammunition boxes, the bottom a number of thick envelopes.

"Diamonds and money in the envelopes, my dear Boris?"

"Diamonds, money and passports—everything someone needs to make a quick exit."

"You look like you have enough to more than tide you over between trips to Zurich. Still favoring euros, Swiss francs and dollars?"

"Of course, but I now have added rubles to my collection."

"Boris, you are the only Russian I have ever met who is an optimist."

Chuckling, he said, "What hardware do you require?"

"Well, a girl protecting herself doesn't want to make much noise."

"Here is a nice Czech gun, a CZ100B. It has polymer construction, so it is lightweight. This one uses nine-millimeter cartridges, and I have a silencer that works with it. Are two clips of nine-millimeter hollow points enough?"

"I will only need one clip, and thank you, Boris." She worked the action a few times, dry-firing the gun. Then she placed the clip in the stack, chambered a round, attached the silencer and dropped it into her shoulder bag. "Incidentally," she said, "I will be stopping off in Cuba on my way back to St. Barth. I must be going now."

"Say hello to our friends in Havana, and particularly to Roberto. I am sure you will be seeing him."

"Ah, yes. I will call you from St. Barth." And with another hug, her tote bag a bit heavier, Sofia set off in a northeasterly direction toward the Parc de la Villette. With long strides, she thought, *How much I like to walk in Paris on a beautiful afternoon.*

One of the places Sofia liked to walk was the area in the nineteenth arrondissement in the northeastern section of the city, where the remnants of the old canal system passed through quiet residential neighborhoods.

It was through such a neighborhood that Sofia and Valerie Pickett walked. Sofia, having arrived at the café after Valerie, suggested a walk rather than sitting at the café.

As they left the café, Pickett made a halfhearted effort at gallantry, complimenting Sofia on her stylish outfit and her elegant gloves. But the way his hand shook and the dark circles under his eyes betrayed a man under stress. "I am sure the police suspect me. Sofia, you have to help me unwind this. I will sell my store and give you part of what I get, but you must help me repay the insurance company. I am losing my mind over this. I am not cut out for this kind of thing."

"Valerie, this is not a place to talk. Let's walk a bit." As they walked along one of the canals, he became more agitated. She couldn't believe someone could sweat that much in the cool early evening. Every few steps, he took out his handkerchief and wiped his brow.

As they crossed a bridge over one of the canal locks, Sofia looked around the quiet neighborhood and paused, as did Valerie, his back to the low bridge rail. With one motion, Sofia raised her tote bag so that its bottom was level with Pickett's chest, put her hand inside, gripped the silenced CZ100 and fired two shots through the bottom of the bag into his heart and two more into his head. Dropping the bag on the ground, she pushed the slumping Valerie over the railing into the lock, and walked off the bridge and along the canal. Looking around, she tossed the pistol into the murky water. She disposed of the tote bag in a trash can behind a small restaurant near the canal. She then entered the nearest metro station and threw one of her gloves in the trash can near the platform and the other glove in the ladies room wastebasket. Exiting the metro at the Place de la Bastille, she walked to the Place des Vosges and her hotel. Changing into a light tan dress and matching sweater, she had an early dinner on the terrace of a bistro near her hotel.

The next morning, after a brief stop at a photography store on the Boulevard Beaumarchais, Sofia was on the Air France flight to Havana. She always was excited to be heading home to Cuba.

CHAPTER NINE
Paris

ABOUT THE SAME TIME Sofia's flight to Havana took off from Charles de Gaulle Airport, Gerard walked into Pierre Abou's office and, removing a pile of papers from the chair in front of Pierre's desk, sat down. "I was looking at your report on the session with Pickett," Gerard said. "We have yet to get the requested information from him. He makes me very suspicious. I want to talk to him again."

Pierre loved the opportunity to surprise Gerard with new information. Waiting a moment to reply and pushing his chair back slightly, he said, "Ah, but it will be a one-way conversation."

"What do you mean?"

"They pulled Pickett out of one of the canals near the Parc de la Villette this morning. He had four bullet holes in him."

"*Sacré bleu*. A robbery?"

"I don't think so. His wallet was in his pocket and an expensive watch on his wrist."

"Any idea when it happened?"

"A barge man found him in a lock a few hours ago, so he just arrived at the morgue. I thought I would go down there and see what the examiners think. But from the description they gave me and his identification, not much doubt it was Pickett. We will get a picture, and I will have our guys canvass the neighborhood, but no one reported any gunshots yesterday or this morning. Those canals get used during the day, so I would suppose it happened late yesterday, or perhaps at night or even this morning. It's a pretty quiet neighborhood."

"So, our big jewelry robbery, which might not have been a robbery, is now also a murder case. Put everything you can on this Pickett thing before the trail gets cold. I want to know about him. Girlfriends, boyfriends, business associates. Was he a gambler? Did he owe money to the wrong people? What was he doing up in that section of Paris? His store is on the Place Vendôme, and doesn't he—excuse me—*didn't* he used to live in the Eighth over near the Parc Monceau? Very strange."

"I just got an interesting call from the Paris office of a big New York-based insurance company, Larsen and McTabbitt," Gerard said. "They had some of the coverage layers on both the Bois de Boulogne and the Pickett robberies. The guy who called me said that on losses of this size, they usually handle the investigation. Something about their resources and expertise. A little pompous."

"And a little late. The Pickett heist was over a month ago, and the Mexican guy was robbed a few weeks later. You would think they would have called us a lot earlier."

"You would. He also told me that they are looking into the Naples robbery."

"My friend in Naples has never mentioned getting any requests from insurance investigators," Pierre said.

Gerard shrugged his shoulders and said, "That is probably because they have not gotten in touch with the Naples cops, either. This is an American company—big, probably arrogant. They want to avoid publicity, and they probably underestimate police departments and overestimate their own capabilities. I am supposed to call one of their senior people at nine in the morning New York time. You know, Pierre, the only common thread in these cases is Sofia Mostov. Maybe she is just a wholesaler and her involvement is a coincidence, but she is no ordinary jeweler. I am going to call the St. Barth chief and ask him to keep an eye on her. I want to know if he hears anything, or if she leaves the island. I have a good feeling about him. I think we can trust him to be discrete. Oh, that reminds me, talking about St. Barth, have you gotten any information on that Catherine York woman?"

"Not yet. I sent the request through Interpol. I should hear something from them or directly from the New York PD today or tomorrow."

"Now that we have a dead body to go with missing jewelry, we will have to cancel today's lunch," Gerard said. "Let's meet first thing tomorrow morning at the morgue. I still want to see Monsieur Pickett one more time."

Late that afternoon, having made some inquiries that confirmed the impeccable legitimacy of Larsen and McTabbitt and the identity of Nick Reschio, Gerard called Reschio. Gerard thought the conversation was stiff, although Reschio loosened up a bit when Gerard casually let drop that he had spent two years in Washington as a liaison to the FBI. L & M had clearly been working on the jewelry robberies but didn't seem to have gotten any further than he had. They also knew about the St. Barth connection. One additional piece of information that Gerard gleaned was that, a little over three months ago, a Miami jewelry store had been robbed and more than $80 million of merchandise stolen. The Miami cops had no suspects. Some of the stolen jewelry appeared to have originated with Sofia Mostov. Reschio was interested in the relationship the French had forged with the Naples police. They decided that it might make sense for Gerard to meet with the L & M people in New York, and they agreed to try to schedule such a meeting in a telephone call the next day.

After the call to Reschio, Gerard called the St. Barth chief and then spoke to Pierre who was at Valerie Pickett's apartment with several officers searching it pursuant to an order from an investigative judge. Then Gerard went home to change clothes. Casually dressed in a blue-and-gray cashmere blazer, gray slacks and a light blue open-collar shirt, he walked across the Pont Marie to the right bank.

As he walked along the Rue Pavée where it intersected with the Rue des Rosiers, he reflected on how much he loved the old Marais district. Here in the cobbled alleyways, the cramped winding streets, the diverse mix of Jews, Arabs, Iranians and others and their shops and restaurants, interspersed with grand seventeenth-century houses, even Gerard could get lost and love the feeling of exploring a city he had lived in all his life. He turned left on the Rue des Rosiers and walked past the delicatessens, the food shops and small synagogues, through the active street life. On one storefront, he could see that someone had painted a crude swastika, which had recently been covered with fresh white paint. His reverie broken, he sped up until he reached the Rue Beaubourg. The Beaubourg itself suddenly loomed ahead, its modernistic design a jarring contrast to the medieval world Gerard was exiting.

He quickly walked past the Place Georges Pompidou and then through what he considered the failed retail and shopping district that had replaced his beloved Les Halles to the Rue Montorgueil. He entered a black-timbered restaurant where Marcel Lefour sat at a corner table on the second floor.

In his early eighties, small and wizened, Lefour with his black jacket, black sweater and ever-present beret looked like he had frequented that restaurant for fifty years. And, in a sense, he had. Except for a brief stint in prison in the 1970s, he had probably never left Paris for more than a few days in his life.

A resistance member, it was a teenaged Marcel who Gerard's father first met when he crept into Paris one night to help prepare the way for the liberation of the city, and it was Marcel who whispered to Gerard's mother that her husband was in Paris.

After the war, the young Marcel parlayed his contacts into a thriving black market business, becoming a middleman in the trade of American cigarettes, stockings, German cameras, radios, liquor and any other desired item that was in short supply.

As the years went on, Marcel transformed his business into the largest fencing enterprise in Paris. He finally got caught, and it was after he was released from prison that Gerard, now a police officer, met up with him again. Professing to have "gone straight," Marcel maintained his, as he would put it, social contacts with his former associates. Gerard kept an eye on him, made sure that an overzealous cop did not mistake Marcel for the criminal he might or might not be, and received a lot of valuable information in exchange.

And did Marcel like snails. So it had become a tradition that the two of them would meet from time to time at one of the many Parisian establishments that served snails. The old and favored restaurant they were in served the mollusks in many ways. Over a plate of escargot prepared with Roquefort cheese with an artichoke on the side, the two men sat, heads huddled together, enjoying a bottle of perfectly chilled Sancerre. Gerard thought some Rieslings went very well with escargot, but he knew better than to order a German wine with Marcel, who never forgot his friends and never forgave his enemies.

Gerard described the two robberies and the murder to Marcel, who listened while eating his snails nonstop. They decided on another order of snails, this time with curry, and a second bottle of wine, a Corton-Charlemagne, a better match with the curry, thought Gerard. Gerard sat back and savored the spice of the curry contrasting with the snails swimming in butter sauce and garlic. This old restaurant was comforting to him and evoked the timelessness of Paris in a way that newer places could not. *In Paris,* he thought, *old restaurants and old men like Marcel didn't change.*

Marcel stopped eating long enough to say that he would check his sources and find out if any large quantities of jewelry or unset stones were showing up in Paris; Moscow, a recently developing market for stolen jewelry; or other locations where Marcel had contacts. As to Valerie Pickett, his name had never come up in the Paris bookmaking world that Marcel knew well, but he would see what he could find out about him.

They parted with Marcel, in his low growl, saying, "I'll get back to you."

Checking his office voicemail before driving to the Paris morgue the next morning, Gerard was particularly interested in a call from the St. Barth police chief. Jean-Claude Sourel had done his work well. When he discovered that Sofia had left the island, he had the tickets collected at the St. Barth airport reviewed, and they showed that she had gone to Paris. Sourel also reported that she had not yet arrived back in St. Barth. Gerard immediately called one of the young detectives in his unit and directed him to find out, by checking hotels, if she was still in Paris. If she was not, he wanted to know the dates of her stay and where she went after she left Paris.

Every time he visited the morgue, Gerard thought that he smelled of formaldehyde and disinfectant for days. At least the old morgue had charm and history. This one, located in the basement of a government building, was antiseptic and a bit too businesslike for him. The green walls reminded him of a prison, where the green paint supposedly had a calming effect on inmates. *The bodies in the morgue,* he thought to himself, *didn't need any calming.* As for Pickett, it was clear that he had been shot at extremely close range and pushed off the bridge. The medical examiner told Gerard that the time of death was between five and eight in the evening. Abou had determined that the last barges of that day passed through the small lock where Pickett's body was found at about 4:30 PM. No shell casings were found on the bridge, and no one in the neighborhood had reported to the officers who were showing his picture around that they had seen Pickett.

The two detectives had lunch at a bistro Gerard liked near the Place de la Madeleine. Following oysters, they each had a sea bream baked in a salt crust, a dish suggested by Pierre because the intense flavor of the crust reminded him of Marseilles cuisine. Gerard dropped Pierre off at the nearby Place Vendôme, where he was going to do another search of Pickett's store.

When he returned to the office, Pierre reported that they could find no record other than the insurance appraisals they already had that provided any information on the stolen jewelry. The records Pickett apparently kept for tax purposes were predictably incomplete, items denoted by number only. Pickett apparently didn't like to pay taxes. His staff claimed to know nothing about his business dealings. They were only clerks, and Pickett was at the store almost all the time. There was no assistant manager. He had no family other than one brother, who lived in Grenoble.

Gerard and Pierre were somewhat glum that afternoon as they reviewed the case in Gerard's office. Pickett's death had cut off a promising avenue, and the Mexican who owned the house that had been robbed was not in Paris. The housekeeper had a phone number in Mexico City for him, but when the detectives called the number, they were told that the owner was away and that his Paris lawyer was handling the details of the robbery. The Mexican police would "get back to them," but Gerard was not optimistic on that front. The guy was obviously wealthy. In Mexico, that meant he was well-connected and that meant they would get little information. The French border police would let him know if the Mexican came back to Paris.

Why would someone want to kill Valerie Pickett? The detectives were debating that question as they began to go through his customer records when there was a knock on the door of Gerard's office. The young detective who Gerard had assigned to check out Sofia Mostov's travel schedule entered the room, greeted Pierre and Gerard, and handed Gerard a copy of Sofia's hotel registration.

"So she was here for one night," said Gerard. "Do you have her travel information?"

"Yes, when she left Paris, she flew to Havana."

"She was in Paris when poor Pickett was knocked off," Gerard said. "Pierre, I was debating going to New York, but now I am definitely going. Those insurance people know a lot about Sofia. You go to Naples and see how much connection to her there is in that case. I will arrange with our embassy in Rome to set things up for you to visit with the Naples police. They will provide a translator. And I know what you are thinking—no, you can't take Isabella with you to translate. I like your wife's cooking too much to have her mad at me. You might also consult your friend, Sherlock Holmes, and see if he thinks that a beautiful blonde jeweler could also be a murderer."

It was a Tuesday, and Gerard called Nick Reschio to arrange a Thursday morning meeting at his office in New York, made the necessary arrangements with the French Embassy in Rome and went home to pack.

———

The next morning, Gerard was on an Air France flight to New York. The department driver who took Gerard to Charles de Gaulle Airport gave him an envelope with overnight faxes, e-mails and phone messages. Opening it, Gerard saw a note from Pierre. The New York police had responded to the Interpol request about Catherine York. The Catherine York who lived at the address Gerard had provided was a senior executive with the insurance firm of Larsen and McTabbitt. *This trip,* Gerard mused, *has just gotten a whole lot more interesting.*

CHAPTER TEN
Cuba

ALTHOUGH SHE HAD MADE the trip many times, Sofia's heart always beat a bit faster as the descending plane flew over the dark red tobacco fields near Cuba's José Martí Airport. She sat up and looked out the plane's window as if this was her first visit to Cuba.

The scene at the airport was chaotic with the notoriously inefficient Cuban bureaucracy doing what it does so well, dealing with chaos by operating at a glacial pace. Her Cuban passport got her through the passport line fairly quickly, with the only delay a long, approving look from the official. *Ah, yes,* she thought, *Cuba, where macho was still thriving.* As Sofia left passport control, she was motioned into a small room where her longtime acquaintance, Pepe, who was a senior airport official, sat. Pepe studied the airline manifest daily and made it a point to meet important passengers, not out of an excess of hospitality but because he could be of help to such people, and he expected to be compensated for his services.

After kissing Sofia on both cheeks and inquiring about her health, he asked how long she would be staying. "Only a few days, but time enough to see some of your photographs." Pepe was an avid amateur photographer, and one of the ways he supplemented his meager official pay was to sell his mediocre work at high prices to those for whom a close relationship with someone who controlled arrivals and departures at the airport was of value. "And this should improve your work," said Sofia as she rose to depart, leaving a leather-trimmed green canvas bag she had bought in Paris that morning on the table. Inside was a new Lecia M-7 camera, 50mm and 135mm lenses to supplement the 35mm lens on the camera, three filters and thirty-six rolls of Fuji 35mm film. Her cheeks kissed again, she walked out. *Maybe the next time,* she thought, *I will bring him some soap and deodorant.*

Standing alone in a bright ray of sunshine that came through the unwashed skylight of the main terminal was Roberto. He wore a white shirt over beige linen slacks, and his tanned skin glistened in the sunshine. *He was,* she thought, *like a beautiful piece of carefully chiseled marble standing in the gloomy arrival terminal.* He walked quickly to her, gave her a long, passionate kiss and, with one arm around her and the other one pulling her bag, led her to his black Acura parked in a "No parking at any time" zone at the terminal curb. With a casual salute to the policeman enforcing the no parking zone, Roberto held the door for her, and they were off.

Driving at his usual breakneck pace, they headed north to Havana. Roberto used his horn to warn slower prerevolution American cars, bicycles and even horse-drawn carts and pedestrians who shared Cuba's roads with the newer Japanese cars that were increasingly frequent around Havana.

Roberto's apartment was in a whitewashed building off Avenue Three, near the bay in Havana's Miramar section. Miramar, particularly near the water, always reminded Sofia of the Havana of her youth. The most posh of the Havana suburbs before the revolution, Miramar was slowly regaining its previous status. Foreign investors; newly wealthy Cubans, many of them government officials; and foreign diplomats all were moving into Miramar, and new hotels and excellent restaurants were starting to appear.

"Welcome to Playa," Roberto said, using his nickname for the neighborhood, "your second home, Sofia." Leaving his car with the doorman, they rode the elevator to his tenth-floor apartment. If the building had been taller or the elevator slower, she thought, he would have undressed her before the elevator stopped.

They almost tumbled into his apartment and then onto his bed with its view of the blue bay. The large windows were open, allowing the ocean breeze to gently flow over their naked bodies.

Sofia and Roberto saw each other perhaps five times a year, mostly in Cuba, but occasionally in St. Barth or in Europe. Each meeting was punctuated with their intense, short and satisfying lovemaking. He was five foot nine, muscular and very active. She loved to watch him when they made love. While Sofia had known many men, she got immense pleasure with Roberto. Perhaps it was the love potion of long absences. Perhaps it was because there were no preliminaries, none of the studied attempted seduction that amused her so with most men she encountered. They each knew what the other wanted and freely gave—one to the other—openly and without self-consciousness.

As they laid in the late afternoon sun on his balcony, their hands intertwined, she thought about what a complex and yet simple man Roberto was. He was her business partner, running what they called the "Cuban branch." He was a fierce Cuban patriot, uncomfortable when he was out of Cuba, deeply committed to Cuban independence and unfriendly to both the United States and Russia, both of which he believed had used Cuba for their own purposes.

And yet he was certainly no fan of the Cuban leaders who he believed had betrayed the revolution against Batista and enriched themselves at the expense of the Cuban people. Sofia did not care about politics, but she had been a spectator in many passionate conversations where Boris Voroshilov and others had tried to get Roberto to acknowledge the inconsistency between his dislike of the regime and the substantial amounts of money he paid to various of its members so that he could run the Cuban branch without interference.

He would respond, "In Cuba, one must pay the *maceta*, whether on the street or in an office. It is a cost of doing business." While he lived well in a country where poverty was still extreme, he provided substantial support to a number of Cubans who were in need, and he supported political activities that would have landed a less generous benefactor of high officials in prison. Sofia thought that he lived too much on the edge, and she worried about him. *But,* she thought as she looked at him naked and asleep, *that was part of what attracted her to him.*

As they showered, he said, "I will take you to an early dinner. You have had a long day. There is a new place over in Kohly. The music there is very good." They talked about her stay. He knew that she liked to walk around old Havana and on the Malecón and remember her early years in Havana. Dinner tomorrow would be with old friends, and the next day they would drive west of Havana to the "office." Then she would fly to St. Barth.

———————

The next day they walked and walked, from the frenzied activity on Obispo, a busy street on the edge of the old town, through the neighborhoods south of the Malecón, where she loved the street life and the music coming when one least expected it around the corner or from a rooftop above. The faded pastels of the buildings, the street vendors—and always the music and the warm breezes—then and then only could she breathe freely and think back on the lonely twelve-year-old who had left Havana many years ago.

The dinner in the home of Roberto's sister had the rare, relaxed feel that comes in a police state when one can be completely at ease with one's companions. In a country that has its own word, *chivato*, for informers, and where each neighborhood has its watch organizations to spy on neighbors who might be opposed to the regime, trusting and open conversation was a luxury.

Some of the dinner discussions were about places Sofia had visited. They asked her about the French attitude toward Cuba. Why wasn't there more French investment and why didn't the French match their rhetoric with more purchases of Cuban goods? And what about America? Everyone there had a relative who had left Cuba for Florida so that the politics of South Florida and its impact on the embargo was on everyone's mind, and everyone had an opinion.

The conversation turned to how the embargo might end, the social and cultural upheavals that would follow, and the issues that would arise from the claims that the Cubans who left the country after the revolution would make on their prerevolution property and assets.

Like so many dinner party conversations around the world, this one ended with no problems solved. Unlike many others, however, the participants had a sense of elation that they could even have the conversation.

On their way back to Roberto's apartment, he said to Sofia, "During that whole conversation on the embargo and the future of Cuba, you were silent."

"I know," she said. "They didn't talk about jewels or money. What time do we leave tomorrow for Pinar del Rio?"

"Sofia, at least, unlike the rest of us, you know exactly who you are."

———

The next morning, Sofia and Roberto headed west to the province of Pinar del Rio, a sparsely populated agricultural region. They followed the *autopista* to its end in the town of Pinar del Rio and then navigated unmarked, rutted roads for another hour. Finally they came upon a cluster of buildings surrounded by a barbed wire fence that showed signs of recent repair. There were a few wooden buildings and three low concrete-block buildings with several cars outside. A long vegetable garden grew next to one of the wooden buildings, and chickens and goats roamed around it. A few shirts hanging on a clothesline provided further signs of rural domesticity. Several yards from the low buildings was a tall square windowless concrete structure. It was surrounded by a sturdy chain-link fence topped with barbed wire. Just beyond the fence was a small stream with a metal and stone dam across it that created a pond.

A visitor looking closely might conclude from the barbed wire fence; the empty flagpole, its chain rattling in the wind; and the block buildings that this tiny settlement had once been a military base. The faded red star on one of the buildings would be a clue that it had been used by the Soviets during their stay on the island. The observer would be correct, but there never were any visitors. If a tourist, having made a number of wrong turns while trying to explore the area, had come upon this place, the snarling dogs and a few inhospitable Cubans, perhaps wearing sidearms, would have made the short stay unpleasant.

This was Sofia and Roberto's Cuban branch. As they pulled up, they were greeted by two large barking dogs, straining at the chain leash held by a burly Cuban. The man had an AKS-74U, a short snub-nosed variant of the Kalashnikov AK-47, slung over his back. As the guard was hugging Sofia and Roberto, two white-coated men emerged and greeted the visitors warmly. One was a dark-skinned gray-haired Cuban, and the other, a middle-aged man with a goatee who spoke Spanish to them with a thick Russian accent. Roberto pulled a large cooler out of the Acura's trunk and opened it, displaying the Russian vodka, caviar, *crème fraiche* and smoked salmon that would be the highlights of their lunch.

They entered one of the concrete buildings, where a few more workers in white lab coats greeted them. The Cuban guard turned the dogs over to two more men, who were both casually dressed. One carried a Walther P99 in a holster at his side.

The building they entered had workbenches and metal cabinets along most of one side. On the workbenches were several high-powered precision drills, as well as hooded optical devices that had air ducts in the top of the hoods. The remainder of the large room was taken up with large bins. At the right-hand side next to the door there was a sturdy door to a metal storeroom. The building had only a few windows high on the walls. It was brightly lit and quite cool. The hum of two large air-conditioning units at each end and several ceiling-mounted fans broke the silence.

"So," said Roberto, addressing the gray-haired Cuban and the goateed Russian, "how is the new generator working?"

The Cuban said, "Roberto, so far, so good. It increases the efficiency of the reactor and gives us higher temperatures and shorter operating cycles. We are able to smooth out the voltage flow from the uneven power these *guajiros* provide us. One would think with all the *baro* we give them, they could do better. The product we made for you last month was good, no?"

"They looked good to me. The test will come in the cutting."

"Sofia, you will send them to Tel Aviv and Amsterdam?" asked the Russian.

"Yes, they will go by the usual routes. I saw Boris in Paris a few days ago, and he sends his greetings. He wants us to toast him with good Russian vodka."

"Ah, Boris," said the Russian, "he helped us a lot when he was here in January. He improved the efficiency of the reactor." The Russian gestured to the tall building. "It is getting harder and harder to get the materials we need. After the World Trade Center attack, the Americans have been cracking down. They are worried about terrorists making a bomb. Our friends in Russia still come through. I wish Boris would have stayed longer, but he doesn't much like the food here now that he has become a Parisian. Most of the old crowd is gone; the Russians who come here now are a lot of loudmouthed boors."

Sofia commiserated with the supply problem and complimented the two senior managers on their work. Walking around, she greeted the other workers, warmly hugging them.

Roberto, watching her, marveled at how a beautiful woman could lift the spirits of the most hardened of men. *Sofia,* he thought, *wore her charm like an insulated coat over ice.*

They toured the facility, with two of the Cubans who had donned white coats for the visit changing to overalls and proudly showing off the new generator.

They laughed as Roberto related the tribulations in getting the generator through the Cuban bureaucracy. The generator was manufactured in Germany and shipped in through Mexico. Thinking that he had paid off everyone who needed to be paid off, Roberto had been in his office not far from his apartment when he got a telephone call from his agent at the airport telling him that there was a problem. "Where is the generator?" Roberto had asked.

"That's the problem," the agent replied. "It is in the air on a crane next to the plane, and the crane operators won't unload it until they get four thousand euros."

"*Pinga*," said Roberto, "that *guapo*, Pepe, was paid enough to take care of those guys." Pepe would not answer his call, so Roberto had to drive to the airport, where he could see the crane with his precious generator suspended between the cargo plane door and the runway. It was lowered only after Roberto's agent doled out four thousand euros. The laughter resumed as Roberto described chasing Pepe around the airport until, with Roberto's hand around his throat, he disgorged four thousand euros from Roberto's original payment.

One of the overall-clad Cubans was the master mechanic of the factory, and the gray-haired Cuban complimented him in front of Sofia and Roberto on how he kept things running in an economy notoriously short of spare parts. "It sometimes takes months to get what we need from Russia, France or Germany, so Jorge saves us much downtime. He can fix anything. Show them your workshop and cars."

Beaming from ear to ear, Jorge took them over to one of the small wooden buildings nearby. Attached to it was a shed with large barn doors. Next to a large workbench, there was a lathe attached to the floor and a metal grinder against the wall. On another wall hung fan belts and a rack of spark plugs among scores of automobile components. Opening up the barn doors, Jorge proudly pointed out a 1947 maroon Pontiac torpedo back, a 1949 black Chrysler Imperial sedan, a 1950 white Buick Roadmaster sedan and, obviously his pride and joy, a 1949 white Cadillac convertible with red leather upholstery.

"And do they all run?" asked Sofia.

"Of course," replied the normally taciturn Jorge.

"Then I would be honored, *compañero*, if you would take me for a ride in your Cadillac," Sofia said.

Jorge looked as if he had been asked to chauffeur a queen, and perhaps, thought Roberto, he had. Jorge almost jumped into the convertible, backed it out of the shed, and after ceremoniously dusting off the passenger seat, opened the passenger door for Sofia with a bow. Off they went.

"I suppose," said the Russian, "that I wouldn't get far if I offered her a ride in my Mitsubishi SUV."

"I suppose that you wouldn't," replied Roberto.

After Sofia returned from her ride, she, Roberto, the gray-haired Cuban and the Russian had a brief business meeting, agreeing that, with the last winter's product about to enter the supply chain, and with inventories in St. Barth, Rome and Tel Aviv, they wouldn't need to start production again until winter. Perhaps that work would coincide with Boris Voroshilov's annual visit.

The whole staff then settled down to a lunch of caviar, salmon, local chicken and vegetables, and, of course, beans and rice, all washed down with vodka, French champagne and beer. Sofia handed out envelopes to each person—"Bonuses," she said—and then she and Roberto started the trip back to Havana.

Not hungry after the large lunch, they made love and fell asleep in each other's arms. They then went into Central Havana for dinner and a late night of jazz and dancing. It was a tired Sofia who headed for the airport the next morning. As he kissed her at the airport, Roberto gave Sofia a rosary. Surprised at this gift from the nonreligious Roberto, Sofia looked at him quizzically. With a smile he said, "My dear Sofia, you are flying Cubana today, not on your own plane, and I thought a rosary might be a more useful safety device than the seat belts."

Sofia's flight made it safely to St. Martin. *Perhaps with the aid of the rosary,* she thought. After the short flight to St. Barth, she showed her French passport to the customs official on duty at the airport and got into the waiting car for the short ride to her villa.

After she left the airport, the customs official picked up the phone and made a short call. "She is back," he said.

CHAPTER ELEVEN
New York

A T TEN THE NEXT morning, Gerard arrived at the Park Avenue offices of Larsen and McTabbitt for his appointment with Nick Reschio. After showing his French police identity card to the guard in the lobby, Gerard was directed to an elevator and told to go to the thirty-first-floor reception area.

After a short wait, a well-dressed woman of about fifty appeared and introduced herself as Mr. Reschio's assistant. She showed Gerard into a conference room, which contained a well-polished mahogany table surrounded by ten comfortable-looking leather chairs. One wall was mostly windows and faced Park Avenue; the other three walls had prints of the Lloyd's of London building, the Lloyd's Partners' room, and buildings in other cities. Gerard recognized a Paris building where L & M presumably had its office and a building in Hong Kong. Coffee, tea and juices were set out on a buffet. Above the buffet, a maritime scene showed several U.S. Navy warships of the sailing age surrounding a ship that flew no flag—*probably*, Gerard thought, *a scene from L & M history.*

A man of medium height with close-cropped hair and a muscular build entered. He was wearing a blue suit, a white-and-blue-striped shirt and a red tie. He introduced himself as Nick Reschio, shook Gerard's hand and seated himself with his back to Park Avenue. As Gerard sat down opposite him, he observed that Reschio did not take the seat at the head of the table. *A good beginning*, thought Gerard. They made small talk for a few minutes about Gerard's flight. Reschio had brought no files with him, and Gerard left his closed briefcase next to him on the floor.

Gerard offered Reschio his card, and Reschio reciprocated. Reschio's card was engraved and providing only the bare minimum of information—name, title, company name, address and phone number. Gerard's card had his title and the colorful emblem of the French National Police, as well as his direct office number, a twenty-four-hour department number, his cell phone, fax number and e-mail address.

Nick looked at the card and said, "There are a lot of numbers on your card."

"Ah, yes," replied Gerard. "You know how hard it is to find a policeman when you need one. I try to make it easier."

Nick smiled. As he was asking Gerard how long he had been in police work, the door opened, and Catherine York walked in.

As he rose from his chair, Gerard tried not to look startled. He focused on what she was wearing. Gerard always noticed what women wore. Her dress was light blue and of a material that clung to her just tightly enough to suggest that this businesswoman was indeed a woman. Gerard remembered the lovely body underneath that dress. She had a sweater around her shoulders that matched her dress. Her dark hair was worn back, and her diamond studs sparkled in the light from the window. She wore a beautiful pendant with rose-colored and blue stones that looked like the work of a Native American artist. The pendant was attached to a platinum collar. The pendant was a nice contrast to the tailored look of the rest of her outfit. The whole ensemble, Gerard thought, contrasted with the indifferent suit and tie worn by Reschio.

Catherine introduced herself and, after she laid several thick files on the table, handed Gerard her card. It told him that she was a vice president of the firm. He reciprocated with his card, and she walked around the table and took a seat next to Reschio. She offered not a flicker of recognition of Gerard. If she recognized him from St. Barth, she was a consummate actress, he thought.

Reschio said that Catherine was one of the firm's senior investigators and was the lead on the series of jewelry robberies. "As you came in, I was asking Mr. de Rochenoir how long he had been in police work. Incidentally, you speak excellent English, how did you learn it so well?" Nick said to Gerard. "I know three words of French. Catherine here has some Spanish."

Gerard explained that he had sometimes accompanied his father to the United States when Gerard was a child as young as nine. His father had traveled in the States extensively, even before the war—World War II, he added with a nod to the relative youth of the two Americans. Gerard's father had been one of Charles de Gaulle's liaisons to the British and then to the Americans during the war. He taught Gerard English and insisted that Gerard continue his English studies in school. "My father had worked and served with the U.S. Army, and he was persuaded that the power and wealth of America would be a major force in the postwar world." Gerard said that he also had spent two years in the States working with the FBI.

"And what about police work?" Nick asked.

"When I graduated from university, I went to work with the French government. The ministry I worked at was involved in national security matters, and I found that I liked complex investigations. The National Police offered me the chance to work more independently on a variety of cases and, to my parent's surprise, I became a cop. After the war, my father worked to reassemble and then develop the family real estate holdings, and he began to invest in industry in France and the United States. I could have gone to work with him, but when I got out of university, he was getting older and slowing down. I took leave from the ministry, traveled and skied, and then joined the National Police. I needed action, and the family business was winding down to the management of investments. That wasn't for me. My parents knew that."

"Do you have a family?" Nick asked.

"Just a sister and three nephews. What about the two of you?"

"I am married, and we have three daughters. Catherine is married to her work, right, Kate?"

"If I am, maybe we should get down to it," she said.

Gerard had a sinking feeling that he could no longer delay confronting his concerns about Catherine. As he was trying to decide how to deal with the situation, he heard Catherine's pleasant voice.

"First, let me say, Monsieur de Rochenoir"—Gerard noticed her use of 'monsieur' rather than Nick's 'mister'—"how much we appreciate your taking the time to come to New York and meet with us. I made inquiries about you of our Paris office. Nick, I haven't had a chance to tell you, our guest is quite a famous French detective. He is well-known for some of the cases he has worked on. In the French press, he is rumored to be part of a secret high-level antiterrorism task force and—maybe best of all—he does all this for one euro a year. He contributes his salary back into a fund to support the families of French police who are killed or injured in the line of duty."

"You, mademoiselle, are too flattering," Gerard said. "Your staff has made me into something more than I am."

"Well, I'm impressed," said Reschio.

Opening a manila file, Catherine said, "Let's get to work. We are dealing with four major jewelry thefts in three countries over a period of only a few months." She summarized their information on the robberies.

After a discussion and a comment from Gerard that he knew little about the Miami theft, Nick said, "All the more reason for us to get together. We need to pool our knowledge. We know very little about the Paris cases and even less about Naples."

Shifting uncomfortably in his chair, Gerard said, "Before we start, Mr. Reschio ... "

"Oh, call me Nick, and I hope I can call you Gerard. You can call Ms. York Catherine—we are informal Americans here."

"Okay, Nick, but this is awkward so I will be direct. I need to talk with you privately."

Catherine looked surprised but immediately said, "You fellows talk. Go ahead. I have some things to do in my office." She got up without glancing at Gerard and left the room.

"Gerard, what is this about? I hope you don't have reservations about working with a woman."

"No, no, not at all. That is not the problem. Nick, are you aware that Catherine was recently in St. Barth?"

"Yes, I know that. How do you know?"

"Because I was there too, working on this case. A person of interest to us is a woman who owns a jewelry store on St. Barth as well as operations in Rome and Tel Aviv. I went to St. Barth to learn what I could about her—this Sofia Mostov. I was observing her store, and I saw Catherine go in and spend a long time there. I recognized Catherine from the St. Martin airport. Then I saw the two of them together on the beach in what I can only describe as an intimate relationship. Sofia Mostov appeared to be massaging her—like so many women on St. Barth, they were both topless. Then they went swimming together. The next day, before she returned to New York, Catherine again spent time in the Mostov woman's store. I can only conclude that they are friends—maybe more. For me to reveal details of our investigation to her under these circumstances is impossible."

"Son of a bitch," said Nick, clapping his hand to his forehead. "This is one of those colossal misunderstandings that would be hilarious—sort of like those English plays my wife drags me to full of mistaken identities—

if the stakes were not so serious. There is absolutely nothing between Catherine and Sofia Mostov. Catherine went to St. Barth for the same reason you did. We saw that the St. Barth operation had sold a lot of the pieces that were reported stolen. Hell, we were suspicious enough to send Kate down to investigate. The Mostov woman thinks Kate is a rich, naive American looking to buy an expensive piece because she got a big bonus. She thinks Kate is an investment banker—we have a small investment bank that is a subsidiary. Our officers are all partners. We make a little money, and it is a great cover for some investigations. Particularly for this job, because every jeweler and Ferrari dealer around worth his or her salt knows that investment bankers get huge year-end bonuses, or at least used to. Kate was supposed to get the confidence of Mostov. Apparently Mostov is some kind of dominating control freak, and Kate played her role well, so Sofia got friendly. Believe me, Kate likes men. She just doesn't have much time for them. But you can ask her about the whole St. Barth thing yourself. She is one hell of an investigator—and a very smart woman. Okay?"

Gerard sat speechless, looking at Reschio.

"I will get her, and you two can compare notes. We have a small dining room downstairs. Nothing too fancy. I will meet the two of you for lunch in about an hour."

As he got up to leave the conference room, Gerard got up as well and said, "This detective jumped to the wrong conclusion. I will apologize to Ms. York. As Sherlock Holmes said, 'Nothing is more misleading than an obvious fact.' I am pleased to work with her. Thank you for the explanation."

As he was waiting, Gerard thought to himself, *Now I am quoting Holmes. I must remember to tell Pierre.*

A few minutes later, Catherine came back to the room.

"Did Nick tell you about our conversation?" Gerard asked.

"Only that you saw me in St. Barth. He said that you would explain. That's all. Just exactly what is going on?"

Gerard repeated the story of his observations of her and Sofia, leaving out only the swimsuit-shopwindow episode.

"You saw the two of us on the beach?" Catherine asked.

"Yes, as I told Nick, I was having lunch at a table on the corner of the terrace when you arrived."

"That's pretty embarrassing. I have never gone topless before in my life. You saw me half-naked. That's a novel way to start a business collaboration."

"Catherine, first let me apologize. The suspicious policeman in me took over. I look forward very much to working with you. Second, you are a very attractive woman. I would know that even if I had not seen you on the beach."

"Thank you. I am not immune to flattery. Apology accepted. Let's get to work. Gerard, while you were on the island, did you visit Sofia Mostov's store?"

"Yes, I met her. She is an interesting woman."

"She clearly likes to be in control," Catherine said. "At lunch she laid out an itinerary for my afternoon of sightseeing and suggested a place for dinner. The next morning before I left, she tried to sell me an expensive piece of jewelry. Does she know you are a police officer?"

"No—I didn't even give her my last name. Nick said that she thinks you are an investment banker."

"She does—a good cover to buy expensive jewelry, isn't it?"

They worked through what they each knew about the robberies. Catherine was startled by the news of Valerie Pickett's murder. They then went through the Miami case. Catherine left the room while Gerard talked on the phone to Pierre, who had just gotten back from Naples. Reschio's assistant waited outside the room to take Gerard to lunch.

The Larsen and McTabbitt private dining room was on the same floor as the reception room. It was really a series of several rooms of various sizes, with only a small general dining room. It was clearly a place to hold business lunches, and Gerard thought, almost shuddering, business breakfasts. Though Gerard had been a hard worker all his life, he was an enthusiastic participant in the French tradition of long lunches. The pleasant wood-paneled dining rooms of L & M were a substantial step-up from the frequent sandwiches-at-the-desk routine of his FBI days. But he considered the American practice of breakfast meetings barbaric, and he had avoided them as much as possible in Washington.

Nick and Catherine were already in the small room to which Gerard was directed. As he was studying the menu and circling his choice, a short energetic baldheaded man entered the room.

Nick said, "Gerard, meet our CEO, Adam Bendel."

Rising to shake Bendel's hand, Gerard observed his perfectly cut gray flannel suit and thought, Oxford, Gerard's favorite American maker.

"It is my pleasure, Inspector," Bendel said. "I have heard much about you from Nick and Catherine. I understand that you ski. That is one of my favorite sports. I have a place in Aspen that I get to far too little, and I skied in Davos this winter—I go there each year for a conference. Where do you like to ski?"

With a shrug, Gerard said, "The French Alps are probably my favorite."

"Yes, they are very nice, but I find the snow more reliable and the runs more challenging in Switzerland, and the Italians seem to have the best food at their resorts. Have you ever gone helicopter skiing?"

Gerard responded that he had done some in Austria. Bendel interrupted him to say, "British Colombia is the best. But tell me, Inspector, besides skiing, what do you like to do when you are not catching criminals? Ha ha."

Nick interjected, "Don't you hunt birds, Gerard?"

As Gerard was about to respond, Bendel said, "I had the chance last year to hunt pheasants in Europe. Did you know, Inspector, that the Romans introduced pheasants to Italy? There haven't been any for a long time, but this fellow in Umbria has a lot of land and is renovating some old farmhouses, and he is reintroducing ringnecks. Some of my Italian friends invited me to join them on the inaugural hunt. Quite an experience—sure beats South Dakota for ambience—but I can't remember the name of the landowner."

"Might it be Count Tassé?" Gerard asked.

"That's it. Have you heard of him?"

"Yes, I had dinner with him in Paris last year. We are thinking of trying to introduce pheasants on our estate in the south of France."

"Oh, really." Bendel then took a bite of his salad and said, "Let's talk about the case." He emphasized how important this matter was to Larsen and McTabbitt.

In each of the robberies, the claim had been promptly paid, as was the practice at this level. The various firms that had different layers of coverage (L & M always having the last layer) were now out a total of close to $300 million. Part of the service that Larsen and McTabbitt provided to other insurance companies was that, if there was a hint of fraud, L & M pursued the matter more exhaustively than any other company in the industry. Although L & M fees were higher than the company's competitors, the high rate of recovery on fraudulent claims meant that its customers' net expense was actually lower than with the competition.

"Rate of recovery," Bendel said. "That's our competitive advantage,

Inspector. When I took over, one of my objectives was to increase profitability by investigating claims in a big way. Nick runs that operation, and Catherine is his ace investigator. Good group. My strategy is working. One of our secrets to success is that we do a lot of our investigative work on our own. Right, Nick?"

Nick nodded in agreement.

"The local cops," Bendel went on, "often don't place the same priority on insurance fraud that we do. No local political advantage for them."

"But," interjected Catherine, "this case is an exception because there are three different countries involved."

"Yup," Bendel agreed. "The more countries or even U.S. cities, the more complex it gets. I understand that both the FBI and Interpol speak highly of you. This case is an exception to the way we work, and you, Inspector, are part of the reason. We look forward to working with you, don't we?" Bendel looked in Nick and Catherine's direction, assuming assent. "It was nice talking with you. I'm on to another lunch—like to make at least two every day."

And with another handshake, he was gone. They were silent for a few minutes—Gerard thought to allow the air to reenter the room. Nick said, "Adam is very good with customers."

"I am sure he is," replied Gerard.

The three of them finished lunch and returned to the conference room. Gerard reported on his conversation with Pierre. The victim of the jewelry theft, an Italian named Guido Antonini, was a tough customer. Affiliated with the Camorra, the Neapolitan mafia, he was not cooperative. He had provided receipts and the insurance records, including appraisals. He questioned why the police wanted anything else. The theft happened at his villa on the Amalfi Coast when he was away. Someone cracked his safe. No staff was present. The alarm system wasn't always turned on, and apparently it had been off at the time of the robbery. He said his staff was loyal and wouldn't be part of a theft. Besides, because he was who he was, only a stranger would do this. Nobody in Naples would have the balls to rob him.

Antonini apparently was miffed at having a French cop present, and when Pierre tried to follow up on the somewhat routine questions of the Naples officer, Antonini pretty much ignored him. This annoyed Pierre, who had apparently suggested to Antonini at the end of the interview that he was always welcome in France, but if he as much as jaywalked, Pierre would see to it that the only French cuisine he enjoyed would be served on tin plates.

As he finished recounting the conversation with Pierre, Gerard shrugged his shoulders. Once the French embassy attaché who accompanied Pierre wrote his report, there would probably be a letter from the ambassador to the chief of police, which the chief would send to Gerard for inclusion in Pierre's file.

"What will you do with it?" asked Catherine.

"File it in my wastebasket, where I have placed other such letters," Gerard said. "Abou is an excellent cop, and, therefore, it should be no surprise to anyone that his record is clean."

Catherine and Gerard planned to review the files on the various pieces of stolen jewelry. Nick would meet them when they finished mid-afternoon for a summary. Before Nick left, Gerard said that he wanted to make amends for his *faux pas* in jumping to a conclusion about a relationship between Sofia and Catherine and take the two of them to dinner that night, if they were free. The New York restaurant, Le Bernadin, he said, had cuisine comparable to the best Paris establishments.

"I'm available. What about you, Kate?" said Nick.

Catherine nodded yes.

"Good," Nick said. "But Le Bernadin, Gerard, do you know how hard it is get a reservation there? We have been trying for quite a while. You have to call a month in advance, and then the only time they have open is like 10:00 PM. Too late for this guy. But if we can get in, could my wife, Amy, join us? She is in the city working today, and we had planned to spend the night at our apartment. She would love Le Bernadin. She's a lawyer, very discrete. We can talk in front of her."

"Let me make a call, and we will see about dinner." Gerard stepped out to one of the private telephone booths in the hall near the conference room and called the French consulate.

When Gerard came back, he and Catherine, now sitting shoulder-to-shoulder, went through the files. A fax from Pierre was brought into the room. It said that there was nothing new to report on the Pickett investigation, but Sofia Mostov had just returned to St. Barth. Also, Marcel Lefour wanted to talk to Gerard. Should Pierre arrange a lunch the day Gerard got back from New York? Pierre knew that Marcel would only talk to Gerard, and never over the phone. As Gerard and Catherine finished their work at 3:30 PM, Nick rejoined them and gave Gerard a folded note. "This was called in for you a few minutes ago," Nick said.

Opening the note, Gerard said, "We have a table at Le Bernadin at eight. I look forward to seeing the two of you there and to meeting Mrs. Reschio." As Gerard left, he shook Nick's hand and kissed Catherine's.

Later that evening, as Nick and Amy walked to their apartment on Central Park South from what they both agreed had been a wonderful meal at Le Bernadin, Nick asked, "What did you think of our French friend?"

"I thought he was charming."

"Oh, you women all think that a guy with a French accent and a great suit is charming. What was charming about him?"

"Nick, I love you with all my heart. You are a great guy. But you don't get charming."

"Okay, what part of it don't I get?"

"Did you notice how little Gerard talked about himself and how interested he was in who Catherine was, what she did, what her interests were?" Amy asked. "When she mentioned art, he asked her about what she collected, the exhibitions she enjoyed. Only in passing did it come out that he had a family collection that his mother hid from the Germans during the war. My guess is it wasn't *Saturday Evening Post* covers!

"He seemed genuinely curious about why I had gone back to law practice and the kind of work I did. Women like men who are interested in them and don't spend the dinner talking about themselves. He asked you about your Marine service. We didn't need three or four macho Marine stories, all of which Kate and I have heard. The guy has skied all over the world. He has been a ski instructor. The blow-by-blow account of your broken leg twenty years ago at Stowe probably didn't enthrall him. Did you notice when I asked him about his work, he talked about how the police forces in France are changing with the addition of more women and then turned it right back to me. He asked me what it was like to be one of the first women in an old firm when I got out of law school and what the obstacles were to me as a woman becoming a partner. That's charming, not hand kissing or flattery—but it didn't hurt to notice what we were wearing and compliment us on it. But enough—you get my point—and you aren't going to change, you big lug."

Then she stopped on the sidewalk and gave him a kiss. "Didn't Catherine look pretty tonight?" Amy said.

"Right, she went home early from the office to change. That lavender dress certainly fit her in the right places."

"Catherine is a beautiful woman. The dress was Armani. Remember, Gerard asked her if it was an Armani?"

"Right. How did he know that?" Nick asked.

"He probably didn't. But if it was, he got an *A* for being with it, and if it wasn't, Catherine would feel good because whatever she paid for the dress, it would have been less than if it was an Armani."

"You folks are way over my head. I think she likes him. He is solid— for a Frenchman. Getting the Le Bernadin reservation on a few hours' notice was pretty impressive, and he is on these jewelry robberies. One of them may have turned into a homicide. We are back to our place, mademoiselle—how's that?"

"Not bad, but, dear, I haven't been a mademoiselle for a few years."

Gerard and Catherine finished their work late the next morning and met again with Nick. The three decided that it might make sense for Catherine to come to Paris in a week or so to look at the crime scenes and coordinate with the L & M Paris office. Gerard said that he and his department would be glad to cooperate, and Catherine said she would decide about the trip next week.

Catherine asked Gerard what time his flight to Paris was, and he replied that he was taking a late afternoon flight.

"Good," she said, "we have time for lunch. My treat."

They went to lunch at a Japanese restaurant on East Forty-fourth where they together sampled a number of dishes. Catherine thought that it had been a long time since she had eaten off the same plate as anyone.

By five thirty, Gerard was sitting in his first-class seat, sipping a glass of champagne and thinking how much he liked Catherine's perfume.

CHAPTER TWELVE
St. Barth

SOFIA WAS NOT HAPPY. She was almost shouting into her cell phone, even though the connection to Cuba was unusually good. "Roberto, that *pinga,* Guido Antonini, has paid us not even one million euros. He owes us twenty million more, and he is making noises I don't like. Now he is worried that the police are suspicious of him because some French cop shows up in Naples and asks him a few questions. This isn't a French case, it is an Italian one, and Guido owns half the force in Naples. I told him that we are getting tired of waiting and to pay his debts. He says in that oily English of his that I should come over, and we will talk about it. What's there to talk about? A deal is a deal."

"At least Perez has paid us, and he seems to be satisfied with the way the robbery of his Paris house was staged," Roberto said.

"My former colleagues are very good at making something that never happened look like it did happen."

"Yes, they are. But if Perez finds out that Antonini hasn't paid us, there could be big trouble."

"You are right about that, Roberto."

"If he finds out—and he will—there will be hell to pay. He will want his money back. It will be a matter of pride with him. He will probably want more than what he paid us. I can hear him now going on about getting paid for his trouble. Perez is not someone to fool around with. And Antonini cannot be trusted to keep his mouth shut if he thinks he has cheated us. We have to deal with the problem."

Sofia, trying to control her anger at Antonini, clenched her phone so hard her hand hurt. "I know. I know. Boris and I are going to Zurich to meet with our tight-assed Swiss bankers. Then we are going to the workshop in Rome. I think I will also go to Naples to meet our friend, Guido, and do a little collecting."

"Be careful. He is a snake."

"I have dealt with snakes before."

CHAPTER THIRTEEN
Zurich

THE SQUARE NEAR THE Baur au Lac hotel in Zurich was bathed in the clear light of a Swiss early summer morning. Sitting at a small table, Sofia and Boris were treating themselves to creamy cappuccino and local pastries. They talked about their upcoming meetings with their bankers and the train trip to Rome later in the day.

Sofia described her phone conversation with Guido. Boris said, "Ah, *plemyanitsa*, you are so focused, so strong, yet I remember the frightened twelve-year-old I met at the Moscow airport on a cold March day."

"Yes, I will never forget that day and how alone I felt until I saw you. And it was so cold. I had never been outside of Cuba, and I had never seen snow, but I was by then cold inside all the time. I hadn't seen my father for a year. Then the call came from you to my mother that he was dead. No other information. My mother screamed and cried for three days. A month later, neighbors came to the apartment with a police officer to tell me that my mother had drowned. No other information. A desultory hug. Some food. And then they left. I sat in that apartment for two days. I couldn't cry. I couldn't walk out the door. I will never forget that feeling. It was as if I was suspended in time and space. My mother was an only child, and her parents were dead. There were no relatives in Cuba. No one. Then the phone rang. It was you. My Uncle Boris."

"I remember that call. I expected a scared little voice. I hadn't been in Cuba for almost a year, and the last time I saw you was a trip to the beach."

"You built a sand Kremlin for me," Sofia said.

"Yes, I didn't realize until later how appropriate my choice of building materials was. Think of it—I was into irony, and I didn't know it! On the phone I heard the voice, not of the girl I remembered, but that of a young woman who spoke excellent Russian with that soft Spanish accent. You still have it, you know."

"My father always insisted that we speak Russian at home. He said that he couldn't be critical of my accent because my Russian was so much better than his Spanish."

"You have always had a gift for language," Boris said. "Your French is perfect. I live in Paris, and when I ordered a meal in a restaurant a few days ago, the waiter asked me how the weather was in Moscow!"

"I can't remember much of that call, but you did tell me that I was coming to Moscow. Then that woman from the Russian embassy came to the apartment, helped me pack, took me to dinner, stayed with me that night and drove me to the airport. I felt your love and caring that day, and I still feel it. But I will tell you something about that flight that I have never before mentioned. Not only was I scared because I was going to an unknown place and I felt so alone, but I had no money with me. Not a peso. Not a ruble. I felt helpless, and I have never forgotten how I felt that day. Maybe that is why I love money so much. But once you took me in, you always made sure I had money in my pocket. And we lived comfortably in Moscow. I never felt poor there."

"In those days, the organization took care of its own."

"Talking about the organization, I have never asked you when you decided that I should join," Sofia said.

"When I saw you at the Moscow airport that morning. In a year, you had grown taller, and you had the carriage and strength of your father. But more importantly, you were tough. No tears, no looking back. In a few weeks, with new clothes and those fur-lined boots you loved, you looked like you had lived in Moscow all your life. By the time you were fifteen, you had taken three years of English in school, were a track star and were becoming a better shot than I was. The sports authority wanted to take you and turn you into one of their super athletes."

"You saved me from discus throwing. These shoulders. I still avoid strapless dresses."

"It wasn't lost on us that you were becoming a beautiful woman."

"Wasn't it when I was about sixteen that you told me what happened to my father?" Sofia asked.

"Probably. I had to be careful. You don't tell a twelve-year-old that her father was a Soviet intelligence agent killed in mysterious circumstances while on a mission to Mongolia."

"You never told me that my mother killed herself. You didn't have to. I knew it the day she died."

"I don't think you grieved until I took you back to Cuba when you were perhaps eighteen, and you looked through those boxes of her stuff."

"With all my jewelry, that bracelet my father gave her is still my favorite. She was beautiful. My father was her life. He traveled all through the Caribbean and Central America. I thought he was a salesman."

"He was—and a good one. He recruited and ran agents all through the region. He was one of the best, and he was one tough guy. I remember once in Nicaragua, the locals were giving us a hard time as we got up to leave a meeting. One of them stood in the door and tried to stop us from leaving. There were three of us and maybe ten or twelve of them. Your dad took the guy down with a knee and a punch. We left."

"My mother was sad when he was traveling, and she came alive when he came back," Sofia said. She set her jaw, and her eyes focused on Boris. "I loved her, but she was weak. I will never be dependent on a man—or anyone else—for my happiness or my support. That is why having a lot of money—more than I could make selling bracelets to tourists—is such a passion for me."

Boris was silent for a long time. Then he said, "We always said that the best agents were orphans, and you became an orphan at twelve and an adult at the same time."

CHAPTER FOURTEEN
Italy

S OFIA AND BORIS TRAVELED to Rome on the train and later that evening checked into the Hassler Hotel near Rome's Spanish Steps. Before leaving Zurich, Sofia had called Guido Antonini. He was delighted that she was to visit him. Guido, who saw every woman he met as a potential conquest, had put Sofia on the top of his list. Short and very fat, Guido often pursued tall, slender women. The maxim that opposites attract generally worked only one way, and not to Guido's favor. However, his approach was to overcome his attraction deficit with money, jewelry, alcohol, drugs and occasional brute force.

Guido asked Sofia if she had ever been to the Amalfi Coast, south of Naples. Sofia had visited that beautiful area on several occasions, and she knew Antonini had a villa in the Positano area. But she said she had not, knowing that her response would produce an invitation to his villa. And predicting how his mind worked, she expected him to tell her that he would send the villa staff away for the night so they would not be overheard discussing their business.

Sofia Mostov had survived and prospered by using all her gifts, including an ability to think one or two steps ahead of the people she dealt with. Boris Voroshilov always told her that she would have been a superb chess player. It was the Russian in her, he said. Antonini followed her script almost to the word, substituting as the expected reason for the staff's night off, "so that we can get to know each other better." Sofia's skin crawled. *The bastard*, she thought, *isn't even couth enough to put up a front.*

Boris, Sofia and the key people from the workshops in Rome and Tel

Aviv spent the morning reviewing designs for new jewelry. They discussed the size and cut of various gemstones. Both workshop managers, Alfredo in Rome and Avi in Tel Aviv, were impressed with the ability of Sofia, as the owner of the companies that controlled the workshops, and Boris, who they viewed as another principal, to procure quickly the gemstones in the varieties, colors, sizes and cuts that were called for in the designs. By the time Alfredo and Avi finished the projects they were working on, Boris said he would provide them with what they needed for the new pieces.

Following the morning meeting, Boris and Sofia had an early lunch at a small seafood restaurant close to the Pantheon. As they walked to the car after lunch, Boris handed Sofia a package. "A woman may need some protection even in a place as beautiful as the Amalfi Coast," he said.

Sofia borrowed a car from the Roman workshop manager on the pretense that she wanted to go to Naples for the day to study some of the jewelry in the Pompeii museum. She headed south on the *autostrada* around Naples to the Amalfi Coast and Positano. Taking her time, she arrived at Antonini's villa at six in the evening. The Amalfi Coast is justly famous for its breathtaking scenery. Cliffs jutted almost straight up from the Gulf of Salerno, and Sofia admired the islands in the distance, picturesque fishing villages on the seashore at the bottom of valleys, and villas built into the sides of steep, rocky hills.

Antonini was waiting for her. His silver Maserati Quattroporte was parked in the driveway. His villa was just off the road that hugged the Amalfi Coast, high on a hill above the Hotel San Pietro. The villa, about five miles from the town of Positano, had a commanding view of the sea and the coast. On a large terrace overlooking the sea, there was a table set out with an elaborate buffet, champagne in a silver bucket, other wines and a large plate of what looked like caviar.

Guido greeted Sofia with a hug that lasted too long and offered her a drink. Not intending to eat or drink anything offered by Guido, Sofia said that she was thirsty from the drive and, for now, would just finish the bottle of water in her large purse.

Guido insisted on giving her a tour of his villa. It was done in excessive amounts of gold leaf and marble. Sofia thought it was filled with enough furniture to have provided some Naples interior designer an early retirement. Guido led her through the villa, his arm around her waist.

He talked nonstop, trying to impress Sofia with how much things had cost. The last stop on the tour was his bedroom. On the second floor of the villa, it was a large room with floor-to-ceiling doors opening onto the terrace, with a view of the sea. The bed was huge and, as Sofia's eyes took in the expansive room, she saw that the ceiling above the bed was a large mirror. One wall was covered with murals depicting men and women, men and men, and women and women in a variety of sexual acts. Guido flicked on a light switch, and the mural was bathed in soft white light which gradually turned to red. He said it had taken the artist six months to complete the mural. He pressed another switch, and a large TV screen came up from the foot of the bed. His bathroom, which he insisted on showing her, featured a large whirlpool bath that also faced the sea.

As they walked out of the bedroom, Sofia thought he would try to throw her on the bed, but he limited himself to running his hand down her back and a bit lower. She wondered how long it would take her to break his arm.

They returned to the terrace, and Guido again offered her a drink and food. He apologized for the informal nature of the meal, but he said—repeating himself—that he had given the staff the night off.

"Guido, before we have what I am sure will be a memorable dinner and evening, we have some business to discuss."

"Ah, Sofia, you put too high a priority on business. We Italians work only to enjoy life, and this is a night to enjoy."

"It is hard for me to enjoy life with someone who owes me more than twenty million euros. You have received your insurance settlement, and you have paid me nothing."

"It is complicated," Guido said. "I have many obligations, and I have to be careful. As I told you, I was visited by the police again, and this time the Italian investigator was accompanied by a French detective who was a really hard type. If I pay you more for the pieces than you invoiced me, I will create a paper trail for the police to follow."

"You haven't even paid the full invoices, and they were for more than one million euros. You remember the plan."

They stood face-to-face on the terrace as the light faded, almost like two boxers in a ring. For a moment the only sound was the surf crashing into the cliffs below the villa. Her voice rising as she fought to control her anger, Sofia went over their arrangement. His records were to be modified so it appeared that much of the stolen jewelry had been acquired from sources other than Sofia. Then he was to have his whole collection reappraised with the explanation that prices had gone up recently. The robbery was to be reported and the insurance proceeds divided fifty-fifty.

"Sending twenty million euros to my Swiss bank accounts will not create a paper trail, since it will come in smaller amounts from various of your Swiss accounts and go to several of mine," Sofia said. "The transactions among the Swiss banks will be covered by bank secrecy. But we have talked about all this before. Now is the time to arrange payment."

"I told you, I have many obligations. The amount of money you want is not available to me now. I paid you almost one million euros. Your costs are covered. Perhaps I can cut you in on some other deals, and you will get your money that way. We can talk more about this in the morning. Maybe by then I will think of a way to get you some more money quicker." He smiled and then said, "But for now, let us eat, have some champagne and enjoy my villa and this beautiful evening. Get comfortable. Take your driving gloves off, and let me take your jacket."

Sofia took a deep breath to try to control her rage and hoped that the gathering dusk obscured her red face.

"Antonini, don't toy with me. This visit is about money that you owe me, not about drinking champagne. I am not leaving until we resolve this—and it won't be in the bedroom of your vulgar villa but right here and right now."

The smile on Antonini's face quickly became a snarl as he started to move even closer to her. With an almost guttural harshness, he said, "I will pay you when I decide to pay you—if at all. Now get out of my house before I put my hands around your lovely neck and ... "

As he approached her, Sofia took Boris's Beretta Tomcat out of her jacket pocket and fired two shots into Antonini's forehead and one into his chest. After confirming that he had taken his last breath, she grabbed his body by the legs, hauled it to the stone wall at the end of the terrace, lifted it up and over the wall and watched as Antonini's body somersaulted down the four-hundred-foot cliff to the rocky beach below.

Taking only a minute to catch her breath, Sofia took a napkin from the buffet table and mopped up whatever bone and brain fragments were large enough to catch her eye. She pocketed the three spent cartridge casings and walked out to her car, her eyes resting for a moment on Guido's silver Maserati.

Four-and-a-half hours later, Sofia parked the car in front of the workshop and walked back to the Hassler to a good night's sleep. Ahead of her was one more day and night in Rome, then a morning train ride to Zurich and the first leg of the three flights that would take her back to St. Barth.

CHAPTER FIFTEEN

Paris

BACK IN PARIS FROM New York, Gerard had arranged to meet Marcel Lefour for lunch. All his meetings with Lefour were over meals. Marcel liked to eat, and he liked that Gerard always paid. The restaurant Gerard chose was located on the Rue Christine in Saint-Germain, just a short walk from his apartment. It met Marcel's requirement of serving food that he considered classically French.

Convinced that fresh air and sunshine was the best antidote to jet lag, Gerard took a roundabout route to lunch. Walking to the east end of the Île Saint-Louis, he crossed the Pont de Sully. He enjoyed the view of the French architect Jean Nouvel's modernist Institute of the Arab World as he crossed the bridge. Peeking into a few bookstores in the university neighborhood just beyond, he walked through the heart of the left bank along the Rue des Écoles until he reached the Boulevard Saint-Michel. The street turned back toward the river, passing the museum of medieval art in the old Hôtel de Cluny. Gerard loved the bustle, the cafés, the shops and Boulevard Saint-Michel itself as it bisected the left bank, following the route of the old Roman road. He then crossed the boulevard and walked through narrow streets roughly parallel to the river until he reached the restaurant. A one-hour stroll through the heart of his beloved Paris rejuvenated him more than a long nap.

Marcel was seated at a table near the front of the restaurant when Gerard arrived. Even though Gerard was early for their reservation, he knew Marcel would be there. No matter how early Gerard was to one of their meals, Marcel was always there first, seated at a good table.

Dispensing this time with snails, Marcel ordered onion soup for a first course and then *andouillete*, a sausage in a mustard and cream sauce. Gerard ordered one of his favorites to start, a salad of endive with crumbled Roquefort cheese, followed by a filet of sole with crayfish. Two half carafes of the restaurant's excellent house wine soon appeared, one a Bordeaux, another a Chablis.

Marcel's soup arrived, the dark golden brown of the caramelized onions giving off a wonderful smell of onions and cheese as Marcel punctured the cheese and bread on top of the crock with his spoon. When the *andouillete* arrived, Gerard couldn't resist tasting the strongly flavored sausage, enhanced by the savory combination of the cream and mustard sauce. Gerard decided that his sole needed a heartier sauce. It seemed a bit dainty compared to Marcel's choices.

"So, what goes, Marcel?" Gerard asked.

"Your jewels have not shown up in Paris, Amsterdam, Rome, Moscow or Marseilles. And I am surprised. With this much stuff, you usually see pieces come into the market soon after the heist. The faster it moves two or three steps from the perp, the harder it is to trace. And you would certainly expect to hear about some of those big stones that weren't in settings. Of course it could have been moved to South America, Vegas or Hong Kong, but it's a lot safer to move hot items first inside Europe—wonderful open borders and all that."

Marcel, thought Gerard, often could get information faster than the police. "What about Pickett?" Gerard asked.

"A real loner—just stayed in his store and sold overpriced pieces to rich people. Had a reputation for unusual jewelry with real big price tags. Bought expensive wines. Had a nice place off the Rue de Courcelles—would hold parties for his customers. But not a guy who gambled, used drugs or chased women, or men, as far as I can determine. Did you find anything in his house?"

Gerard smiled. "Now, that's police business, but if you are asking about the stolen merchandise, it wasn't there."

"Okay. Gerard, tell me how much do you know about the guy who got ripped off for the big stash over in the Sixteenth?"

"You mean Francesco Perez? We haven't been able to interview him. He's a Mexican, super rich, he has places in Mexico City, down near Acapulco, Miami and New York, plus the big Paris house. We have been talking with his lawyer here. He is supposedly an international investor— probably not too clean."

"And that's it?"

"Yes," Gerard said apprehensively—he was thinking that Marcel knew more about Perez than he did.

"I thought you were such an ace cop," growled Marcel as he dug into his *andouillete*, sopping up the sauce in hunks of bread. "Not clean doesn't begin to describe Perez. Your guy is a big-time dealer, has a major piece of the white powder business out of Colombia as it passes through Mexico. He ought to call his places here and in Miami and New York, Casa Money-Laundering."

"We suspected something, but we had no reason to check him out. He doesn't appear to do any of his business here. All the paperwork on the jewelry was perfect—photos, insurance appraisals. It looked like a professional burglary—maybe too professional," Gerard mumbled almost to himself.

Marcel ate vigorously and signaled the waiter for a cheese plate and more red wine. Gerard sat quietly for a few minutes. "You know, Marcel, this case is starting to smell worse than that cheese you like so much."

"Tomme de Savoie is a damned national treasure. Your father loved it, and he was a French patriot. When he was in London, I think what he missed most about France other than your sister and sainted mother was the cheese. He once told me that the British couldn't even make a decent stilton cheese—and they invented the stuff. He would send back the stilton cheese in London restaurants—their own cheese. What a man he was."

"Maybe the reason I don't like that cheese is a form of youthful rebellion. The son separating from the father and all that stuff."

"I wouldn't know. My father took the initiative and separated from me and my mother when I was five years old—the son of a bitch."

"Well, Marcel, what smells is this: Three of the largest jewel robberies in Europe for many years. Two from private owners. One a mafioso from Naples, now the other apparently an international drug dealer. The third is from a jewelry store, and the jeweler was just murdered. Very high-end jewels, and much of it sourced from the same supplier. The American insurance investigators told me that there was another robbery of a Miami jeweler that may be part of the same pattern."

"You better check to see if the Miami guy is connected to Perez. This Perez is a real bad guy."

They finished lunch, and Gerard walked directly to his office. He went through paperwork that had accumulated in his absence while impatiently waiting until it was eight thirty in the morning in New York. As he picked up the phone to dial Catherine's office, he felt an excitement out of proportion to the news about Perez. *This American woman,* he thought, *has a delayed effect on me.*

When Gerard finished telling Catherine about his conversation with Marcel, she immediately made the connection between Perez's Miami condo and the jewelry store robbery. She was going to think about how to proceed, and she reminded Gerard about the firm's reluctance to share much information with local police departments; they were particularly cautious with the Miami PD.

"Ah, so I should be flattered that you are cooperating with us," Gerard said.

"Oh, stop fishing for a compliment. Nick thinks you are great and, as you I am sure picked up on, he is not a fan of your country."

"And you?"

"You just don't stop, do you? I like your taste in restaurants." And then she added, "And in ties, too."

"Why don't you hold off for now on calling the Miami police," Gerard said. "Let me see what I can find out from the FBI. If Perez is the player that Marcel thinks he is—and his information is usually very reliable—they will know about him. Have you considered further coming to Paris?"

"No, let's see how this case develops in the next few days."

Feeling disappointed at her response, Gerard finished the conversation. He sat at his desk staring at the phone—feeling something that he hadn't felt for a long time. He admitted it to himself: *I miss her.*

CHAPTER SIXTEEN
East of Rennes, Brittany

IERRE AND JEAN-MICHEL TOURNIER, a detective who worked with Pierre and Gerard, approached Valerie Pickett's farmhouse in the late morning. They were followed by a car with two gendarmes from Rennes. Set at the edge of a meadow and bordered by woods, the farmhouse was a small, restored, old Breton stone building. It had one story with a steep roof and a garden and terrace off to one side.

The house was several miles from the nearest town and, they estimated, about an hour-and-a-half drive from the French coast and the area around Saint-Malo.

"A nice quiet place to rest from the rigors of selling expensive jewelry to rich people," said Pierre. "Look, Jean-Michel, he even has a swimming pool."

The detectives knocked on the door while the Rennes officers walked around the back. Confirming that no one was in the house or in a small outbuilding on the property, Pierre motioned to Jean-Michel to place the official notice authorizing the search on the door and waved off one of the young gendarmes who was about to remove the hinges of the locked front door.

"One of my specialties," said Pierre as he expertly picked the lock and opened the door.

Donning gloves, the four policemen began to search the house, opening drawers, feeling walls for hidden safes, examining the attic and removing items from cabinets. The house had three bedrooms, a kitchen, a living area and a room off the living area that could be a study, except that it had almost no furniture in it. The officers probed each upholstered piece, looking for anything that might be hidden in a cushion or seat back.

As the two gendarmes headed out to search the garage and outbuilding, Pierre stood looking at the one room that was almost bare. "Jean-Michel, what seems strange about this room?" Pierre asked.

Looking around, Jean-Michel shrugged his shoulders and said, "Nothing, it is just an empty room."

"But why would this room have so little furniture, and why should it have what appears to be a newly refinished wood floor and baseboards?"

"I don't know," responded Jean-Michel. "Maybe there was some damage."

"Perhaps, but it seems out of place to have a rug in the middle of the floor with a table. Every other room in the house has a lot of furniture in it. It looks like it was recently redone—and has no apparent function. Why would someone come in here to sit? If Pickett redid the room and was going to buy new furniture, why wouldn't he leave it empty until the new furniture arrived?"

Jean-Michel interrupted, "Who knows what was on Pickett's mind? We will never know what his decorating plans were. We should see how our colleagues are doing and, if they find nothing, consider our next steps."

Pierre scratched his chin and mumbled something. Jean-Michel said, "What did you say, Pierre?"

"Oh, nothing. I was just thinking about Holmes always saying to be wary of the obvious." And then walking, into the room, Pierre said, "Help me move this table and rug." The table, chairs and rug moved off to one side, Pierre sat down on his knees and felt the area. "Jean-Michel, please ask the Rennes cops to come in here and bring that big toolbox they put in the trunk of their car."

With the three other officers watching him, Pierre began to pry up the floorboards that had been under the rug. Asked what he was doing, Pierre pointed out that most of the wood flooring in the room ran in a series of one-piece planks from one wall to the other. He showed his observers that, under the table, six of the planks had been cut so that for each plank there were three pieces of wood, carefully joined together. Now all four of the officers worked quickly to remove the centerpieces.

Underneath the removed flooring, there was a cavity, and in the cavity, a large metal box tightly wrapped in plastic. They lifted it out, and Jean-Michel took several photographs. They carefully removed the plastic wrapping and opened the metal box. In it were a number of black felt bags, many bearing the name, *Valerie Pickett, Bijoutier.*

Pierre opened one and took out a heavily jeweled bracelet. He opened another and held in his gloved hand three large diamonds. He examined several other bags, each containing a piece of jewelry or an unset stone.

No one said a word. Then Jean-Michel hugged Pierre. "You saw what no one else saw. What is it you always talk about? Deduction. That was deduction."

"Thank you," said Pierre. "While I would be surprised if this is not the supposed stolen merchandise, we won't be sure until we check it, piece by piece, against the inventory produced by Pickett. I don't want to do that here, so we will immediately take this box to Paris."

Pierre called the police office in Rennes and asked them to send more officers to secure the scene and maintain a watch on the house. The two gendarmes would remain. He and Jean-Michel would leave for Paris.

When Pierre was finished giving instructions, he sat down for a moment and took a long drink of water. Then he said to himself, *Thank you, Mr. Holmes, and now I will breathe.*

As Gerard was preparing to leave the office, the phone rang. Pierre Abou's familiar Marseilles accent came through the receiver. "You remember the Holmes story about the barking dog or the dog that didn't bark. Was it the 'Hound of the Baskervilles'?"

"No, it was 'Silver Blaze.' You are calling me from your car phone to talk about Sherlock Holmes?"

"Actually, something even more important. When I was searching Pickett's farmhouse, I noticed a room that had only a few pieces of furniture in it, and the floor looked new. That seemed odd. Why an empty room with only a table, two chairs and a rug? And I thought of the Holmes story about the dog. What did Holmes call it—a 'curious incident'?"

"Okay, Pierre. Yes. Holmes called it a curious incident of the dog at night, and the police inspector said something like, 'The dog did nothing in the night.'"

"And then Holmes said, 'That was the curious incident.'"

"Very good, Pierre, but might I ask where you are going with this?"

"Since it was curious that there were only these chairs, a table and rug, I moved them. Some of the floorboards looked different than the rest, so we pried them up. Underneath there was a large metal case tightly wrapped in plastic. It was—how do the Americans say it?—the jackpot. I don't know if it is all here, but I think it is likely that most of the jewelry stolen from Pickett's store was buried under the floor in his country house."

Gerard was silent for a minute. *"Incroyable.* A great piece of police work, Abou. Where are you now?"

"Just west of Rennes. I have Jean-Michel with me. The Rennes cops are securing the farmhouse."

"Okay, I will have you met by some escort cars. I will call you as soon as I have the rendezvous point. I will try to have them meet you before you get to Le Mans."

Gerard made a call to arrange Abou's escort. While he had no reason to suspect that someone would try to intercept Pierre and the jewels, the police might have been observed searching Pickett's house. Nothing about this case was predictable. If there was to be a move on the jewels, the most likely place would be when Pierre and Jean-Michel were stopped at a traffic light or slowed by traffic. Gerard chose to have two marked police cars, lights flashing and sirens blaring, meet Abou and escort him, one in front, one bringing up the rear. The three cars would proceed to Paris at high speeds and be met by two additional motorcycle officers to lead the convoy through the always-congested Paris streets, made even busier because it would be rush hour.

Gerard asked for the department's senior evidence registrar and another detective to join him when the cars arrived. His assistant, who was also about to leave for the day, walked over to a shop on the Île Saint-Louis, just across the Pont Saint-Louis, and brought him back a sandwich, which he ate at his desk. The day that had begun for him over the Atlantic was not likely to end soon.

CHAPTER SEVENTEEN
Paris

FOR PARISIANS AND VISITORS alike, the sound of sirens and the sight of a line of speeding cars with flashing lights is just another component of the urban scene. So the three police cars and two motorcycles speeding through the city probably registered only in that section of most urbanite's consciousness reserved for the barely noticed routine of daily life. But for Gerard, the sight of the little convoy pulling into the garage of the police headquarters building was intensely exciting. He hugged Pierre, whose crooked grin spread across his entire face, as two officers loaded the heavy lead box onto a dolly and wheeled it through two security doors to an elevator and into a small windowless room. With the box on the table, Gerard motioned to Pierre to open it. The small room was crowded with Gerard, Pierre, the senior detective Gerard had asked to be present, the evidence registrar and the registrar's assistant, who had a camera.

None of the people in the room talked—later Gerard wondered if anyone had even breathed—as Pierre undid the box's latch. The box was filled with black felt bags of various shapes, most of the bags imprinted with the logo of Valerie Pickett's store. As each bag was removed by the registrar, wearing white gloves, it was dusted for fingerprints, and then the process was repeated for each piece of jewelry. The contents were then photographed and compared to the insurance list from the theft and Pickett's inventory.

The first piece was a pendant the shape of an oak leaf, with white diamonds and sapphires set in platinum. The whole piece was outlined in black diamonds, the same material as the leaf stem. Each white diamond appeared to Gerard to be cut to reflect the light of the adjacent sapphire, each of which was cut in the cabochon style, so that they appeared dome-shaped.

The next piece was a necklace of sapphires of different colors, created as a series of butterflies. There was a large white diamond in the center, connected by gold rings set with small diamonds. Gerard counted ten butterflies composed of a total of thirty sapphires. Each butterfly had a red center sapphire, but the surrounding sapphires were shades of blue, green, pink, violet and even gray stones.

Several bags revealed unset stones, including large blue and yellow diamonds and some large rubies that Gerard estimated were four or five carats and of a color he thought to be almost vermillion.

After each piece was photographed and inventoried, Gerard and the registrar signed the list, the other senior detective witnessed their signatures, and the pieces were placed in department evidence boxes along with the now-empty lead box which Pierre had dusted for fingerprints in Pickett's farmhouse. Everything was then hauled off to the secure evidence rooms in the bowels of the building.

The whole process took several hours. At the conclusion, it was obvious that every piece reported stolen was in the lead box. Gerard, now thoroughly exhausted, went back to his office and called Catherine in New York. It was three in the afternoon in New York, and her assistant said Catherine was out. Did she have a cell phone? Yes, and Gerard called the number. Catherine answered it after several rings; he could barely hear her over the sound of traffic.

"Where are you?" he asked.

"On Fifth Avenue, walking back to the office."

"How far from the office?"

"About ten minutes. Why do you ask?"

"Can you call me at my office as soon as you reach yours?"

"Sure," Catherine said. "You are working late."

"I know. Please call as soon as you reach your office. It is very important."

Those minutes were among the longest in Gerard's life. And actually, they were almost thirty minutes. Catherine, like most New Yorkers, had underestimated the time it took to get from one New York location to another, whether on foot or by subway or taxi.

Gerard felt his eyes start to close when the sound of the phone ringing startled him.

"It's Catherine. What is so important?"

Gerard described the find at the Pickett farmhouse, Abou's initial determination that it was a significant cache of jewelry and his surmise that it was indeed the stolen jewels, the trip to the department, the inventory and the conclusion.

"It must have been incredibly exciting to open that box."

"Catherine, I have never experienced buried treasure, but that is what I imagine it must feel like."

"Well, it was buried, and at $80 million, it is sure a treasure."

"The question is, who are the pirates?" Gerard said.

"Indeed—and how do we get our $80 million back? Well, this does it. I'm coming to Paris. I can't leave until Sunday, but I will send you my schedule tomorrow. I want to give your man, Abou, a kiss."

It was dark as Gerard made the short walk to his apartment. Gerard stopped and looked at the great cathedral. He would never tire of the lights illuminating the stones of Notre-Dame's flying buttresses, bathing them in an almost ethereal soft light that made the stones look white. The Rue Saint-Louis was almost deserted, and he heard his footsteps echoing off the walls of the buildings that lined that ancient street. He had made that walk so many times over so many years. Tonight he felt alone. He was glad Catherine York was coming to Paris.

CHAPTER EIGHTEEN
New York

THE RESTAURANT ON GREENWICH Street in Tribeca was one of their favorite meeting places. Judy Weiss had been a close friend of Catherine's since college. They were at ease with each other and could share intelligence about who was doing the best pedicures in Manhattan in one breath and talk about New York politics or the gallery scene in the next. As Judy juggled being a mother, a wife and an investment banker, Catherine was there to support her. When Catherine went through the breakup of a five-year relationship, Catherine called Judy her "sanity net."

Their routine was that Judy would walk to the restaurant from her Wall Street office and, after a long dinner, they would take a cab home together. Judy's Park Avenue apartment was only a few blocks from Catherine's apartment.

Catherine was always interested in the exploits of Judy's two young sons, and Judy had a reminiscent interest in Catherine's single life. Catherine was working on a complex financial fraud case, so Catherine was particularly eager to get Judy's Wall Street insights.

As they finished that topic, Judy said, "How is your social life?"

"If you consider gallery openings, an occasional party and business entertaining a social life, it's great."

"No new men?"

"No. And I am not looking. I like my independence—no pouting, passive-aggressive Howard to tiptoe around."

"Catherine, you have to forget about Howard. He was a jerk. It was always all about him. He could never get over the fact that you were a lot more successful—and interesting—than he was."

"You know, I am over him. I really am. It was painful. I don't deny that. And sometimes I have pangs about what it could have been. But I think I am a pretty optimistic person, and I try to live each day and not look back. It is lonely sometimes, but I hate the dating scene."

"You've given up on men?" Judy asked.

"No, not really, but I wouldn't get serious again with someone I didn't want to spend the rest of my life with. I'm not unrealistic—I know all relationships involve compromises—but right now, at least, I don't have the energy to make the journey from the guys I seem to run into along the way to Prince Charming."

"Relationships sure do involve compromises. I love Mike, and our life together is wonderful. Yet there are days that I am really pissed at him."

"I think you just defined a good marriage."

The conversation turned to their meal and the New York restaurants that were their current favorites. They talked a bit about some of the deals Judy was working on and swapped some investment ideas.

Catherine said that she was going to Paris on business.

"Is that the same case you said that French detective was coming to New York on?" Judy asked.

"Yeah. Talking about restaurants, he took Nick, Amy and me to Le Bernadin—got the reservation on a few hours notice!"

"Pretty cool."

"I think he was making up for considering me some sort of criminal." Catherine related the St. Barth episode, which Judy thought was quite funny.

"So what's he like—the tough cop type?"

"Actually, he is not at all what one would expect. He's older—probably sixty or so, very handsome and distinguished-looking. You should see the way he dresses. And—get this—he is a dollar- or euro-a-year man. Comes from an old French family—does police work because he likes it."

"Well, you described him, but what is he like? How do you feel about him? You know, Catherine—feelings."

"Judy, we worked together for a day and a half. He was professional in the office and quite nice at dinner, but I don't have any feelings about him—one way or the other."

"Will you see him in Paris?"

"Of course, there has been a breakthrough in the case, so we will be working on it. It's business—that is all!"

CHAPTER NINETEEN
Paris

THE NEXT MORNING, GERARD truncated his usual Saturday morning routine of a leisurely stroll through Paris and, after working out, walked to his office. Abou had gone back to Pickett's Paris apartment with two of the department's investigators to search it again and to interview some of the neighbors.

Talking to Abou on his cell phone, Gerard said that, in the excitement of yesterday, he had forgotten to tell Abou that he had received a message from the St. Barth chief that Sofia Mostov had left the island. Her ticket was to Zurich; she was due back on St. Barth early next week.

"What is she doing in Switzerland for almost five days?"

"I don't know, Pierre. Maybe it takes her that long to count her money. Call me when you are finished. Oh, I also got an e-mail from Catherine York, the New York insurance investigator. She is coming to Paris. She'll arrive Monday morning and come to our office in the afternoon. Any response on the Mostov fingerprints I got off those photos from St. Barth?"

"No. No matches yet."

Monday morning, Gerard was at a senior staff meeting when a clerk handed him a note. It was from Pierre:

"I just got a call from the Naples detective I am working with. A fisherman found Guido Antonini's body yesterday at the bottom of a cliff below his villa on the Amalfi Coast. At first they thought

he had fallen, but when they examined his body in Naples, they found three bullet holes in him."

After staring at the note for a few minutes, Gerard excused himself from the meeting and went to Abou's office. "Pierre, what do you make of this latest twist in our case?"

"One thing for sure, it is not good for your health these days to have your jewelry stolen."

"Do the Naples police have any theories?"

"A big shot in the Camorra gets whacked. I am sure their view is that it is an internal Mafia thing, and good riddance to Antonini. He wasn't winning any popularity contests with the Naples cops anyway."

"It doesn't sound like you think they are going to pursue the jewelry robbery or the murder investigation very vigorously," Gerard said.

"Yeah. It probably falls below the latest purse-snatching in the Quartieri Spagnoli on their list of priorities."

"I am going to make some calls to senior people there. We need action from them. I don't believe in coincidences anyway, and this second murder is no coincidence."

"Let's see—we have left an American jeweler and our Mexican drug lord. If one of them gets knocked off, we have another example of that globalization you are always talking about."

"Abou, stick to police work. You will never make it as an economist. But I am going to meet with some of our narcs to see what they have on Francesco Perez. I should also hear from the FBI today. We can see where we stand when Catherine York comes by this afternoon. And, again, you and your friend Sherlock Holmes did one excellent job finding the buried treasure."

Abou was beaming as Gerard left his office.

The American Airlines Boeing 767 from New York arrived in Paris on time. Catherine was met by a driver from the Larsen and McTabbitt Paris office, who took her to the hotel that the Paris manager had booked for her in the Eighth Arrondissement, near the Avenue Montaigne. Excited to be in Paris after an absence of a number of years, Catherine quickly unpacked, showered and changed clothes, choosing a light green silk pantsuit and black low-heel shoes. The waiting driver took her to the Paris office.

What Catherine didn't know was that the choice of a restaurant for lunch with the Paris office manager and his key lieutenants had been a subject of significant office debate, second only to the choice of hotel for her stay. Concerned that selecting a famous grand hotel such as the Ritz, George V or Crillon would send the wrong message to the New York headquarters but also worried that Catherine might not like the one they chose for her, they had finally settled on a small and elegant hotel where several fifty euro notes would assure an especially high level of personal service. For lunch, the debate was between a place with a large outdoor terrace just down Avenue Matignon from the office and a restaurant on the Rue de la Trémoille close to her hotel. They finally decided on the Rue de la Trémoille because of the ambience of a small room and the excellent food and service.

After lunch, Catherine was driven to the Île de la Cité and the police headquarters opposite the ornate gates of the Palais de Justice and shown to Gerard's office. As she entered, she saw Gerard behind his desk and another man sitting in one of the two chairs in front of the desk. Gerard stood up and kissed her hand. He wore a pearl gray suit of lightweight cashmere with a white shirt and a tie with broad gray and pink stripes. She noticed his cufflinks were made of black onyx. She glanced out of one of the windows behind his desk to see the facade of Notre-Dame. *Quite a view from an office window,* she thought.

The other man, who had also risen as she came in, was short and almost swarthy in complexion, with a stocky muscular build that showed through his wrinkled brown sports jacket. His nose looked like it had been broken more than once and, when he smiled, his broad grin was lopsided.

Gerard introduced Pierre Abou, and after some preliminaries about her trip over, they began to discuss the case. Abou's English was limited but passable, and he sometimes spoke in an odd stilted way that came across to her as almost British in expression. Catherine noticed that Gerard allowed Pierre to bring her up-to-date on the murder of Guido Antonini and describe in detail the discovery of the jewels at Valerie Pickett's farm. He only interrupted to help Pierre express himself in English.

Gerard then filled both of them in on the most recent information on Francesco Perez from both the FBI and the French narcotics officials. Gerard's FBI sources confirmed Marcel's information. Perez was known to be a major figure in the Mexican drug trade. He was a behind-the-scenes figure who kept a low profile and was thought to specialize in the financial management of the cartel. Investing proceeds, setting up bank accounts and laundering the cartel's large amounts of cash were among his activities that the FBI was watching. In the United States, he was active in Miami.

The French authorities knew about Perez as well. He had purchased a large and very expensive house in Paris and filled it with high-quality art, all bought through dealers in Paris, London and Rome over a relatively short period of time. In addition, Perez had furnished the house with expensive antiques, also purchased in large quantities from dealers. He was rarely in Paris, and French authorities did not believe he was involved in the Paris drug world, so they had not paid much attention to him. After Gerard's visit, that would change.

Gerard asked Catherine where she was staying and how long she planned to remain in Paris. She said that she would stay as long as necessary to move the investigation along. "After all," she smiled, "I packed light, but I am in Paris, so it would not be a bad thing if I had to buy some clothes."

"Your office made that easy when they selected your hotel," Gerard said. "You are a five-minute walk from the couture center of the world."

"My stay just got longer."

"Good. Let's look at some treasures."

The three of them went to a secure area in the headquarters complex. An armed guard looked for a moment at Catherine's temporary pass and for a couple of moments at Catherine herself before they were buzzed through. Once they were seated in a small room, the evidence boxes were brought in. Catherine looked at each piece, comparing it to her list and to the descriptions in the files she had brought with her. At one point, while looking at a necklace of blue and yellow diamonds, she said, "I can't resist. Gerard, would you help me with this please?" She put it on and looked in the small mirror in the room.

Seated back in Gerard's office, Catherine had her fourth cup of French coffee of the day. *Jet lag or not,* she thought, *this stuff is strong.* Looking around Gerard's office, she commented on how pleasant it was. "If it weren't for that display of handcuffs between the windows behind you, one wouldn't know that they were in a policeman's office."

"That is the point of the handcuffs. A number of people who sit in your chair, Catherine, are not happy to be there. When they answer my questions, it is hard for them not to be aware of the handcuffs."

"Gerard is a very effective questioner," Pierre said. "The iron fist in the velvet glove type. I myself prefer to dispense with the velvet glove."

"We have taken Pierre out of Marseilles, but we will never take the

Marseilles street cop out of Pierre," Gerard said. "The only person who pushes him around is his wife. Pierre, show Catherine pictures of your family."

As Catherine said what handsome boys Pierre had, that broad lopsided grin appeared. It got even broader when Gerard said that it was fortunate that they looked like their mother. Catherine was feeling increasingly comfortable with this unlikely duo.

She said that she would like to have the jewelry examined by one of their experts—would that be possible? Gerard replied that such an examination could be done, but it would have to occur in the headquarters building with police present. The police would bring a binocular microscope and a gemological refractometer for Catherine's expert. She wanted to call her Paris office, which was arranging for the expert, and her New York office as well. Gerard's assistant showed her to a conference room.

After she left, Gerard said to Pierre, "What do you think?"

"She is very pretty and very strong."

By the time Catherine was shown back to Gerard's office, it was late in the afternoon. Gerard was sitting behind his desk reading a report. He rose to greet her. As she sat down, she said that the Paris office had gotten in touch with someone in Amsterdam who they had used before in European jewelry investigations. He could fly down tomorrow morning and be available in the afternoon. Gerard said that the instruments would be delivered in the morning and that the Dutch expert could start his work in the afternoon.

Catherine asked him what he thought of the murders. Gerard responded that the Italian police were now getting engaged in the Antonini matter, after he and the French police chief had applied some pressure. There were apparently no witnesses. Antonini's villa had no close neighbors. The police knew that he had given his staff the night off, but they had prepared a lot of food, so Antonini must have been expecting guests. When the staff came back the next morning, the place was open, the lights were on, Antonini's car was there, and he was gone. He had not spent the night in his bedroom, and that information, plus the report of the Naples medical examiner, meant that he was killed sometime the previous evening. No one heard anything. The Italian police dusted the place for fingerprints, but they had waited too long, and the staff had cleaned the villa by the time the police got to work. Gerard would send Pierre or another detective to Italy in a day or two to look over the scene and keep the pressure on the Italians.

As for Pickett, the French police were not making any progress.

Although the neighborhood was residential, no one heard any shots. The only person who might have seen Pickett was a café waiter and, if it was Pickett, he was alone. The discovery of the stolen jewels raised several questions as to why he was killed.

Gerard and Catherine sat together and listed the possibilities:

1. It was a random killing or a botched robbery attempt.

2. Pickett was killed because of something in his life unrelated to the jewel robbery.

3. He had an accomplice in the robbery who killed him and planned to take the jewels.

4. There was some other kind of falling out among thieves.

"His prints are all over the jewels and the bags," Gerard said. "There are no other prints, although someone could have handled them with gloves. Pickett got nervous and upset when I questioned him, and Pierre put more pressure on him when I was in St. Barth."

"Talking about St. Barth, wasn't Sofia Mostov in Europe at the time of Antonini's murder?"

"Yes, although at this point all we know is that she was in Switzerland. But she was definitely in Paris when Pickett was killed."

"Could you find out if she was in Italy, or at least if she left Switzerland?"

"Catherine, that's a good line of inquiry. We can ask the Swiss police to check hotel records. We can also check with the airlines and see if someone with her name flew from Switzerland to Italy. But she has a French passport and French identity card, so if she drove or took the train, she could have entered Italy easily, and there wouldn't be a record. I will ask the Italians to check hotel records in Naples and Positano."

"What about Rome?"

"Why Rome?"

"Doesn't she have a workshop there?" Catherine asked.

"Yes."

"Maybe she visited it when she was in Europe during that five-day period. She is supposed to get back to St. Barth tomorrow, isn't that right? She didn't have time to go to Rome when she was in Paris a few weeks ago, so maybe she went there this time. It makes sense for her to stay in touch with her business. I don't know Italy; how long would it take to drive from Rome to Positano?"

"Three to four hours—maybe more if the traffic is heavy around

Naples or getting out of Rome," Gerard said. "But how do we know she even knew Antonini?"

"We don't, but a lot of the pieces he reported stolen had come through either her St. Barth or Rome operations, so it is likely that they met."

"It is a long stretch to think she killed him. Why knock off a good customer? Same thing for Pickett. What reason is there for her to kill him? It is pretty circumstantial to leap to that conclusion just because she was in Europe at the time the murders took place."

"Perhaps. But I don't believe in coincidences, do you?"

Gerard smiled and shook his head.

"Besides, Mr. Policeman, do you have any other suspects?"

"Touché. Catherine, you would make one fine detective. You should talk to Pierre about his favorite detective, Sherlock Holmes."

"Why Sherlock Holmes? I don't think I have ever read any of his stories."

"Logic, my dear Catherine, logic," said Gerard, smiling. "Holmes had great deductive skills. We could use him now. Anyway, I will have some checking done in Switzerland and Italy, and I will also have a talk with my new friend, the St. Barth police chief, and see what he knows about Sofia Mostov. You must be tired. Let me drive you back to your hotel. On the way, if you want, I will give you a quick tour of the robbery locations. Are you hungry? Would you like an early dinner?"

"Thanks. Let's do the tour, but I want to get to sleep early. I will have something to eat at the hotel."

As Catherine got into Gerard's BMW, she said, "Doesn't look like a police car." Gerard smiled, but didn't reply. He took her first to the Place Vendôme and, as they drove along the Rue Saint-Honoré, he said that this was a street of wonderful shops. Definitely worth a long stroll. He turned left into the Place Vendôme and then right into the curved street that ran along the seventeenth-century facade facing Napoleon's column in the center of the Place. The column was made, as Gerard pointed out, of the melted cannons the French had captured at the battle of Austerlitz. He pulled up in front of the shuttered windows of *Valerie Pickett, Bijoutier.*

Gerard stopped his car, although there were signs Catherine was sure said "no parking." Taking a key from his pocket, Gerard opened the center compartment of the car and took out a red light, which he placed on the dashboard. He plugged the light into the cigarette lighter outlet and turned a switch so the light came on and flashed.

"*Voilà*, it is now a police car," Gerard said.

Before he closed and relocked the center compartment, Catherine saw a bracket holding a holster and a pistol.

They looked at the store. Gerard flashed his police identification to a guard and took Catherine into the courtyard behind the facade. He pointed out where entry to the building had been forced.

Catherine said, "According to my report, the thief got in through Pickett's office on the second floor above the store."

"Yes, if there was a thief. With Pierre's discovery, this supposed robbery is turning into an insurance fraud case. Later, if you like, we can go into the store. It is closed for business now. Would you like to take a short walk?"

"It would feel good to stretch my legs a bit."

Catherine hadn't been to Paris for so long that she had forgotten how beautiful the Place Vendôme was. They walked along the sidewalk, looking into the windows of the world-famous jewelry stores lining the street. They joked about how, at each window, everyone else saw beautiful jewelry, while she saw a potential insurance claim, and he saw a potential crime scene. They crossed the Rue de la Paix in front of the Charvet store. In the windows, Catherine saw some familiar-looking ties.

"You shop here, do you not?" she asked.

"Why, yes, you are observant."

"See, I would make a good cop. But would I have to carry a gun?"

"Only if you wanted to shoot someone."

They walked into the Ritz Hotel, where they decided to have a drink in the garden. Gerard asked her, given her interest in art, if she would like to visit some galleries during her stay and if she was planning to see any museums. Catherine said that it depended on how much free time she had. While she was in Paris, she had agreed to review some European cases the Paris office was working on, since Nick did not like to travel. They walked through the long gallery of the hotel, passing a line of display cases showing samples of what was for sale in Paris' finest shops. Off the lobby on the Rue Cambon side of the hotel, Gerard showed Catherine the bar that Hemingway frequented and the location on the street where Princess Diana set out on her fateful drive.

They left the hotel through the Place Vendôme entrance and walked past the Justice Ministry headquarters, where Gerard said he had a meeting tomorrow morning. He showed Catherine the mark in the wall that was one of the original measurements of one meter. He said that it was one of several that were put in Paris after the revolution to facilitate conversion to the metric system.

"A strange monument," she said.

"This is France. We celebrate all our victories, even if they are a single straight line; it is our defeats that we ignore but cannot forget."

They went back to the car. Gerard kept the light flashing with the comment that traffic was heavy and drove along the Champs-Élysées and around the Arc de Triomphe. Catherine gripped the door as Gerard maneuvered the big BMW around the circle that surrounded the Arc through what seemed to her to be a dozen lanes of traffic. Some cars deferred to the flashing red light; some didn't. Soon they were parked on a tree-lined street of large walled mansions. Gerard pointed out Francesco Perez's house and described how the burglar might have gained entry. Then they went back to Catherine's hotel. Gerard stopped just short of the entrance to put the red light back in its compartment, remarking that he wouldn't want the hotel staff to wonder why she was being transported in a police car.

As he parked in front of the hotel and the doorman came out, Catherine thanked him for the tour and agreed to have dinner with him the next evening. Since he would be out of the office in the morning, she was to arrange with Pierre Abou for the Dutch gemologist to examine the jewelry.

Then he was off. As Catherine picked up her key and went to her room, there was a spring to her step. She thought, *I enjoy being with that guy*, a thought that returned to her during her early and solitary dinner in the hotel's small dining room.

CHAPTER TWENTY
Paris

THE DUTCH GEMOLOGIST ARRIVED at the Larsen and McTabbitt office mid-morning. Catherine greeted him, and they sat down in the office's conference room. Tall, skinny and balding, he had a goatee and wore a waistcoat with a long gold chain across it. His name was Henrik Van Bilt, and he seemed to her a bit old fashioned. *Probably a good thing in a jewelry expert,* she thought.

They worked through lunch, going over the inventories of the stolen jewelry. They had sandwiches brought in, to the disappointment of the office manager, who was looking forward to another long Parisian lunch on the company.

The L & M driver then took Catherine and Van Bilt to the Île de la Cité. Van Bilt carried a black case containing his personal binocular microscope. Pierre met them at the entrance. Van Bilt's microscope attracted extra attention as they went through security. They went to the same small room Catherine had been in yesterday. As promised, there was a large binocular microscope on the table, along with a rectangular instrument with a single eyepiece and a lamp that looked like it belonged in an operating room.

Van Bilt, who had not altered his initial glum expression, actually smiled when he saw the instruments. "Good," he said in his heavily accented English. In addition to him and Catherine, there was a uniformed policeman, who Catherine assumed was present to make sure that neither she nor Van Bilt made off with any pieces of jewelry.

Pierre then said that he was required to tell them that they would be handling evidence in two crimes, one of which was murder, and that tampering with, altering or removing any piece of evidence was itself a crime.

Pierre said that the examination could now begin. Van Bilt took out each piece one at a time. He placed it on a felt cloth and examined it under the strong light. He would look at each stone under the microscope, sometimes use the refractometer by putting the lamp behind it, placing some kind of liquid he had brought with him on the prism of the instrument, then putting the stone on top and looking through the eyepiece. With each piece, he would mutter in Dutch and make notes on the inventory sheet that described each stone and piece of jewelry.

After about an hour Abou left the room. The uniformed policeman sat still as a rock staring at Van Bilt. Catherine wished she had brought a good book. Finally, Catherine thought, *These guys are like camels, but I need to use the restroom.* She said as much in her fractured French to the policeman who, without taking his eyes off Van Bilt, pushed a button under the table. A policewoman came in shortly and escorted her out.

At four, Pierre returned and sat down. Catherine whispered to him, "Help, I am trapped here." Pierre smiled and got up and left. Shortly thereafter, Gerard came in, accompanied by a uniformed officer.

"Dr. Van Bilt, how are you coming?" Gerard asked. "How much longer before you are finished?"

Van Bilt replied that he would need tomorrow morning to complete his work and would be able to make a report in the afternoon. Gerard suggested that Van Bilt work until 6:00 PM and then resume at 9:00 AM the next morning.

Catherine said to Gerard, "Thank you for rescuing me. The guy is working for me, and I have to observe him, but he is not into dialogue."

Gerard's assistant brought Catherine to the building entrance where a taxi was waiting to take her to her office.

Later, as she stood in her hotel room, she wondered what to wear to dinner. Gerard had said that, since the weather was so nice, they would have dinner on the terrace of a restaurant. She settled on her old standby—a simple black dress with a deep V-neck and a shawl of violet and black if it got chilly. *What necklace to wear?* She decided on her pearl necklace and matching earrings. She was glad that, at the last minute when she was packing for the trip, she had decided to include a few of her nice pieces of jewelry, even though the insurance executive in her knew the dangers of traveling with expensive jewelry. *Oh, well,* she had chuckled to herself, *it's insured.*

She was dressed and ready to leave at seven forty-five, even though Gerard was not to come by for her until eight fifteen for their eight thirty dinner reservation. As she stood in her room, looking out the window at the Eiffel Tower in the distance, she had to acknowledge that she was excited. This wasn't a business meeting. It was a date. In Paris with an interesting man. She almost called Judy but instead turned on the television set.

At exactly eight fifteen, the phone rang, and the front desk clerk announced that Monsieur de Rochenoir was in the lobby. Catherine glanced in the mirror quickly before making her way downstairs. Gerard was waiting for her, having changed from his gray double-breasted suit of the day to a black suit with a lavender shirt and a multicolored tie she was sure was from Charvet. The material was a lightweight summer cashmere. *Gerard,* she thought, *must have single-handedly raised the per capita cashmere consumption in Paris.*

His BMW was double-parked in front of the hotel; Gerard obviously addressed Parisian parking restrictions by ignoring them. They drove a short distance to a restaurant in a garden off the Champs-Élysées. The maître d' clearly knew Gerard, shaking his hand and then leading them to a secluded table on a terrace where chestnut trees reinforced the sense of an oasis in the city.

Catherine commented on the beauty and privacy of the location. Gerard said this restaurant was particularly special on summer evenings, and he hoped that she would enjoy it.

He ordered two glasses of champagne, which she thought was about the creamiest and best champagne she had ever had. For her first course, she ordered foie gras, while he had salmon carpaccio with caviar. When Catherine asked for a glass of sauterne to accompany the foie gras, Gerard suggested a different wine. He said that this foie gras dish was prepared with Banyuls, a late-harvest red wine, and that she might enjoy a glass of the same wine. It was, he said, from the coast of France near the Spanish border. She took his advice and, after a few minutes of tasting the foie gras and the wine, had to agree that it was a wonderful pairing. They lingered over the first course, sharing each other's dishes.

Gerard asked her about growing up in Wisconsin and what it was like to go east to Harvard and then to New York. She talked about her father and mother and two brothers.

Catherine asked Gerard about his family. He told her about his parents, that the apartment he lived in had been theirs and how, after his mother's death, he took over the apartment. His sister preferred the family estate in the south of France, where he visited her each August. He had retained a small house at the edge of the property.

They talked about their siblings. With two older brothers, Catherine said that she had been a tomboy and explained that term to Gerard, who had looked at her quizzically. She asked him about his relationship with his sister. It was not close, mostly because she was eight years older than he was. She was born in 1938, and the continued expansion of the family was delayed by the war. His father had been a French army officer, at odds with the establishment over preparations for the war with Germany that many thought was coming. In 1940, when France fell, he had gone to England with de Gaulle and the Free French and had not seen his wife and daughter for four years.

Looking across the table straight at him, Catherine asked, "Was it hard to move back into your parents' home?"

"You are very direct, Catherine York. Yes, it was strange. When my mother died, I had been in the department for only a few years. I had an apartment in the Fourth Arrondissement in east Paris. It was near what is now the Picasso Museum, in an area full of artists, small cafés, music—not as bourgeois and upscale as that neighborhood has become. My parents' apartment had been in the family for many years. It was in a very desirable location. It was larger than I needed. But I couldn't bear to sell it out of the family, so I took it over. I did a lot of renovation to make its décor modern and to my taste. The only room I didn't change was the kitchen."

"Why not?"

"I don't cook."

They laughed.

During the conversation, dinner arrived. At Catherine's request, Gerard had ordered for both of them—cod crusted with black truffles and served with braised endives. They had discussed which wine to order and agreed that a light Pinot Noir would work well with the delicate fish, the flavorful preparation of the truffles and the endives braised with butter and cream. They both were delighted with the rich aromas of the sauce.

They resumed their conversation with Catherine asking Gerard, "Since you think I am so direct, try this question. Why haven't you ever gotten married?"

"We French often answer a question with a question. Why haven't *you* married?"

"Because I haven't found the right man."

"To the point again, Catherine." He smiled and lifted his glass to toast her.

They talked about their work and then the conversation moved almost naturally to relationships in their pasts, to the difference between living in Paris and New York, and to art exhibits and plays they had each recently seen. They discovered that they both played tennis but that Catherine liked to ride horses and Gerard didn't. He talked about his time skiing and teaching skiing. She had been a varsity swimmer in college.

Dessert was crepe suzettes, followed by Calvados brandy.

"Mr. Policeman, isn't there a law in France against giving a girl too much wine at dinner?" Catherine asked.

"If there were such a law, I would enforce it only selectively."

As they sat at the table, thoroughly engaged in each other's company, Catherine looked at her watch and said, "I can't believe that it is almost midnight. We have been here almost three and a half hours. And we haven't discussed the case!"

"It's late, and I should take you back to the hotel. But now let me be direct. I have enjoyed this evening immensely. I would like to take you to my favorite restaurant for dinner tomorrow night. And then we can discuss the case."

Catherine looked at him for what seemed to Gerard like an eternity and then said, "It's a date."

The next day Pierre, Gerard and Catherine gathered in the same small room at French police headquarters to hear Van Bilt's report. The three of them were seated across the table from the Dutchman as he adjusted his glasses and spread out his notes and inventories. Catherine wondered if this hot, poorly ventilated and brightly lit room was also used to grill suspects. It seemed well-suited for interrogation.

"First, I must tell you that the jewelry pieces and unset stones that I have examined match exactly the insurance inventory you have provided me," Van Bilt said. "Then I must caution you that my conclusions are only tentative. More tests with equipment I do not have with me, such as spectroscopic and density analysis, as well as ultraviolet light examination, would be necessary before I can be more definitive."

"Definitive about what?" Catherine interjected.

"Definitive about whether the gems here are legitimate."

The room went silent. Catherine spoke up first, almost shouting, "Legitimate—what do you mean by legitimate?"

Van Bilt stood up, interrupting Catherine, put both his hands on the table and said, "What I am trying to say is that it is possible—no, it is likely—that every one of these stones, set or unset, is fraudulent. That is—they are not natural. They have been fabricated."

There was stunned silence. Van Bilt sat down and let out a huge breath. "More tests, more tests are needed to be certain," he said to no one in particular.

"If you are right, this is fraud on a major, unprecedented scale," Catherine said.

"It is precisely the scale that first raised my suspicions. The early stones I examined, I thought, were exceptional. Such color, so few inclusions. One can produce a precious gem synthetically that is very close to the chemical composition of a real stone—it can even have colors that are true to the real gem, but to the eye of the expert, it doesn't look natural. Transparency is not right, inclusions aren't right. Inclusions, after all, are part of the natural process of forming a gemstone. The better stones have fewer inclusions, and stones like emeralds can be identified to their region of origin by the type of inclusion. But to see so many stones that are almost perfect—in thirty-five years as a gemologist, I have never seen this. I will show you."

Catherine and Gerard, and occasionally Pierre, looked at a number of unset stones as well as stones in jewelry pieces under the binocular microscope. Van Bilt pointed out features as they looked.

Van Bilt said that fraudulent white diamonds were particularly hard to detect but that he was certain testing with a thermal conductivity meter would support his conclusion because the synthetic stones will conduct heat to a much lesser degree than diamonds. Anxious to continue, he then said that, while white diamonds were generally much more plentiful than colored stones, in this collection there was a surprisingly high percentage of clear stones that he would classify as exceptional.

Van Bilt and Catherine briefly discussed how the diamonds would be classified under international and U.S. standards. Gerard asked what the grades meant, and Catherine said that all of the diamonds were of the highest classification possible. "Unheard of, really, isn't it, Dr. Van Bilt, for a single collection to have all stones of this quality?"

"Yes, yes, but the point I also want to make is that here there are so many diamonds that are colored—and colored very singularly—yellow, pink, blue, even violet and a red stone—and they are of exceptionally high refractive index."

Gerard looked puzzled.

"What I mean," Van Bilt said, "is that they reflect light very well. It gives them the sparkle that people love—and pay for—in diamonds. It is not only their refractive quality but their hardness that creates luster. Yes, hardness. I did a hardness test under the scope, trying to place these stones on the Mohs' scale—that is the way we measure hardness. Diamonds, being the hardest of minerals, have a measurement of ten. These stones are very close to a ten, harder than corundum, which is a nine."

"In our office you looked at the inventories of the other three robberies. Were diamonds, and particularly colored diamonds, represented about equally in those collections?" Catherine asked.

"Yes, I think so," replied Van Bilt. "Diamonds, rubies and sapphires were the predominant stones by far, as I remember. Also emeralds."

"And with this collection, you have the same concerns about the stones other than the diamonds?"

"Yes, take rubies, for example," Van Bilt said, his voice rising with excitement. "There are a lot of easily identified imitation rubies out there, although many who buy rubies—and opals, as well—in Southeast Asia find out too late. We see a lot of doublets, where a slice of corundum is colored to imitate the desired ruby or opal—black opals are frequently the target—and attached to the synthetic ruby or opal by colorless cement. Fake emeralds are made in a similar way, except the color comes from a middle slice of a green substance.

"But these stones are quite different. They are complete. The rubies have excellent color, transparency and few inclusions. But the inclusions that are present all seem to follow a similar pattern. If someone looked at just one stone, the inclusions would appear natural, but looking at a dozen, all perfect—it just can't be."

Gerard asked Van Bilt if he had any theories as to how these stones could be fabricated. Van Bilt responded by saying that people have been trying to make imitations of precious stones for thousands of years. "The Egyptians used glazed clay to imitate turquoise almost six thousand years ago. And there are turquoise stones in this collection of high apparent quality—very similar to the superb turquoise from Iran. The Romans used colored glass to imitate emeralds. Real gemstones have been treated with heat, have been stained, have had cracks filled—all to enhance their value. The issue has always been heat and pressure, how to get intense heat and high pressure, emulating the natural conditions under which gemstones are formed. And how to create stones of the proper hardness, how to suffuse them with color, how to duplicate the natural imperfections that characterize true gemstones. Recently, radioactive particles and lasers have been introduced as people try to adapt technology to the task of creating imitation gemstones that will pass as real."

Van Bilt sagged back in his chair, seemingly exhausted by his examination and his discourse.

Pierre, who had been quiet, then said, "If Dr. Van Bilt is correct, and if the jewelry stolen in the other three robberies are also fake … "

Catherine finished his thought, "Then we are facing one of the largest jewelry insurance frauds ever."

"And," Pierre said, "two murders."

"So far," added Gerard.

The room was quiet as each person contemplated the implications of Van Bilt's conclusions. Gerard and Catherine exchanged glances. Gerard left the room and quickly returned with two uniformed officers and the detective in charge of the evidence area. Catherine thanked Van Bilt for his work, and Gerard said that he would be escorted out of the building by one of the other officers. Gerard said that Van Bilt's report was so extraordinary that he would arrange for a Paris gemologist the police had worked with before to examine the jewels as well.

Gerard, Catherine and Pierre returned to Gerard's office. Gerard stood with his back to them, contemplating the facade of Notre-Dame out of his office window. The late afternoon light produced a soft reddish glow on the old stones. He turned and began talking.

"The Swiss police say that there is no record of Sofia Mostov staying in a hotel in Zurich or Geneva or Lausanne. I think Catherine's intuition that she might have gone to Italy is worth following up on. Pierre, can you light a fire under our Italian friends and see if she stayed in a hotel in Rome, Naples or on the Amalfi Coast? I think we have enough reason to question her staff in Rome. Besides, we need to know what goes on in her Roman workshop."

A woman entered the room and handed Gerard a note. "Good," he said, "our gemologist is available to work with us. If Van Bilt is right, and he certainly seems to know what he is talking about—we will know more on Friday after our expert is finished—there is a factory somewhere where this stuff is turned out. If the Italians cooperate, Pierre, you should go to Rome and look at the workshop and interview the employees. If Sofia was in Rome, they will know. Meanwhile, we need to search Francesco Perez's house. Maybe you will get lucky again. Get that rolling. I have to go to a meeting of a task force that doesn't officially exist over at the Interior Security Ministry, but before I leave, I will ask the St. Barth chief what he knows about this Sofia. We need to get smart about her quickly."

Catherine added, "And I am going to have some comparative analyses done of these stolen jewelry inventories. How many three-plus carat rubies in total were stolen and how many came through Sofia? Nick is going to fall through the floor when he hears we may have been cheated out of perhaps as much as $300 million. And what about earlier jewelry theft claims we have paid? This is turning out to be one big problem."

CHAPTER TWENTY-ONE
Paris

THEIR DINNER RESERVATION WAS at eight thirty. Catherine decided to go shopping after spending a few hours at the office, and she found a dress at a shop on the Rue Saint-Honoré that seemed perfect. It was deep violet, with a low-cut, tight fit that said, *This is a dress for going out; don't wear me at the office.*

Reschio was out of town, due back tomorrow. When she couldn't reach him on his cell phone, Catherine left him a long voice message. When they talked tomorrow afternoon, she should have the second gemologist's conclusions, at least tentative ones, but she doubted they would differ much from Van Bilt's.

She didn't know what restaurant Gerard was taking her to, only that he was calling at the hotel at eight fifteen. When he arrived, in the double-breasted medium blue blazer and blue slacks that he had worn earlier, he said that his meeting had lasted longer than he had thought. A colleague had dropped him off at the hotel. They would take a taxi to dinner.

Gerard seemed preoccupied, but his mood changed as the taxi sped down the Champs-Élysées through the Place de la Concorde. The car turned onto the Rue Saint-Honoré and then made a right, passing the shop at which Catherine had bought the dress.

The taxi stopped at a busy intersection, and Gerard led her away from the Rue Saint-Honoré through an elegant entrance into what appeared to her to be a park. As she walked, Catherine saw that the park was really a large garden, long and surrounded by uniform four-story buildings. The first floors on two sides were a series of arcades, which appeared almost shadowy in the slowly growing dusk. Rows of tall, symmetrical windows graced the upper stories.

As they walked through the garden and then along one of the arcades, they looked in the windows of shops that sold vintage clothes, old medals and even toy soldiers. Gerard told Catherine a bit about the history of the Palais-Royal. A triumph of eighteenth-century architecture, it now housed government offices, he said. It had been home to a number of members of French royalty—Louis XIV had even lived there as a youth.

Catherine thought that the walk to the restaurant through this wonderful garden had to be about as romantic a prelude to dinner as she could imagine. They were surrounded by beautiful buildings at dusk on a summer evening, and the many flowers that lined the pathways scented the air. She was glad she had bought a new dress.

As they approached the end of the garden and the entrance to the restaurant, Gerard pointed at the busy Rue de Beaujolais a few steps from the restaurant's entrance. He said that he had wanted her to walk through the Palais-Royal to get the sense of approach through perhaps the most elegant of Parisian spaces.

The dining room was beautiful, with one wall containing windows facing the Palais-Royal. Two of the walls were partially mirrored, and panels between the mirrors contained paintings in a classical style that looked like they had been in the room for a hundred years. The dark wood of the wainscoting below the mirrors, the soft light from the chandeliers, the gentle colors of the paintings, the perfectly set tables, each with a single pink rose in a silver vase, all created a sense of warmth and anticipation for the evening ahead. They were escorted to a corner table.

"Welcome to Le Grand Véfour," Gerard said. "This restaurant is very old and historic. Napoleon and Josephine, Victor Hugo and many other notables dined here, and their names are on plaques at the tables they favored, or so is the myth of the place. We are sitting at a table favored by Honoré de Balzac—at least, that's what the plaque says. The beauty of a restaurant this old is that there is nobody alive who remembers where any of these people actually sat. We do know, however, that Balzac liked a good meal."

Again two glasses of champagne appeared. *Even better than last night's,* Catherine thought.

As they raised their glasses, Gerard said, "To your stay in Paris, and to our new friendship."

They clinked glasses, and Catherine thought, *To our new friendship indeed. Judy, where are you when I need you?*

After a discussion of the relative merits of the champagnes of last night and the one they were drinking, Gerard asked her, "What were the results of your review of the inventories of the stolen jewels?"

"Dr. Van Bilt's recollection was quite accurate," Catherine said. "Each collection has roughly the same percentage of white diamonds and colored diamonds, with the emphasis on the rarest colors, as well as big rubies, sapphires and emeralds. There are also turquoise and silver necklaces and bracelets; the turquoise is described in the appraisals as being of Iranian origin. Perez had an emerald brooch that was supposedly early eighteenth century. The grades of the stones are pretty similar across all four lots."

They were both silent for a few minutes, and then Catherine laughed and said, "You are thinking about Sofia Mostov's store in St. Barth, are you not?"

Gerard replied, "Yes. In addition to your other skills, you also read minds?"

"That's my secret," she said with a smile.

Gerard tipped his glass to her. "To secrets—sometimes most delicious if shared."

He then went on, "Our gemologist will start his work early tomorrow morning, and I asked that he give us an interim report in the afternoon. I think the Italians will cooperate and let us question the Mostov Rome workshop staff as early as Friday afternoon. Still no report on whether Sofia stayed in a Rome hotel, but, just before I came to your hotel, I had a very interesting conversation with the St. Barth police chief. When I asked him what he knew about Sofia, he replied that it was a small island and she was a well-known person there."

Gerard paused to inspect his champagne glass, took a sip and continued. "Sourel said that he thinks Sofia was originally Cuban but left the island as a youngster and lived in Russia—perhaps with her father, who was Russian. At some point she acquired French citizenship. She travels a lot to Cuba—he doesn't know if she has a Cuban passport—and to Europe, as well. He knows that she has a facility in Rome that he thinks is both a workshop and a sales office. A lot of merchandise is shipped from Italy to St. Barth. She is not married. Apparently, she never has been. She has frequent visitors from Europe and Cuba. Her St. Barth operation is reputed to be the largest volume high-end jewelry store on the island and maybe in the Caribbean. From Italy, she sells merchandise to jewelry stores on other islands in the West Indies. He didn't know about the volume of such sales. Her business is owned by several levels of corporations that are not French—probably Swiss. She has lawyers that he knows about in Switzerland and on the island."

Gerard continued, "Then he told me something particularly interesting. He said that there is a rumor on the island that she was once involved with the Cuban or Russian intelligence service. He said it is only a rumor, but he does know that she is an excellent pistol shot because sometimes she comes to the pistol range on the island that the police use."

"Hmm, it seems as if we have a woman of mystery on our hands."

"Yes, perhaps, or perhaps the kind of mystique that is good for business. We should be able to search Perez's mansion tomorrow. But enough business—a beautiful evening, a beautiful restaurant and a beautiful woman in a beautiful dress—let us order."

They began with a cold artichoke and then shared a dish of ravioli filled with clams. They shared a mussel soup cooked with saffron, which Catherine suggested because she had never had anything like it.

"Well," said Gerard, "it is a bit heavy for summer."

"Maybe," said Catherine, "but I am starved."

As he was eating his soup, Gerard said, "You were right, this is excellent. The mussels have an intense flavor, and the saffron fragrance contrasts in an interesting way with the mussels."

"Think of it as a Wisconsin special," Catherine said. Gerard toasted her.

Gerard had a chicken dish as a main course. At his suggestion, Catherine had thick cuts of lamb prepared with a ground espresso-bean rub, a dish that she had trouble imagining but no trouble enjoying. The perfectly prepared lamb seemed to infuse the coffee beans and excite both her taste buds and her sense of smell.

The wine Gerard ordered was a first-growth Pauillac. Catherine said that it had flavors of black currants. "These wines are big and complex, maybe too much for the chicken, but perfect for your lamb."

"Well, thank you, Gerard, for choosing a wine that is so delicious with my food. Tell me, what do you think of California wines?"

They discussed the relative merits of French and California red wines. She liked the fresh, upfront flavor of the California Cabernet Sauvignons, Pinots and Meritages and found some of the French reds to be less satisfying—interesting, but lacking in rich flavors.

Gerard thought the French aged some of their wines too long. The

British aged theirs too long for sure. There was wine in his cellar that his father had laid down in the 1940s, but some of the old Bordeaux, in particular, decanted and savored, offered a subtlety that he found wanting in many excellent California wines. "To appreciate our wines," he said, "one must train the palate." They agreed that they needed to do some serious comparative tasting in the future.

Catherine laughed and pointed at him playfully. "Gerard, it sounds like we are making plans."

"And why not?" he replied with a smile and a twinkle in his green eyes.

The wine discussion led to the topic of why French-American relations were sometimes difficult. Catherine, who had been a history major in college, talked about how important French assistance was to America as it struggled to free itself from England. The French ideas of the enlightenment were central to the Declaration of Independence; Thomas Jefferson remained committed to France throughout his presidency. A lot of American anti-French feeling, she said, was in response to perceived French attitudes about America.

"A very complex topic," Gerard responded. "We are proud of our culture, our language, our history, our customs and, yes, our cuisine. Do you know that the recipe for the bread you are eating at dinner is set out in legislation? No one can call their bread 'traditional French bread' in France unless they follow the recipe. Foie gras has been declared by legislation a 'national treasure' to prevent animal rights activists from challenging it.

"But I think our relations with America will always be somewhat difficult. We try to maintain our culture and language, but American styles and language and commerce are so pervasive that we sometimes feel our very essence being threatened. Perhaps our reaction to what we perceive as your openness and power is to back off and appear reserved."

As Gerard talked, Catherine sipped the almost opaque red wine and thought how complex it was, just like Gerard. She wondered if his comments about French attitudes toward Americans were a subtle message for her. Then she heard Gerard say, almost like the interruption of a dream, "I didn't mean to go on for so long." He began asking her questions about her life in New York.

Catherine interrupted him. "Gerard, I am flattered that last night and again tonight you asked me so many questions about myself. Men usually spend most conversations talking about themselves. But you reveal so little of yourself. You seem so guarded."

Gerard shrugged, took a sip of wine and said, "I suppose I am a bit reserved."

"That's all you can say? I am not going to let you off that easily. What was Gerard, the child, like growing up? Did you have a lot of friends?"

"I don't think much about it, but I kept to myself a lot as a child. My parents were older than most of my schoolmates' parents. My father took me on business trips. We went to the United States several times."

"Were you close to him?" Catherine asked.

"He seemed to be interested in me—my schoolwork for example—but he was—aloof, I suppose, is the way one could put it. He encouraged me to read and taught me to ski, but he didn't have much interest in my social life."

"And your mother?"

"Catherine—a lot of questions." He laughed.

"I have told you all about my parents and about growing up in Wisconsin. I just want to keep the conversation from being too one-sided."

"She was beautiful. I remember her as always elegantly dressed. She took me on walks and to the opera. But she spent a lot of time with her friends. There were maids, governesses. We didn't spend a lot of time together as a family except when we went to the country in August. As I look back—which I don't often do—I think I spent a lot of time alone. But, I am used to asking the questions—answering them is not something I am accustomed to doing."

"As you were talking, I was thinking how interesting it is that you ended up as a policeman."

"What is interesting about that? You think I was more suited to be what—a banker?"

"No, it is not that it seems unusual that someone of your obviously wealthy childhood would go into police work, but what I was thinking about is that police work fits with your protected, guarded nature. Why did you choose police work, anyway?"

"It seemed logical at the time," Gerard said. "I didn't start out as a street cop—perhaps that I wouldn't have done—but I moved from one ministry to another, and police work seemed more interesting to me than the work I was doing. I don't like to be bored—and at the level I was able to enter it was, and remains, intellectually challenging. Besides, I get to meet such beautiful women."

"Nice try at diverting me. I haven't thought much about it, but it seems that it could be a good fit for someone who is a bit of a loner. After all, you have a badge and a gun between you and the rest of us. A convenient wall."

They sat silently for a few minutes—almost as if exhausted from the conversation. Catherine said, "I hope that I wasn't too persistent and prying."

"Not at all." Gerard looked at her and smiled. "I like that you are interested in me. Who knows? I may tell you my whole life story, except I am fearful that you would think of me as an aging, boring guy."

"No chance of that."

They left the restaurant into a soft, warm June night.

Gerard said that it was only a short walk to his apartment, where he could get his car and take her back to her hotel. They walked through the Tuileries, along the river side of the Louvre and over the Pont des Arts to the left bank of the Seine. They stopped on the bridge and looked at the Eiffel Tower in the distance and the lights of Paris reflecting off the surface of the water. In an act as natural as it was uncharacteristic, Catherine took Gerard's hand. They walked hand-in-hand along the river and then around the Pont de la Tournelle to the Île Saint-Louis. The Parisian night was beautiful, and Catherine felt she had known him for a long time. He asked if Catherine would like to see his apartment. She said she would.

Chapter Twenty-Two
Paris

THE NEXT MORNING, AS the breeze from the river came through the windows of Gerard's bedroom, Catherine turned to him, kissed him and said, "Your mustache tickles."

"I will trim it."

"No, I love it. And what was that talk last night about being an old guy?"

"The American singer Toby Keith has a line in a song where he says something like, I ain't as good as I once was, but I'm as good once as I ever was."

"We did it twice."

"Okay, I will write to Mr. Keith and suggest that he change his song, but I don't think he will pay much attention to me."

"I can't believe you listen to Toby Keith songs, but you never cease to surprise me, Mr. Policeman. Since I didn't exactly bring a robe, do you have a shirt I can put on? I will see if I can make us some breakfast."

"Of course, my shirts are hanging in that closet, but I am afraid you will not find anything with which to make breakfast."

Catherine went into the closet and came out wearing a light-blue shirt. "Gerard, you have more shirts, suits, jackets, slacks and ties than most clothing stores!"

"If there is ever a clothing shortage, I will be prepared."

Catherine wandered through the spacious apartment and found the kitchen. The apartment had a contemporary yet timeless feel. There were parquet floors in the Versailles pattern, large windows and French doors, beamed ceilings and large old doors, a huge red marble fireplace, and plaster walls. The walls' warm hues of brown and off-white were protected from nail holes by picture molding all through the apartment. The furniture was modern. There were colorful oil paintings on the wall that Catherine wanted to look at much more closely to confirm that they were as amazing as a quick glance led her to believe, but the large kitchen was a wonderful contrast. It looked like it had not been changed since the 1930s. She pulled on the old latch handles and opened the refrigerator, which was almost empty except for a bottle of Veuve Clicquot champagne, tomato juice, a carton of eggs, several bottles of water, a melon and a package of prosciutto.

Catherine opened one of the cabinets and found it full of cans and bottles of prepared food. There were cans of cassoulet and bottles of duck in a mushroom sauce from Hediard, a famous Parisian grocery store that she recognized, bottles of vichyssoise and gazpacho, cans of sardines and fish soup.

Gerard walked in.

"Look at all this food," Catherine said. "I thought you didn't cook."

"I don't, I heat."

Looking at some cans, she said, "Gerard, are champignons mushrooms?"

"Yes."

"Would you like scrambled eggs with mushrooms and bacon?

"That would be good, but I don't have any bacon."

"Yes, you do. Show me where the plates and the coffeepot are. I see the pans. Give me ten minutes, and we will have breakfast."

While Gerard watched and made coffee, Catherine sautéed the mushrooms, lightly fried the prosciutto in olive oil, made scrambled eggs, cut up the melon and served breakfast for the two of them.

"American ingenuity," he said and thanked her.

After breakfast, Gerard helped her clean up and went to take a shower before driving her back to her hotel.

When he came out, Catherine was wearing last night's violet dress and looking at two paintings. "They are Matisse, are they not?" she said.

"Yes," he said. "Do you recognize the work on the other wall? It is a Braque. My parents bought a number of cubist pieces. They also collected Mondrian and some Miro."

"And that is quite a Picasso in the dining room."

"There is another in the study, along with two more beautiful Braques.

My mother hid the collection in the basement during the occupation. She was afraid that the Germans would seize them. The Picasso in the dining room was slightly damaged, but Picasso himself supervised its restoration."

"Your parents knew him?"

"Oh, yes."

"Who did that black-and-white piece in the hall?"

"Kasimir Malevich."

"Wow! What about some of these other works? I recognize Motherwell, de Kooning, Frankenthaller."

"You have a good eye. That blank space is an Ellsworth Kelly that I have loaned to an exhibition. There is a Jasper Johns in the other room and another you might have missed in my study."

"Did you buy these paintings?" Catherine asked.

"Some of them. Most were acquired by my parents. There are also a number of newer French artists that I have been buying—in my bedroom."

"Somehow I didn't notice."

"My father spent some time in New York in the midfifties, and he thought the New York painters were doing exciting things. Challenging all the accepted norms. So he bought some of their work. I bought a few pieces when I was living in the States, but by then prices had gotten quite high. I still buy work, but I am running out of wall space. We have three Picassos, and my sister has the third one in her place in the south of France. I would love to show you the apartment in a more leisurely fashion, but we both have work to do. I also have an interesting wine cellar in the basement. This little island is my neighborhood. Could I ask you, yet again, to dine with me tonight? It would be informal, and we would eat here on the island." He looked at her and gently kissed her.

They stood together, looking at each other and then Catherine said, "Gerard de Rochenoir, you are becoming an addiction. Yes, let's do dinner tonight. Now take me to my hotel, where I will try to pretend when I ask for my key at nine thirty in the morning that I am not wearing the dress I had on when I left for dinner last night!"

CHAPTER TWENTY-THREE

Paris

GERARD BEGAN MAKING CALLS to his contacts in the French intelligence service to determine if they had information on Sofia Mostov. He then accompanied Pierre and several other officers as they searched the Perez mansion. Marcel had told Gerard about the art and antique furnishings Perez had purchased, but the number of items and their apparent high value still surprised him. After several hours of searching, there was no sign of the jewels, nor had the narcotics officers found what they were looking for.

The only find of interest was a gun safe in the basement that the Perez housekeepers, a French-speaking Mexican couple who had proper residence permits, said they could not open. Two technicians from the department were called to work on the safe.

The housekeepers said that Perez had not been in the house for several months. They couldn't remember when he had last been there. Did he come alone? the police asked. No, he was generally accompanied by several men. That was about all the officers could get from the housekeepers before Perez's lawyer, called by the housekeepers, showed up.

Gerard had encountered the aggressive and officious attorney before. After an unpleasant exchange over the search, Gerard left Pierre to explain to the lawyer why he could not accompany the police as they searched and what the penalties were for interfering with an authorized police investigation. Gerard concluded that the lawyer was blustering so that the housekeepers would report to Perez how strongly he had represented Perez's interests.

Gerard had a lunch meeting at a restaurant in Neuilly with several of his colleagues to discuss a case. After lunch, he drove to the laboratory of Alain Frankel, the gemologist retained by the department. Frankel's laboratory was in a modern building in the La Défense development northwest of Paris.

From his car, Gerard talked with Pierre, who was still at the Perez place. Pierre reported no progress on the search for jewels. The Perez lawyer was still there, although he had stopped insisting on following Pierre around after Pierre had threatened to handcuff him to a chair.

"Now, Pierre, you wouldn't have really done such a thing, would you?" Gerard asked.

"No, I don't have handcuffs with me—although I have some in the car. Besides, Perez's ace lawyer has been on his telephone for the last twenty minutes. He really got excited when we opened the gun safe and found two Uzis, six handguns, a twelve-gauge shotgun and enough ammunition to mount a small revolution."

"Ah, Pierre, the armory may explain one thing that puzzles me—why didn't Perez have any alarms or motion detectors on the second floor? The answer, perhaps: since he had armed guards with him, he wasn't concerned about someone getting in through the second floor and doing him harm. Everything in the house was insured fully, and since he bought all that highly expensive art and furniture not out of love for French art and antiques but to launder drug money, he put in the minimal security he needed to satisfy the insurance company and to alert his security guys if someone tried to penetrate the perimeter. My rough estimate is that he has ten to fifteen million euros in art, antiques and rugs, and he has probably never seen half of it. He wasn't concerned about burglars but about other gangsters who might be coming after him. Okay, I will see you at the office after Catherine and I meet with Frankel. Don't break any of Perez's antiques."

When Gerard entered Frankel's conference room, Catherine was waiting. Kissing her hand, he complimented her on the beautiful soft red suit she was wearing.

"Dior. I went shopping this morning again. I didn't pack for a stay of more than three days so I have the perfect excuse to buy more clothes, although I doubt Nick will agree with me putting this outfit on my expense account."

Alain Frankel entered the room. He wore a white lab coat and was of medium height with red hair. His tiny glasses with round lenses seemed a bit incongruous with his broad face.

Gerard introduced Catherine as an American colleague, not wanting to bring in the insurance angle yet, and asked Frankel to begin.

Frankel began with the disclaimer that Catherine thought they must teach in gemology school to the effect that his report was only preliminary. He had only worked on the material since this morning, and he said with annoyance, looking at Gerard, "Every time I want to take a piece from one room to another, your watchdogs require me to note the piece, and then they accompany me. It isn't efficient."

"We like to maintain an unbroken chain of custody on evidence, Dr. Frankel. It makes the courts happy. But thank you for doing this work on such short notice. I hope we have not inconvenienced you too much, but it was important to the most senior levels of the police to get your help because we have such a high opinion of your work. I understand that your conclusions are only tentative. On that understanding, please share them with us. As in all our work with you, this is, of course, strictly confidential."

Catherine observed Gerard's handling of Frankel and thought, *Here is a man who has a way about him that results in people saying yes even if he hasn't asked the question. Charm,* she thought.

Soothed by Gerard but looking a bit suspiciously at Catherine, Frankel began.

"I have considered this collection as a whole, reviewed the inventory provided to me and examined a number of individual stones. As we agreed, in a couple of situations I removed stones from set pieces, being careful not to damage the necklace, bracelet and the like.

"There are more tests to perform," Frankel continued, "but I would say that I find it hard to believe that someone could assemble a collection of stones this perfect and of this size without the precious gem world hearing about it.

"If I were to examine just one piece—say, a large yellow diamond—I would assign it a rating based on color and purity and make an estimate of country of origin. In the normal process, such stones would not be suspicious, particularly if they have gemological certifications and appraisals by reputable jewelers. But each one of these stones is of very high apparent quality. If a diamond is not legitimate, it can still sparkle to the layman, and some jewelers, using just an eyepiece, will see them as real. That is because diamonds have such a high refractive index, as is also the case with carefully crafted fakes. A normal refractometer can't measure it. If the stone is in an emerald cut rather than a brilliant cut, which is the case with many of these stones, there is less fire or sparkle, and this contributes to the difficulty of distinguishing between real and simulated stones to the nonexpert or the hurried or the improperly-motivated expert. Staying with diamonds, the inadequacies of the refractive measurement can be offset by measuring thermal conductivity, weight, reflectivity, density and hardness.

"Then the expert, who has looked at many diamonds over the years, develops a sense enhanced by observation under proper instruments. Internal reflection can be observed and compared, such as the light coming from the table facet. And of course there are different evaluations with different cuts—side-by-side comparisons, for example, of a brilliant-cut diamond and an imitation by carefully tilting the diamond and comparing it with the known simulated stone. I could go on about diamonds and discuss the special issues with colored stones. I could also discuss analysis techniques with rubies and emeralds and other stones—for example, the turquoise pieces in this collection."

Catherine and Gerard looked at each other as Alain Frankel continued without any indication of stopping.

Gerard spoke up. "Dr. Frankel, your expertise is impressive, and I am sure we will spend time with you in the future going over your findings in detail, but this afternoon we must have just your preliminary conclusions so that our investigation can go forward."

Frankel shifted his weight in the chair, wiggling his pen in one hand and gesturing with his left. He paused for a moment and looked at the ceiling.

Catherine thought that he reminded her of a teacher, frustrated at having to explain something to uncomprehending students.

He resumed. "All of these pieces—I stay with diamonds for now—are very close to authentic diamonds on all the tests I have been able to perform, but they fall short on a statistical analysis. They have been produced in some way so that crystalline formations seem to have been grown. One stone, as I said, would pass muster with most gemologists."

But not you, of course, Dr. Frankel, thought Catherine.

"But these stones, with so uniformly few inclusions, with such consistent color, coming out consistently just below diamonds in hardness and density, but indistinguishable in refractive qualities and in reflectivity and, startling enough almost in thermal qualities—" Frankel paused, took a deep breath and exclaimed, "These stones cannot be real.

"In the rubies, the color of these stones is excellent, and the inclusions characteristic of natural rubies have been expertly reproduced, probably by using a technique of very high heat and then cooling. The higher the heat, the more natural-looking the inclusions, and the harder it is to distinguish authentic stones from those that are fabricated. I am surprised that whomever did this found a way to achieve the high temperatures needed to create these pieces. An indication of problems with these rubies is the similarity when comparing the color and inclusions of several of them side by side. I should also note the size of these stones. There are four, either set in jewelry or unset, that are six to seven carats, and another three at four to five carats. Stones of this size are very rare.

"Now moving on to sapphires—to get to what is called the bottom line—"

Gerard interrupted again. "Are you saying that the diamonds and rubies you have examined appear—I know you want more time—but appear to you, as an expert, to be fraudulent?"

"Well … "

"Please, Doctor," said Gerard, "I know your conclusion is tentative, but could you answer my question yes or no?"

"All right, if you insist, yes."

"And your answer is the same with respect to sapphires?"

"Yes it is," Frankel said.

"And of emeralds?"

"I haven't had a chance to do much work on the emeralds in this collection yet, but most fake emeralds are doublets. These aren't doublets. So the way to determine synthetic emeralds—and there are a lot of them out there—is by examination of inclusions to determine if they are natural and to see if there are other characteristics inside the stone that are consistent with it coming from nature.

"On a quick look, these emeralds appear quite good, but the inclusions and other natural patterns seem very similar, so while one stone might pass by most gemologists and jewelers, to see several displaying this pattern and being part of the same collection raises concerns. I will be able to be more conclusive on emeralds, on the turquoise in the collection and the other pieces, probably by the end of the day Monday."

"Thank you, Dr. Frankel. We must leave now. Have a pleasant weekend.

My men will secure the jewels," said Gerard. He shook Frankel's hand, as did Catherine.

Back in Gerard's office, Pierre reported that the Italian police had checked hotel registers and had determined that Sofia Mostov spent three nights in Rome. The second night was when Antonini was killed. There were no airline records, Pierre said, of Sofia flying to Rome from Zurich, and no rental car records in Zurich. She probably had spent a few hours in Zurich and then took the train from Zurich to Italy. The train would not have left a trail.

Gerard responded that Catherine's hunch was right.

"Maybe we should hire her into the department," said Pierre.

"No, we could never afford her," Gerard said. "Her taste in clothes is too expensive. You are probably right about the train. Hard to trace, and the Swiss wouldn't rent her a car, anyway, if they knew she was going to drive it to Italy. So the hotel was the Hassler?"

Pierre nodded yes.

"She lives well," Gerard said.

"And the web of circumstance draws tighter."

"Pierre, you are even starting to sound like Sherlock Holmes. The evidence is pointing to her in two murders. But why—where is the motive?"

Pierre said there were no records of her staying in Naples or on the Amalfi Coast. The two detectives decided to arrange with the Italian police for both nation's police to do a joint interview with the employees of Sofia Mostov's Rome workshop as soon as possible.

Gerard left his office, thinking how much he was anticipating spending the evening with Catherine.

CHAPTER TWENTY-FOUR
Paris

BEFORE CHANGING INTO HER latest Paris acquisition—a chocolate brown pantsuit made out of a fitted crepe material—and leaving for Gerard's apartment, she called Nick.

He greeted Catherine's call with his usual joviality, a mood that changed dramatically when she described the conclusions of the two gemologists. "Kate, you can't be serious! You are telling me that we have paid out over three hundred million dollars in phony claims? You shouldn't have asked me if I was sitting down, I should be lying down! Dammit, are you sure?"

"Nick, these two guys are expert gemologists. We have used Van Bilt a number of times, and the French expert is the foremost gemologist in France, according to Gerard. We could get a third opinion, but I think it would be a waste of time."

"They are real bad guys. How could they make stuff that passed so many appraisals and apparently looked so real?"

"We don't know. Gerard is working on that angle. All we know now is that every one of Pickett's pieces is fraudulent, that they all came through Sofia Mostov, and that the Perez, Antonini and Olsen collections are similar to Pickett's. We know that Antonini was a customer of Sofia, and I would guess that we will find out the same thing about Perez and Olsen, so we have to assume that their claims are fraudulent as well."

Reschio's voice no longer seemed to Kate to leap out of the phone. "You are logical as always. I haven't gone over the Olsen inventory yet, but Perez bought most of the stuff he said was stolen from Mostov's St. Barth store, her Rome operation or from Pickett or Olsen. What a monumental mess.

These people have taken us big-time. I will have to review every jewelry claim we have paid for the past—I don't know—ten years. I wonder how long Mostov has been in business?"

"Gerard can find that out," responded Catherine, "but going back ten years makes sense."

"Does Gerard have any sense of the likelihood of finding any more of the stolen stuff?"

"I don't think so. The French police searched Perez's place in Paris. They turned up a lot of newly acquired expensive antiques and art, and a lot of guns, but no jewelry."

"Well, your discovery really changes things. We need to meet with Gerard soon and figure out our next steps. Oh yeah—how is Gerard?"

"At what?"

"Oh, I get it, so you are socializing a bit with our French colleague."

"Perhaps."

"Now I really can't wait for you to get back. Let's meet with Gerard as soon as possible in New York. And we should probably go to Miami, make nice to the Miami cops and talk with Olsen."

Catherine said, "I should be able to get back to New York in a day or two. I need the final reports from Van Bilt and Frankel."

"Okay. What about Gerard?"

"He is going to Rome soon to interview Sofia Mostov's Rome staff and look around her operation there."

"So, you won't go to Italy with him?"

"No. Gerard doesn't think that the Italians would take too well to an American civilian sitting in on an interrogation. So I will see you in a few days, and I will suggest to Gerard that he come to New York after he is finished in Rome. Incidentally, since I have stayed in Paris longer than I planned. I had to buy some clothes. Prepare yourself to have L & M pay for my upgraded wardrobe."

"Oh, great. St. Barth. Paris. Handsome, rich French detective. New clothes. We should use you to recruit new women hires."

"What if they ask about you?" Catherine asked.

"Tell them that I am suave and dashing but a bit square."

"Pretty good self-analysis—at least on the square bit. Oh, I haven't said much to the Paris office about what is going on. All they know is that we had Van Bilt appraise some stolen stones."

"Smart girl. We can't let this get out until we understand it more fully. It could really screw up the market for jewelry insurance policies. On that subject, now I need to tell Adam the bad news. Then he will be on the hunt for someone to blame for this. The good news is that he will be distracted from bothering us as we try to figure this out."

Catherine then called Judy Weiss.

After some general catching up on Judy's kids and work, Catherine described some of her new clothes.

Judy said, "I can't wait to see them. I wish I were your size so I could borrow some. Now I have some extra motivation to lose the ten pounds I have been trying to get rid of since my first kid was born. So, when are you coming home, and how are things going with your French detective?"

"Okay, let me ask you an advice column kind of question. An American woman of forty, focused on her work, a committed Manhattan type, never been married. A French guy who is sixty, focused on his work, has lived in Paris most of his life, family lived in Paris, never married. Do you think a relationship could work between the two of them?"

"Advice to the lovelorn—baloney. What is going on over there?"

"A lot," Catherine said. "We have been spending serious time together."

"Just work?"

"No."

"Nights as well as days?"

"Yes."

"So someone has bloomed in the Paris summer," Judy said.

"Yeah, I guess so. It has all happened quickly. We have spent a lot of time together, and I feel alive and happy when I am with him. Instead of my usual thing of always thinking ahead, I am just living in the moment. We have today. I don't know if we can have a tomorrow."

"You sound like a Cole Porter song."

"I feel like a Cole Porter song."

"Catherine, I think it is terrific. You are so—so orderly and controlled— you needed something like this. And you sound like you are quite conscious of where this relationship is and what the pitfalls are. When do I meet him?"

"The way this case is going, he will probably come to New York again pretty soon."

"And when do you come back?"

"Right now—over the weekend. We can talk more when I get back."

"You are darned right about that," Judy said. "Love you. Take care of yourself."

Catherine called her parents in Wisconsin and, after a brief conversation about how they were doing and when she might come to Wisconsin, she took a shower—a singing one.

Catherine decided to walk to Gerard's apartment from her hotel. With map in hand, she walked alone through the soft Paris evening, down the Champs-Élysées, around the Place de la Concorde, across the Pont de la Concorde and along the river.

The river of so much history on her left, the ancient quarters of Paris on her right, she felt her senses opening up in a way they had not for many years.

How much of this was Gerard, how much the effect of this place, how much the excitement of unraveling what was likely to be the biggest case she had ever worked on? She considered all of these questions as she walked. What she did know was that she was feeling alive—and she liked it.

Gerard had barely closed the door of his apartment when they fell into each other's arms. Later, after they showered and dressed, he looked directly at Catherine.

"Why such a serious expression?" she asked.

"My life is so ordered. While I have had relationships with women—I like women—those relationships have always been subordinate to the way I lead my life. Its rhythms. Its predictability. Perhaps its—how would I say it in English?—its formality, or better—its structure. Then you come along. Suddenly there is passion. There is laughter. And there is conversation that is not superficial but gets behind my outer person—someone I have always guarded. And I am relating at many levels to another person. Someone I think about when I am not with her. Someone I want very much to be with. Again—an American colloquialism—I am trying to figure it out."

"Gerard, you are too damned rational. Let's live in the moment. Tomorrow will come soon enough. And I can't believe that Catherine York, who most men seem to think is too buttoned up, is talking that way."

"Ah, I prefer you unbuttoned."

"Good. Let's take a walk. Show me your island."

They walked along the narrow street that bisected the Île Saint-Louis, a street that Catherine thought had the intimacy of an alley, but an alley lined up to the sidewalk with small elegant shops. Gerard commented on some of the shops and restaurants. They went into a store with a marvelous collection of marionettes and another that sold duck in all of its edible forms. Gerard walked Catherine down a side street and showed her a plaque on an apartment building, many of whose Jewish inhabitants had been killed by the Nazis.

"Some of these people were friends of my parents," Gerard said. "Every time I stand in front of this building, my heart breaks a little."

He then took her to a small Japanese restaurant close to his building. They talked about Japanese food and their meal in New York.

"We had tea at that lunch. What do you recommend we drink tonight?" Catherine asked.

"Ah, a question that needs thought. What complements or even contrasts these interesting flavors? Many people drink beer or sake with Japanese cuisine, but I think that beer, at least, can overwhelm the delicate flavors and is really a reaction to the perceived saltiness of some dishes."

"What do you recommend, oh Master Sommelier?"

"You asked, so I will give you more information than you probably want. I like various light whites or even sherry with raw fish dishes. Tempura requires a tarter white, and if one orders teriyaki, a Beaujolais is quite nice."

"Gerard, all of these dishes are on this menu. How many wines can we order with one meal?"

"If I had to choose one, and this would be a subject of debate among some, it would be a wine called Condrieu. I will order it so it can be opened and brought to the proper temperature. This wine is from a quite small area on the high banks of the Rhone River. Most people think of the Rhone valley as a red wine region, but this white wine is wonderful. It is subtle and somewhat hard to find, and it doesn't age well, but I think you will like its round taste. It has an aromatic, floral bouquet that I like with Japanese food and with some Chinese food—another interesting cuisine to match with wine. There is even a late-harvest Condrieu that goes well with strongly flavored cheeses. Another white wine that I like with Asian food is from near Avignon: Châteauneuf-du-Pape—also crisp and aromatic. But I have gone on too long."

"I love to hear you talk about wine. If I can remember anything, I will impress my friends with my new sophistication. But, Gerard, my dear, I would prefer the lecture with the wine, not before it."

"I thought the anticipation would heighten your interest."

"Hah. There are some pleasures that are indeed—shall I say, amplified—by anticipating them. That is one reason I walked to your apartment earlier and declined your kind invitation to pick me up at the hotel. But when a girl is thirsty, she is thirsty."

"I will remember the distinction you have so elegantly made," Gerard said.

They then turned to the case. After a few minutes, they decided to schedule a telephone conference the next day with Nick Reschio to decide on their next steps. Gerard was planning to accompany Pierre to Italy soon to interview Sofia Mostov's Rome employees and to look at her establishment. The Italians were cooperating, said Gerard. They would decide tomorrow about Miami. But Catherine would return to New York over the weekend, and Gerard would likely join her next week.

As he drove her back to her hotel, they talked about what they might do together in New York. As Catherine waited for the hotel elevator, it struck her that a new element had been added to the relationship: They were making plans for a tomorrow, or at least a next week.

CHAPTER TWENTY-FIVE
Paris

GERARD AND PIERRE SAT at a corner table in a small restaurant awaiting Frankel's arrival for lunch. They were in Neuilly, a leafy suburb of Paris north of the Bois de Boulogne and not far from Alain Frankel's laboratory. They discussed their upcoming trip to Rome at Sofia Mostov's workshop and the telephone conference that was scheduled later that afternoon with Catherine York and Nick Reschio.

Frankel entered the restaurant and looking around furtively as he walked quickly to the table.

Pierre muttered, "He seems to think he is a secret agent of some kind."

The two detectives had read Frankel's final report, but he insisted on summarizing it for them. He stated, looking around at the surrounding tables, that he was certain that all the gems found in Pickett's Brittany farmhouse were fraudulent.

"You can speak up a bit, Dr. Frankel," said Gerard, pouring a glass of Criots-Bâtard-Montrachet for Frankel, who sniffed it and commented positively on its fragrant aroma. "We have chosen this table so that our conversation will not be overheard."

They ordered lunch, and Gerard asked Frankel if he had ever seen stones that were so perfectly made.

"No, and as I have said, it is the extent of the collection—all perfect—that first aroused my suspicions. It is almost impossible to amass such a collection of legitimate stones. If, as you have implied, there are other similar collections out there, well … " Frankel shrugged his shoulders and took a gulp of wine.

"Abou, what does Sherlock Holmes have to say about this mystery?" Gerard asked.

"Who is Sherlock Holmes?" asked Frankel.

"Oh, just a consultant to our department," responded Gerard.

"If, as Dr. Frankel says, it is impossible for Pickett's gems to be real, we have eliminated the impossible," Pierre replied. "As Holmes once said, with the impossible eliminated, what remains, no matter how improbable, must be the truth."

"Pierre, you are amazing," Gerard said. "I don't even know that Holmes's saying. Well, we must now search for an explanation, no matter how improbable. Dr. Frankel, you must have some theories as to how these stones were fabricated."

"I have thought of nothing else for the past several days. I have done research; I talked with an expert in mineral chemistry." Noticing Gerard's raised eyebrows, Frankel said that he had revealed nothing of the specifics, just posed hypothetical questions.

"So, you have a theor—?"

Responding even before Gerard could finish his question, Frankel said that he did. Such stones, he was certain, could only be created under very high pressure and very high temperatures.

"What technology is available to create such conditions?" asked Gerard.

Frankel paused, took another swallow of wine and looked down at the table, then he replied, "The only way to create such stones is to use the heat and pressure generated by an atomic reactor."

After another silence, Pierre uttered, almost under his breath, "Holmes was right, improbable, but perhaps true."

The lunch quickly finished. In the car on the way back to police headquarters, Pierre asked Gerard if he had any idea how Sofia Mostov could gain access to an atomic reactor.

Gerard said, "I do have an idea, but I have to make some inquiries before it can be more than just an idea."

CHAPTER TWENTY-SIX
New York

CATHERINE WAS IN NICK'S office along with Adam Bendel, going over her report on the case, when Nick's assistant came in and handed him a message. "It's Gerard, calling for you, Kate," he said.

"Good, let's put him on the conference phone," Catherine said.

"I am off to another meeting," said Bendel, "but please let me know what our distinguished French friend has to say. This case is becoming very serious, and it has the potential of making our clients and insurance partners very unhappy. We need to get to the bottom of it quickly before rumors start getting out." With that, he quickly got up and left the room.

Catherine and Nick looking at each other, rolling their eyes at Bendel's stating of the obvious. They heard Gerard's cultured, *"Bonjour,"* come out of the Polycom conference phone on Nick's table.

"Bonjour, Gerard, *et comment allez-vous?"* said Nick.

Gerard replied in French that his health was excellent and that he had some interesting news to report.

"Okay, Gerard," said Catherine, "I don't know where Nick got even that much French, but I doubt it if there is any more coming."

"Now, Kate, my daughter is studying French in college, and she gave me a little help over the weekend. Gerard, how was Rome?"

"We achieved the element of surprise on the manager there. The Italians handled that piece well. We searched the storage areas and workrooms and the retail section." Gerard went on to describe the morning in Rome. "The manager was quite nervous," he said. "But there was no indication that the

144

location was anything more than a workshop where a piece of jewelry can be assembled or worked on. But I have important news on the question of stone production, and I will come back to it in a moment. The most interesting development in Rome was that the manager said that Sofia was in Rome, as you surmised, Catherine, after her stay in Zurich. Further, Sofia borrowed the manager's automobile for a day, supposedly to visit the Pompeii museum in Naples, and had it on the night that Guido Antonini was murdered. The car was back when he went to the workshop the next morning. The manager claims that he never checked the mileage, but we finally got the Italian police interested."

"Did the manager talk much about the work they did in Rome?" asked Nick.

"Ah, yes. Designs generally come from Sofia by mail or fax or from her drawings when she is in Rome. But they also come from someone else who accompanied her—a Russian, named Boris, who she conversed with in Russian and French."

"So, she speaks Russian," Nick said.

"Yes, consistent with what little we know about her. The manager says he does not know where Boris lives. He also occasionally delivers stones to them. Otherwise, they get them from Sofia—generally from St. Barth. Pierre pressed him hard—he can snarl in Italian—and it is pretty clear that Boris lives in France—probably Paris. We have a description of him, and we will attempt to put a name to the description; however, Boris apparently operates secretively. Doesn't leave many tracks."

Then turning to what he said was another major development in the case, Gerard said that he and Pierre had met over lunch with Alain Frankel, the French gemologist. Not surprisingly, Frankel was now certain that all the stones found in Pickett's Brittany farmhouse were fraudulent.

"And he said that the only way to create such stones would be by using the heat and pressure generated by an atomic reactor," Gerard said.

Nick sputtered, "Now nothing about this case would surprise me. How the hell could Sofia Mostov get her hands on an atomic reactor?"

"I am working on that question," Gerard said. "I also think I know how we might get more information about the mysterious Boris."

"Are you going to fill us in on your next steps?" asked Nick.

"Not yet," said Gerard. "This will be a bit delicate. What are the two of you planning to do?"

"It's time to bring the Miami police into this. We need to question the jeweler who supposedly was robbed down there, but I suspect we won't get much out of him," said Catherine.

"Perhaps not," Gerard said, "but we already know that he purchased a lot of pieces through Sofia Mostov and that the inventory of the items stolen was quite similar to the French and Italian—"

"And," interrupted Catherine, "we also know that Perez was a customer of his."

"Right," said Nick, "he fits the pattern."

"Yes, he does," said Gerard, "and I agree that we should talk to him. Since I am coming to New York, I would be glad to accompany you to Miami on my way to St. Barth. I think it's time now to meet with Sofia Mostov, take her into custody and do a thorough search of her house and place of business."

"You can do this?" asked Catherine.

"Of course," said Gerard. "She is a French citizen living in what we consider France. I will talk to the St. Barth police chief, and he will be sure she doesn't leave the island before we get there."

"When will you come to New York, Gerard?" asked Catherine.

"I will leave tomorrow morning, so I will be there early afternoon your time. I think that I will bring Pierre with me. He has never been to the United States, and he will be very useful in St. Barth."

"Ah," said Catherine, "Nick, you will like Pierre. He is your type."

"What is that supposed to mean?" growled Nick.

Gerard said, "I can't imagine what she is talking about. I will see you in your office tomorrow afternoon. You should also consider, as you probably are, getting your FBI involved. I am sure you have good contacts with them, but let me know the name of the lead agent so that I might inform my friends in Washington about this as well."

Shortly after she returned to her office, Catherine received another call from Gerard. He told her that he would be staying at the Mark Hotel, which was quite close to her apartment, and they made arrangements to have dinner after he arrived.

Chapter Twenty-Seven

Paris

A FTER TALKING WITH CATHERINE, Gerard allowed himself a moment of anticipation of their meeting the next day. He acknowledged to himself that he was having trouble getting her out of his mind. He then had his assistant place a call to a senior official with the French foreign intelligence agency. Gerard asked the official if he knew whether, when the Russians were active in Cuba, they might have developed any atomic reactors on the island, probably small ones.

The official replied, "Interesting question. I remember hearing a number of years ago that the Americans were concerned that the Russians might try to manufacture small nuclear warheads in Cuba, but I don't think that anything ever came of that worry."

"It would be helpful to know what your people both here and in Havana think about this," Gerard said.

"I will make some inquiries and let you know what I find out."

"Thank you," said Gerard. "This information is very important to us." He then asked whether or not the organization was aware of two former KGB agents, probably retired from the service, and he described Boris and Sofia.

CHAPTER TWENTY-EIGHT
New York

PIERRE AND GERARD ARRIVED in New York early the next afternoon on the first of the daily Air France flights from Paris to New York. Taking one look at the mass of people from two earlier international flights still in the line for non-U.S. citizens, Gerard decided to utilize the special line for official visitors. He steered Pierre in that direction. Pierre muttered that it would probably take longer to get through the airport line than it would to fly over the Atlantic.

After leaving the airport, Gerard and Pierre proceeded to the Larsen and McTabbitt offices. As they waited in a conference room, Gerard reflected on how things had developed in the case and in his personal life since the first meeting in this same conference room only a few weeks before. As Nick and Catherine entered the room, Gerard arose and, somewhat awkwardly, shook Catherine's hand.

Reschio burst out laughing and said, "For God's sake, Gerard, hug her."

Catherine looked at Gerard and said, "Mr. Policeman, I think you are blushing."

Pierre chuckled and said in his heavily accented English, "Blush, I have never seen him do that before."

Catherine, summing up the case, said that the three big unanswered questions were how the fraudulent stones were created, who benefited from the insurance fraud and how the Paris and Amalfi Coast murders were connected to the case.

Gerard said that he now had information on the first question and hoped to have some more information tomorrow morning. He then recounted the conversations he had before leaving Paris with, as he put it, "an associate."

"Sofia, as you know, was born in Cuba," Gerard said. "Her father was Russian, almost certainly a Russian intelligence agent, and her mother was Cuban. When she was a teenager, she moved to Russia—we are not sure why—and then she went back to Cuba to live for several years. The trail gets cold but is consistent with her working for Cuban or Russian intelligence."

He said he had learned that when the Russians were deeply involved in Cuba in the 1960s and 1970s, they attempted to develop one or two small atomic reactors there, probably with a military application in mind. They never got far, either because saner forces in the Soviet government stopped the project or because they were not able to finish it before they abandoned Cuba.

"It is likely," Gerard said, "that one of those reactors is actually in operation and may well be the source of the fabricated stones. The stones could then be worked into jewelry pieces in Cuba, Rome and perhaps other locations and fed into the market through Sofia Mostov's quite impressive international network of customers and outlets.

"Sofia's Rome workshop," he continued, "was apparently a destination for wealthy customers who wanted unusual and expensive pieces. The Italian police think that some of these customers found the purchase and resale of expensive jewelry an effective way to launder money. And the more we learn about Valerie Pickett's customers, the more global and shadowy they become."

As Gerard finished, Nick said, "Wow. Our insurance investigation is now an international criminal conspiracy. Where do we go from here?"

"We still have to connect all of this to Sofia," Gerard said. "That is now the focus of the fraud and murder investigations."

Nick said that, from his experience, it always made sense to "follow the money." The money had come from the insurance settlements to Valerie Pickett, Francesco Perez, Guido Antonini and Harald Olsen, the Miami jeweler. Gerard added that, since it was unlikely that Sofia defrauded all four of them by selling them jewelry which they thought to be genuine, it was likely that there was a further flow of money from each of the four of them back to her.

"Unless we can get the bank records of one or more of them, we are not going to be able to trace the money from them to Sofia," said Nick.

"Yes," responded Gerard, "we are up against Swiss bank secrecy, although the Italian police have identified two recent transfers from Antonini to a Swiss bank account, both in the several million euro range. Since the insurance proceeds to Pickett were paid directly to his Swiss bank, the trail is cold there."

"Yup," said Nick, "we paid Perez in Switzerland and in Mexico but haven't been able to get any information from the Mexican banks. With your contacts, Gerard, you might have better luck."

"So far we haven't been able to get any information out of Mexico," said Gerard. "But the best trail may well be in Miami since, as I understand it, you made a wire transfer to the Miami jeweler's American bank account."

"That's right," said Nick. "We always pay claims in the United States to American banks because of the banking regulations regarding funds transfers. We can probably get information about any transfer made by the Miami jeweler from his bank, although we will need a warrant for that."

"I think you ought to proceed to do that," said Gerard, "but we should probably wait until after you have had your interview with the Miami jeweler, or you will put him too much on notice."

They agreed to leave for Miami the next day, with Gerard and Pierre going on to St. Barth.

After Gerard and Pierre left, Nick turned to Catherine and said, "Gerard's assistant, Pierre, certainly looks like one tough character."

Catherine said, "That's right, I thought you would like him."

"After one look at him, I feel quite confident that you will be well-protected, so I think you ought to consider going on to St. Barth with Gerard over the weekend. It would be good to be there when they put the arm on your pal, Sofia. Just don't forget to come back."

"Thanks, Nick. I will think about it."

Gerard and Pierre returned to the Mark. Pierre set off on a walk around Manhattan, map and French/English phrasebook in hand. Gerard had what he imagined was what people meant when they talked about walking with a spring in one's step as he took the short walk to Catherine's apartment.

Her apartment was on an upper floor of a prewar building. Facing south and west, it had a view of midtown Manhattan as well as the tops of Central Park's trees. The walls were white and the wooden floors covered with a variety of colorful rugs. Each room had several brightly-colored abstract oil paintings interspersed with black-and-white photographs. The furniture was modern, except for an exquisite lacquered Chinese table in a shade of deep red. Catherine said it was an eighteenth-century piece. Gerard thought the decor conveyed a sense of controlled modernism, with the paintings providing a wonderful visual contrast to the white walls.

Her bedroom looked west, and the late afternoon summer light highlighted the soft whiteness of the linens and comforter on her bed. Gerard's tour of the apartment ended there. He embraced her and caressed her with his hands and lips even as she was still dressed. She felt a shiver of anticipation as she gently placed her hands on the top of his head.

Their lovemaking was intense. Catherine said to him later that they had only been apart for a few days, and it felt as if it was weeks. Gerard kissed her, and Catherine said, "I love the kiss, but I would also like to get through that cashmere shield you wear to find out what you really think about us. You notice I have avoided those words every man dreads from a woman—do you think we have a future?"

Gerard said, "I don't dread those words at all. It's just that things have happened so fast, and this case is so complex, that I think I am still living in real time. This future is something we have to talk about and work out together. On one hand, it's so complicated. There is an age difference. We work in different countries. We live in different cultures. On the other hand, it's very simple. I am happy when I am with you, and when I'm not with you, all I can think about is being with you."

Later, as they sat at Catherine's dining room table after a meal of a pear and Roquefort salad, Catherine's green pea soup—which she confessed she had learned to make in an Italian cooking class, and grilled quail, they began to talk about the case.

"But before we get to the case, I must compliment you on this wonderful wine. Our burgundy and your Pinot Noir are both made from the same grape, but this California winemaker has created a marvelous red wine. And your quail, my dear Catherine, was superb."

"Thank you," she said. "I learned to cook game from my mother because my father and brothers were such avid bird hunters. However, I think my quail is better than my mother's, largely because she only uses the birds she gets from my dad or my brothers. Not only are they full of buckshot, but the dogs have chewed on them. I get my quail from a wonderful shop just up Madison Avenue from your hotel. My secret touch is to add a little truffle oil after the birds are cooked."

"The truffle oil adds a flavor that lingers wonderfully on the tongue. I look forward to meeting your mother, and you can be sure that I will compliment her on her quail if she prepares it for me—even if I can detect teeth marks of the dogs and pieces of shot."

Catherine laughed and said, "Ah, yes, Gerard goes to Wisconsin. It would be an interesting meeting. As to the wine, thank you. Let me continue our conversation about wine from last week. This Pinot is made by a winemaker in his seventies. My wine-store friend says that the maker views his age as an incentive to make wine that is food-friendly, not too tannic and accessible soon after bottling. I suppose when you are in your seventies, you don't want to wait twenty years to enjoy your wine."

"I agree," said Gerard. "Only the English seem to want to leave wine to their heirs. I want to drink it all when I can. Leave them money. Let them buy their own wine. As to your American wine, Catherine, I find it quite wonderful, but my taste buds are not the only of my senses that you have awakened. When I think of us, I like the symbolism of wine that one does not have to grow old to enjoy." He leaned over the table and kissed her. They looked at each other in silence for a long time.

Catherine told Gerard about Nick's suggestion that she accompany Gerard and Pierre to St. Barth. Gerard thought for a few seconds and said that returning to St. Barth with her would be wonderful but that there may be some danger. She might have to stay a bit more on the sidelines than she would like.

"I will go with you, and I am sure that I will be safe," Catherine said. "Besides, the last time you and I were there at the same time, you thought I was some kind of arch criminal."

"I clearly will never live that down," Gerard said. "Now I must return to the hotel to get a good night's sleep."

CHAPTER TWENTY-NINE
St. Barth / Paris

Sofia described the police visit to the Rome workshop to Boris over the phone.

"There is nothing good about this," he said. "That the French police are involved may mean that they are on to the Pickett mess. Did Alfredo describe the French detectives to you?"

"Yes, he did. There were three of them. And one stands out in my mind. Tall, slender, well-dressed, with short graying hair and a mustache."

"Why do you single him out?"

"Because several months ago a Frenchman who matches that description came twice to my store," Sofia said. "You and your colleagues taught me to notice everything and to trust nothing except my instincts. My instincts were to be on guard with him. I saw him watching me at lunch as well."

"It probably was the same guy. I will ask questions in Paris and see if I can find out who he is. Meanwhile, I think I will consider a little vacation. Paris may be hotter than usual this summer."

"Yes, Francesco Perez called me. The French police searched his Paris house several days ago. They wouldn't tell his lawyer why, but his lawyer talked to some people who should know, and the lawyer thinks it may be about the robbery. Perez also says that the French government has made inquiries to Mexican authorities about access to his bank records. Perez says that what the French eventually get won't help them, but he is not a happy customer right now."

"Have you talked to Roberto?"

"Yes, we are keeping the branch shut down, and he said that he is going to add a few guys to the staff to discourage anyone from snooping around."

"Good," Boris said. "Tell him to keep in touch with his government contacts. The French have some intelligence agents in their Havana embassy. You also might send another contribution—a large one—to our banker friends in Zurich from your French and Italian accounts. Roberto should consider doing the same. Be careful. And I saw a report about storms in the Atlantic. How is the weather there?"

"You know it is hurricane season. There is some big stuff brewing. Too early to tell if it is coming this way."

"Okay, *plemyanitsa*, I am leaving my office. Talk to you soon."

Sofia smiled as she visualized Boris shambling out of a phone booth in the Gare du Nord.

CHAPTER THIRTY
Miami

L ATE THE NEXT MORNING, Nick, Gerard, Pierre and Catherine sat in a small room at Miami police headquarters with a slender dark-haired police lieutenant named Ramon Martinez.

Martinez had open in front of him the Miami police file on the jewelry store robbery. He expressed surprise that a jewelry store burglary was probably part of an international criminal conspiracy.

"We may have a major insurance fraud on our hands, and there is more," said Gerard. "We are investigating a murder in Paris that is somehow part of this, and we are assisting the Italian police in connection with a murder near Naples of an Italian gangster who was also involved."

"You mentioned Francesco Perez," Martinez said. "We know him here in Miami. His fellow Mexicans have stuck their hands into the drug business that flows through Miami. With Perez, with French and Italian connections, with these funds transfers, this matter is well beyond my jurisdiction. What is the FBI saying about this?"

Nick, who had earlier outlined the matter for Martinez over the phone, responded, "They are interested and, fortunately, they know Gerard because he worked with them in Washington, D.C., several years ago."

"Really," said Martinez as he gave Gerard a long look. "I will meet with the agent in charge. He can take the lead in getting a warrant that will enable us to review the jeweler's bank records."

Catherine, who had said nothing, was watching Martinez as his hard dark eyes moved from the department file to each of his visitors. She thought that he was the embodiment of street smarts. It was a good idea for

Gerard to tell him of the murders, she decided, because she knew Martinez was wondering what they hadn't told him.

Gerard had requested that no mention be made of possible Cuban involvement, nor did he want anyone else to know of his plans to question and detain Sofia Mostov.

"The Miami PD will cooperate with the FBI, of course, but once they get involved, we will stand aside. It is their show. What is your next move?" asked Martinez.

Nick responded that they would like Martinez to accompany Catherine to the afternoon meeting with the Miami jeweler. She would ask the jeweler about the origins of the stolen jewels. Perhaps Martinez could probe him about the events of the supposed burglary.

"I did ask him about the details when I interviewed him after the burglary," Martinez said. "And we examined what we thought was the crime scene. Frankly, there was little evidence. No forced entry. No prints. No witnesses. The security system was disabled and the safe opened by someone who knew what he was doing. I figured it was some kind of inside job. We have talked to employees, former employees, alarm company people, building maintenance and security, and anyone else we could think of. No leads.

"The jeweler, Harald Olsen, runs a swanky shop on Worth Avenue with a lot of South American and Mexican customers. He has appraisals and invoices for what was stolen. Looked like he had a lot of money into the stuff. So we kind of dismissed him as a suspect. Why would someone steal his own jewelry?"

"That is what we hope to find out," said Catherine.

Martinez and Catherine's interview with Olsen took place in a cramped office at the rear of his spacious store on Worth Avenue in Palm Beach. Olsen was tall, with pale blue eyes that Catherine thought were as cold as some of the jewels she had noticed in his store. He sat behind his desk and looked directly at Catherine and Martinez when answering questions. He did not change his facial expression. Conveying a slight annoyance at the interruption of his day, Olsen said that he didn't know what he could add to his previous answers in interviews with Martinez and the other Larsen and McTabbitt investigator.

Martinez asked him about his purchases of the stolen jewelry.

"I buy from only a few suppliers whom I trust and with whom I have long-term relationships."

Catherine asked if one of those suppliers was Sofia Mostov. Olsen said yes.

"Why her?" Catherine asked.

Staring at Catherine, Olsen said Sofia had access to the exceptional pieces his customers wanted and could have custom pieces made.

"Do you visit her in St. Barth?" Catherine asked.

"Of course I do. That is where I make many of my selections. Why is that relevant to the theft of my jewelry? I haven't heard a word about any progress in recovering the pieces or catching the thief."

Martinez, ignoring his comment, asked Olsen for a list of his customers.

"That question, Lieutenant, seems as irrelevant to the investigation of the robbery as the one Ms. York asked about my travels."

"Is that a no?" Martinez asked.

"Lieutenant, my customers are a confidential matter. I don't see how they are your business."

"Is Francesco Perez a customer?" Martinez asked.

"My customers depend on my confidentiality and discretion. That is one of the reasons I am successful." Olsen continued to fix his gaze on Martinez and Catherine. "I do not want to keep either of you from your jobs of finding my jewelry and identifying the perpetrator, so I hope you won't mind if I return to my work." Olsen stood up and said, "My assistant will show you out."

Catherine said, "Thank you, Mr. Olsen. If you have anything to add to the insurance side of the investigation, I will be at the Mandarin Oriental until tomorrow. We paid your claim promptly; we would like your help."

Olsen looked at her and left the room without replying.

CHAPTER THIRTY-ONE
Mexico City / St. Barth

FRANCESCO PEREZ WAS SITTING next to the swimming pool of his well-guarded villa in a suburb of Mexico City when one of his many cell phones, one with a security device embedded, rang.

"Olsen, to what do I owe the pleasure of this call? Do you have a rare necklace that I can place around the throat of a beautiful woman?" His joviality quickly turned to anger as he listened to the jeweler's account of the interview with Martinez and Catherine.

"They asked about me, did they? And she said if you had anything else to tell her, she could be reached at the Mandarin Oriental? What does she expect—that you will call her and tell her you forgot to claim a $2 million bracelet? What is her name? She is just trying to squeeze you. So is the cop. But I am the one being squeezed, and I don't like it. Thanks for the call. Maybe you should take a trip somewhere for a few weeks. Get out of Miami. It is hurricane season. And use your shredder on any documents and records that have my name on them."

———

Perez called Sofia in St. Barth, reaching her in her car. After she pulled off the narrow St. Barth road, she listened to an angry Perez.

"They tear apart my Paris house. My Paris jeweler gets whacked. Then, they question my Miami jeweler and want to know if I am one of his customers. They have Pickett's records, I am sure, and the dummy probably has my name listed as a customer. Sofia, my dear, dealing with you is getting complicated."

Sofia, calm as usual, had him go over what Olsen had told him about the interview. Perez mentioned that Catherine had asked about Sofia. "What did Olsen say the insurance investigator's name was again?" she said.

"Catherine York. She said that he could call her if he remembered anything else. Such bullshit! Why do you ask?" Perez asked.

"Because a few months ago, a Catherine York visited my store here and expressed an interest in buying an expensive piece of jewelry. She spent considerable time looking at a number of pieces, but she never got back to me. She said she was an investment banker. Gave me a card."

"Business cards are cheap."

"Did Olsen say what she looked like?" Sofia asked.

"What am I, a cop? I don't think he described her. Maybe he said she was an American, dark-haired."

"I am sure it is the same woman."

"Well, I don't like this one bit. We need to talk to her and find out what is going on, how much she knows. I have survived and prospered this long by knowing more—not less—than the people I am up against. I will call you if I find anything out that you should know."

Perez then made a call to Miami.

CHAPTER THIRTY-TWO
Miami

Several hours later, Pierre, Gerard and Nick were in the lobby of the Mandarin Oriental, waiting for Catherine to come down from her room and join them for dinner. As they admired the view of Biscayne Bay through the floor-to-ceiling windows, Nick looked at his watch and said that it was unusual for Catherine to be late. She was, he said, one of the most punctual people he had ever known.

"I will call her on the house phone," offered Gerard. As he walked toward the desk, he saw one of the hotel security men, easily identified by the ubiquitous earpiece, motion to a colleague. They both moved quickly toward a stairway next to the elevator bank. Motivated by instinct, Gerard took out his police credentials and asked the security man what the problem was.

"Some kind of commotion in the garage. A woman struggling with some guys." Shouting at Nick and Pierre to follow him, Gerard ran past the guards down the stairs to the garage. Nick and Pierre followed close behind him.

As the three entered the garage, they saw a man standing next to a car and heard a muffled shout behind him. As they ran for the car, they saw Catherine struggling with two men who were trying to shove her into the backseat of a large black Audi sedan. Pierre, ahead of Nick and Gerard and moving fast, kept close to the line of parked cars. A man standing guard fired a shot at Pierre, who ducked behind one of the parked vehicles. The bullet shattered the rear window of an adjacent car. The shooter tried to get a second shot off, but Pierre blocked his gun arm and struck him in the face with the full force of his head, which he effectively used as a battering ram. His black pistol flying onto the concrete floor of the ramp, the shooter slumped against the Audi as Pierre finished breaking his nose with a right uppercut.

The man holding Catherine threw her viciously into the backseat of the Audi, banging her head against the roof in the process. Turning to face Gerard, the man reached into his pocket for his gun. Gerard delivered the toe of his shoe to the gunman's groin and followed the kick with a karate chop, driving him to the floor. Nick tackled the third assailant and was wrestling with him on the floor when Pierre came around the back of the car, kicked the would-be kidnapper in the head and pinned his arms behind his back.

Gerard removed the second gunman's Glock, and Pierre disarmed the third one just as the two hotel security officers arrived.

Gerard and Pierre, using their neckties as well as Nick's, secured the hands of the three Mexicans. The guards—confused and a bit scared— tried to make out what had happened. Gerard was in the Audi's backseat, checking on Catherine and using his handkerchief to try to stop the bleeding from the gash on her forehead.

Pierre kept one of the Glocks pointed at the Mexicans while Nick, soon joined by Gerard, tried to explain to the hotel security men what had happened. Two Miami uniformed police officers, summoned by the hotel security, showed up with guns drawn. They asked Pierre to give them his weapon, which he did.

Gerard and Pierre showed their French police identification to the Miami officers. The detectives and Nick began to talk. Several onlookers, who had come to retrieve their cars, were waved off by the police, who were further confused by one of the Mexicans saying that they were the victims of an attempted carjacking.

As Nick was muttering about chutzpah, Catherine, who had been sobbing in Gerard's arms, suddenly said that she was the victim of a kidnapping. She told the Miami officers to secure the three Mexicans, who were trying to wriggle out of their necktie restraints, with handcuffs and call Ramon Martinez.

Appreciating the opportunity to call a higher authority, one of the officers called Martinez. The detective arrived within twenty minutes, preceded by two more uniformed police officers.

After hearing the report, Martinez smiled—Catherine thought for the first time since she had met him—and said, "My life was calm—at least by the standards of a Miami police detective—until you folks showed up. The officers will take these three downtown and book them. Catherine, we should have that cut checked out at the hospital, and then I will take statements from the four of you. Officer Barnes here"—he gestured to one of the uniformed officers—"will get statements from the security officers."

Several hours later, Catherine, Nick, Gerard and Pierre were seated in a corner of the Mandarin Oriental bar with Ramon Martinez, discussing the excitement of the past few hours. Gerard was unruffled, as always. Pierre was suffering only a headache from delivering what everyone agreed was a world-class head butt to the gunman who, Martinez said, was in the hospital under guard being treated for a broken nose and concussion. Catherine had a large bandage on her forehead.

A hotel security guard was stationed where he had a clear view of anyone approaching the corner where the group sat. At the hotel entrance, there was a Miami police car with two officers.

Martinez said, "Your three friends weren't doing much talking, and a lawyer showed up pretty fast, but they are clearly connected to the Mexican cartel that has become active in Miami. That means Francesco Perez is involved. They are mean hombres."

"But why go after Catherine?" Nick wondered aloud.

Gerard responded, "We put a lot of pressure on Perez in Paris by searching his house. Then his Paris jeweler turns up murdered. The Miami jeweler is probably connected to him, and I am sure he told Perez about the visit from Catherine and Ramon. I doubt if they intended to kill Catherine"—he looked at her with a slight and tender tilt of his head—"but they probably would have questioned her in an unpleasant way to find out how much she knew and tried to scare her off. These people are not subtle."

"Makes sense," said Martinez. "Perhaps we will find out more after we search Olsen's store records."

"When can you get a warrant?" asked Nick.

"Tomorrow. You and I are meeting with the feds in the morning. But they could slow things down."

"I sure hope not. Once Gerard and Pierre arrest Sofia Mostov, records and people might start disappearing."

"On that note," Martinez said, "we should probably let tomorrow's travelers get some sleep. With that hurricane brewing, you folks might have a tough travel day. We will keep two officers here through the night. The three of you will also get a police driver to the airport tomorrow—all compliments of Miami taxpayers. But seriously, be careful. These are bad guys we are dealing with."

"Thank you for everything, Ramon," said Catherine as she got up from the table, giving him a kiss on the cheek. After hugging Nick, she went to the elevator, leaning slightly on Gerard's arm.

CHAPTER THIRTY-THREE
Miami/St. Barth

THE NEXT MORNING THE three of them were driven to the airport by a Miami detective named Martha. She drove, Catherine observed, with the same disdain for traffic laws Gerard displayed in Paris. *It must be a police thing,* Catherine thought.

The American Airlines flight to St. Martin was on time. After a bit of badinage about who had the hardest head, Catherine and Pierre slept. Gerard reflected on his telephone conversation that morning with Jean-Claude Sourel, the St. Barth police chief. Sofia Mostov was still on the island, but a hurricane brewing in the Atlantic was heading in the direction of St. Barth. After today, it was likely the St. Barth and St. Martin airports would shut down until the storm had passed.

Gerard also thought about how his life had changed since his last visit to St. Barth. The woman he had first seen at the St. Martin airport was now asleep in the seat next to his, her head resting on his shoulder, her shiny, deep black hair contrasting with the light pink of his Charvet shirt. *What a smart, beautiful and interesting woman she was,* he thought. What lay in store for the two of them over the next few days and beyond?

They were the only passengers on the plane to St. Barth from St. Martin, although the small St. Barth airport terminal was crowded with passengers heading to St. Martin, Guadeloupe and other islands from which they could fly to destinations away from the hurricane.

Sourel met them at the airport. As they got into Sourel's car, they did not notice the tall dark-haired young woman on her cell phone under the extended roof of the walkway that ran along the street side of the airport.

————————

At the same time the group was leaving the airport, Sofia called Raul Rentas on her cell phone. Rentas answered her call in his small rented house in the little town of L'Orient, about a ten-minute drive from the St. Barth airport. A former Cuban air force pilot, he had jumped at the chance several years ago to move from flying old Soviet-era MiGs to Sofia's Pilatus PC-12. He adored Sofia, for whom he provided personal security as well as being her pilot.

"Raul, I just got a call from the airport and we will have to leave soon. How close is the hurricane?"

"I am following the storm on television and monitoring the airport radio. About an hour ago, the storm turned to the west, and it looks like it is headed for the island. It may be coming ashore near Pointe à Toiny, but nobody knows for sure. They are closing the airport in about an hour."

"We are going home," Sofia said. "Any problem with fuel or range because of this weather?"

"No, no, señorita. We have fuel on board to go fourteen hundred nautical miles."

"Okay. We leave whether or not the airport is open. I have to go to the store. Then I will put some stuff on the plane. You get the plane ready for a quick takeoff. I will call you in about an hour. And, Raul, don't leave any information about the trips we have made or any other information linked to me in the house. Use that shredder I gave you, and take the shredded pages to the dump."

"Yes, señorita, I will take care of everything."

Sofia pulled on her rain parka and drove her VW Golf into Gustavia. Observing the eerie quiet of the harbor, now almost completely emptied of boats, she entered her darkened store through a side entrance and took a large duffel bag into her office. Opening a safe hidden behind a cabinet, she removed several notebooks and a number of trays of uncut stones, all of which she put into the duffel. She removed several pieces from the other store safes, as well as items from the display cases. After she had filled the duffel bag, she opened her desk drawer and took out a Ruger seven-shot revolver loaded with .38-caliber, hollow-point bullets. She also grabbed a small case divided into two compartments, each holding fourteen bullets, one set of .38-caliber and one of .357 caliber. The Ruger's chamber could take either.

Boris and others with whom she had worked used to banter with her about her preference for revolvers over semiautomatic pistols in her houses and stores. Her response was always the same. "If I am going on a mission and I have worked with the automatic, fired it, cleaned it, loaded the clips myself, then I feel confident using it. But in the store or the house, the gun may sit for months. If I need it in one of those places, it is an emergency. I will likely be on the defensive, not taking the initiative. In those situations, I don't want to think about whether a round is chambered, fuss about the safety and, above all, face a jamming situation. I want reliability." As in most arguments with Sofia, she generally had the last word.

Putting the pistol in her purse, she reset the store alarm and walked to her car. She put the duffel into the back of the Golf and drove through thick rain and rapidly growing darkness. The roads from Gustavia were nearly deserted as she went over the island's hilly spine to a small road that paralleled the airport's only runway on the north. The private planes that used the airport were parked next to the road, behind a white picket fence. Sofia parked the Golf along the road, tossed the duffel over the fence, scaled the fence and carried the duffel to the PC-12. After hoisting the duffel into the plane, she returned to her car. It was getting quite dark as she drove up the high hill to her villa, which had vistas northeast over the bay toward Pointe Milou and west to the Caribbean.

As he drove the travelers to their hotel, Sourel said that he would pick them up in about an hour. They would then proceed to Sofia's villa. They would arrest her and bring her to the police station in Gustavia, where she would spend the night. Sourel was concerned that the hurricane, which had turned to the island, would strike it in full force during the night.

"They are all unpredictable, but this is worse than usual. And it is a big one—picking up speed as it comes out of the Atlantic. The worst of it missed Guadeloupe, but it is battering Antigua now. People here are securing boats or moving them southeast into the Caribbean, covering glass windows with plywood and closing storm shutters."

"But the rain has stopped," said Catherine.

"Yes, it comes in bands, but the next one will be heavy and bring high winds. Then it will get only worse," Sourel said.

The dark clouds dancing in the sky, the unseasonably early darkness, the closed storm shutters, the activity of people boarding up windows and the light traffic on the road added to the sense of an impending storm. As they drove, Sourel talked on his radio. Pierre asked if they were sure Sofia would be at her villa. Sourel said that he had people watching the villa and her store.

"We will arrest her where we find her," the police chief said. "She is not going anywhere in this storm."

They reached the hotel, and Sourel gave Pierre and Gerard yellow-hooded slickers with *St. Bart Police* in large letters on the back. He looked at Catherine, and Gerard said, "You can give her one, too. She wants to be there, but she will stay far away from any action. That bandage on her forehead is the result of a too-close encounter yesterday with some guys who may be connected to the Mostov woman."

Sourel, who had all but ignored Catherine up to this point, looked at her with interest and handed her a parka. "You can keep this. It will be a much better souvenir of your visit than a T-shirt."

"Thanks," said Catherine, "it will look good with the black slacks that I may have to wear for a few days if the shops here close because of the hurricane."

Sourel handed the two detectives Glock-17 pistols in shoulder holsters, each with two extra clips fully loaded with 9 mm bullets. As he left, a gust of wind knocked several large fronds off the palm trees outside the hotel entrance.

The hotel bellman showed Catherine and Gerard to their villa and Pierre to his. Catherine and Gerard entered and found flashlights and a case of water in their room. The bay outside their room was foaming with waves, and they heard the sound of hammering as the staff affixed plywood panels over the hotel restaurant's windows.

Catherine barely had time to appreciate the Christian Liaigre furniture as they intently watched the weather report on one of the two flat screen televisions in the villa. Gerard translated the announcer's French, but Catherine didn't need a translation to understand the satellite images of the hurricane and to see its position northwest of the island of Barbuda. The storm's counterclockwise rotations were sending it on a course directly toward the small island she was on.

As she pulled on a pair of black slacks and reached for her walking shoes, she watched Gerard check out the action on the Glock pistol.

"You know, Mr. Policeman, this is our first trip together, and we are in a beautiful hotel on one of the most romantic islands in the world. If I told my friends only that, they would be green with envy. But if I went on to tell them that this island is about to get hit by a hurricane, my outfit is a yellow police parka, we are about to arrest a dangerous international criminal, and instead of kissing me, my lover is checking out his gun—well, they might not be so envious."

The wind picked up, and the rain pelted the roof and windows of the villa. Gerard put the Glock back into its holster and walked over to Catherine, sweeping her into his arms and kissing her gently over her bandage, on each of her eyes and then on her lips. He unzipped her slacks and pulled her close to him. She could feel the strength in his hands.

A half hour later, they hurriedly climbed out of the villa's king-size bed and got dressed. Gerard said that it was the most pleasurable prelude to an arrest in his entire career.

CHAPTER THIRTY-FOUR

St. Barth

N OW BACK IN HER villa, Sofia was also watching the television weather report. Her cell phone rang. It was Raul.

"I am at the airport," he said.

"I can barely hear you over the wind."

"They are moving planes into the hangars or trying to tie them down. The control tower is shutting down, and they are putting plywood over its windows. Everyone says that the storm has taken people by surprise. It is moving faster than anyone thought it would. Antigua and Barbuda are pretty torn up. What do you want me to do?"

"Stay with the plane," Sofia said. "Don't tie it down. I want to get out of here, but I have to do a few things first. I will be there in about thirty minutes. Keep your phone on, and keep watching the road to my villa."

She took out a different cell phone and dialed Boris in Paris. "Sorry to wake you up in the middle of the night, but I need to talk with you now."

"No problem, *plemyanitsa*. Boris never sleeps, he just closes his eyes. What is the weather like there? There was a news report about a possible hurricane hitting the island."

"Not a possible hurricane, Boris; it is coming. Rain, big winds, and it is getting dark. I am getting out with Raul. We have maybe an hour before we can't leave, although it is going to be close."

"Why the hurry? Why take a risk?"

"Things are heating up. Perez called me a little while ago. I think the French cop I told you about is working with that American bitch. She is an insurance investigator. Can you believe that? Anyway, she and some Miami cop questioned Olsen in Miami. Perez freaked out and had some of his guys try to snatch the American so they could find out what she knew. His guys bungled it. Apparently, two French cops and some other guy who was with her stopped them. Perez's guys are in jail in Miami. He is furious, but he shouldn't have been so damned impulsive.

"I had heard a few days ago that a big shot French detective was coming to the island, so I have had someone watch the airport," Sofia said. "The detective showed up today from Miami. It's the same man who was here a few months ago and who was at our place in Rome. He brought another guy with him from Paris—probably the other cop who was in Miami. And get this—the York woman is with them as well. They were picked up at the airport by the local police chief. Now, why would they come to this island in the face of a hurricane? Not for a vacation. I bet they came to visit me, and I am definitely not receiving visitors."

"I understand. You are smart to leave," Boris said. "Don't delay. You do not want to be trapped on the island by a hurricane. As for me, I told you I was thinking about a vacation from Paris. I just couldn't decide where to go. Now I know. I will leave tomorrow but, with the weather in the Caribbean, I may not be able to get to Havana right away. So I might go by way of Moscow. It is time for a visit. And I will take the train, which will enable me to bring a lot of my things without worrying about airport security."

"A very good idea. I am going to call Roberto. If we can get out, I should be at his place in time for breakfast. You call him, too. Let him know how I can get in touch with you. And, Boris—you should go to Moscow. It has been too long."

"Be careful, *plemyanitsa*."

From a safe, Sofia pulled out French, Cuban, Russian and Canadian passports and six thick packets of currency. She placed them in the backpack, followed by her purse and, finally, a 9 mm Beretta pistol with five extra clips. For a moment she fondled the gun—it was the one she practiced with regularly. She turned on all the lights in her villa in the rooms on the side of the house farthest from the garage and then turned off all lights nearest the garage. Peering at the road that intersected with her driveway through her night-vision binoculars, she could make out a car that she recognized as belonging to the St. Barth Police Department. It had two people in it.

She called Raul.

Sourel picked up Gerard, Pierre and Catherine at the hotel. The hotel attendant tried to shield them from the rain with an umbrella as they ran to Sourel's car, but the wind turned it inside out immediately. Not wanting to wear their police parkas in the hotel, they struggled into them in the car.

Sourel said, "She returned to her villa about an hour ago, and she is still there."

As they passed the airport, Sourel pulled into a parking area where there were two Land Cruisers with St. Barth Police markings. Sourel suggested that he, Gerard, Pierre and one of his uniformed officers ride in one Land Cruiser, which would be used to make the arrest. The other Land Cruiser, which had three uniformed officers in it, would provide backup. Catherine would ride in the second vehicle and be transferred to the car watching the villa with two more of Sourel's officers.

Sofia's villa was on a cliff, so it would be difficult for her to elude them by going out the back. Two of the officers in the second Land Cruiser would precede Sourel's car, drop off Catherine, park on the road intersecting with Sofia's driveway, and then station themselves on either end of the house. Then Sourel, Gerard, Pierre and a uniformed officer would make the arrest.

Two officers had automatic weapons under their parkas. Noticing Pierre's apparent surprise at the heavy weaponry, Sourel said that he thought Sofia was alone, but he couldn't be sure. He was sure that she had weapons in the villa, and she employed both a pilot, who could be armed, and two security people at her store.

Gerard and Pierre looked at an aerial photo of the villa spread out on the dashboard of Sourel's Land Cruiser. The villa had two doors facing the road. Pierre suggested that Sourel knock on the door of the main entrance with Gerard next to him. The policeman with them would be stationed at the second door, and Pierre would stand a few feet back so as to observe both doors and communicate with the officers at the sides of the house and the two in the car with Catherine.

As they drove the short distance from the airport lot to the villa, Catherine thought that the rain intensified and it got darker with each minute that passed. The car's windshield wipers could barely clear the rain off the window before the next sheet of water covered it. The Land Cruiser with Catherine and the three officers went first, and it turned onto the same road paralleling the runway that Sofia had used a short time ago. A few yards before the white picket fence bordering the airport, the road branched to the left up the hill. Sofia's villa was on the road above the airport.

The first Land Cruiser, its lights off, stopped to drop Catherine off. The two officers opened the door of the sedan for her as she slid into the backseat. The big car then made a U-turn and parked behind the sedan. The two officers made their way up the villa's driveway, fighting to hold their footing in the wind and rain. Reaching their positions, they called Sourel on their radios, and his Land Cruiser pulled into Sofia's driveway. The space in the center of the circular driveway was planted with trees, obscuring the view of the unlighted side of the house, where the garage was.

CHAPTER THIRTY-FIVE
St. Barth / Cuba

STANDING JUST INSIDE THE darkened garage, her eyes pressed against her night-vision binoculars, Sofia Mostov watched through the heavy wind-driven rain, her eyes fixed on the St. Barth police car parked on the narrow road that intersected with the driveway to her villa. She watched and reflected on some of the lessons ingrained in her years before by her KGB trainers: careful observation is the essence of the craft; watching those who think they are watching you may be the difference between success and failure; stealth is always the goal; violence should be avoided and, if necessary or part of the mission, should be as subtle as possible—poison rather than hands, hands rather than knives, knives rather than guns, guns rather than bombs. Do not hesitate; act swiftly and aggressively; seek the element of surprise and the cloak of darkness.

Sofia talked on her cell phone with her pilot, Raul. He also had night-vision binoculars and was peering through the open door of the Pilatus as it sat just off the runway of the darkened St. Barth airport.

"How much longer do we have before it will be impossible to take off?" Sofia asked.

"Señorita, the tailwinds are increasing, perhaps gusting to eight or even nine knots. A tailwind of more than ten knots would make taking off too dangerous. The crosswinds are harder to gauge, but they are also increasing rapidly. The hurricane will hit this island soon. We cannot wait much longer."

"The Paris cops and the locals will come here shortly. There is a car watching the villa. I need to be gone, but I do not want to meet them on the narrow road to the airport. Do you see anything?"

"It is hard to see with the rain and the wind. The plane is shaking. But, *sí, sí*. There are headlights—two cars—they are heading down the hill on the road that runs next to the airport. They have stopped. They are not continuing toward the beach. Now they are turning up the hill toward your villa. They are big cars."

"The big cars are police Land Cruisers," Sofia said. "Even if they block my driveway, I can get around them. With only two cars, they won't block the road. They won't expect me to try to leave the villa in this weather, and if they try to stop me, it will not be good for them. Get ready; I will be at the plane shortly."

Through her binoculars, she watched as the two Land Cruisers turned around in the road next to the villa. One parked behind the sedan, and she saw two figures in yellow ponchos leave the car. Both people were bent over against the driving rain. One police officer struggled along the hill below her garage; the other headed toward the far side of the house. *So,* she thought, *flankers. What do they think I am going to do—climb down a three-hundred-foot cliff in a hurricane?* The second Land Cruiser pulled into her circular driveway, its blue and red lights flashing.

Dressed in a black parka and black fatigue pants, Sofia slipped into her Golf, a short-barreled Uzi loaded with a twenty-five-round clip slung around her neck. She edged out of the garage, accelerating just as the police car approaching her villa was obscured by the lush vegetation of the driveway's center island.

She had switched off the dome light earlier, and she turned from her driveway onto the road without touching the brake pedal. She drove without headlights into the rain-filled darkness, hunched forward so far that her face was almost against the windshield, the Uzi bumping against the steering column. Her black-gloved hands gripped the steering wheel so tightly that her hands hurt. She called on the memories of having driven that road over many years to guide her.

With the darkness and the driving rain, the first police officers to suspect that a car had left the villa were in the backup sedan parked on the road. One of the officers in the sedan shouted into his radio that he thought a car had left the villa. The officer next to the garage had heard nothing in the howling wind. Sourel responded that the sedan should drive down the road and look for Sofia's Golf. He ordered the three officers to hold their positions and watch the villa while he, Gerard and Pierre followed after the sedan. Anyone who tried to leave the villa was to be arrested.

As Sofia crept through the curve leading to the intersection with the airport road, she felt a sickening thud as the right side of her car slipped off the narrow strip of concrete into the ditch on the side of the road. She wrenched the wheel sharply to the left and accelerated. The underside of her car loudly scraped the sharp edge of the road as she regained traction. Looking up, she saw the airport tower, now totally darkened, outlined by the quivering lights of St. Jean beyond. As she reached the airport road, she flashed her headlights twice to alert Raul, turned the Golf sideways so it blocked the road just before it intersected with the airport road and threw her keys into the bushes. Carrying her two bags, she ran the short distance to the white picket fence separating the airport road from the private plane parking at the airport. The only planes visible were two tightly tied-down Cessnas and her Pilatus on the active runway pointed toward the bay.

As Sofia was running for the plane, the police sedan came down the hill fast. The sedan's headlights picked up the dark shape of the Golf, stopped where there should not have been a car. Too late, the driver slammed on his brakes and the sedan slid on the rain-slicked road, colliding with the Golf. Sourel saw the collision and was able to stop his Land Cruiser in time. He, Gerard and Pierre hurried to the sedan and helped the three occupants out, shaken up but not hurt except for a bruised forehead on the officer in the passenger's seat. They ran to the airport fence.

Sofia climbed into the plane and sat down next to Raul, who immediately revved the engine, released the brakes and headed down the runway toward the bay. The wind buffeted the plane as it took off, straining for altitude.

As the Pilatus turned on its running lights and gained altitude over the bay, Sourel pounded his fist into his hand. "She is on that plane; I know it. I will call St. Martin and see if they can track it on their radar."

"Go ahead," said Gerard, "but I know where she is going. Tell them to look in the direction of Cuba." As he watched the lights of the plane disappear into the darkness and rain, he put his arm around Catherine and said, "We have not seen the last of her, and she has not seen the last of us. Let's get back to the hotel before this hurricane strikes."

Stripping off her soaking parka and huddling in her seat, Sofia could hear the roar of the big Pratt and Whitney engine as the plane left the runway, and she involuntarily shuddered as churning waves splashed over the fuselage and her window. Raul fought for altitude. He muttered, "Help us, God," in Spanish as the tailwind and crosswinds seemed to act together like a giant hand, preventing the Pilatus from climbing. The waves outside Sofia's window suddenly receded as the plane lurched to the left, throwing her hard against her shoulder harness. The right wing was forced to what seemed to be almost a vertical angle. The tip of the left wing was just above the leaping waves.

Somehow the plane got back to level, and Sofia realized that she probably had not breathed since climbing into the plane. Looking out to her right, she recognized the outline of Pointe Milou, the peninsula that marked the end of the bay and the beginning of the Atlantic, and she realized that the lights of the houses on Pointe Milou were below her. They were safely in the air. She looked over at Raul. He smiled through his sweat-drenched face and muttered in Spanish, "Goodbye, St. Barth. You need a longer runway."

As the Pilatus climbed, Sofia felt herself almost bounce in her seat as the wind continuously jolted the plane. She could see the deep red on the radar, where the heavy rain was now almost directly behind them to the east. Raul headed the plane almost due west, keeping them well south of Puerto Rico.

"Nobody will come looking for us in this weather, and I am hearing little traffic," he said. "What few planes are up here are heading west, away from the hurricane. We will stay on this course until we are south of Jamaica, then turn to the northwest on a course toward Cienfuegos, where there is a military airport I used to fly out of. You will be much less visible there than at the Havana airport. I will radio the Cuban controllers only when we are about an hour out, although it won't make the Cayman controllers happy that we ignored them."

"I will call Roberto after you make contact with Cuba."

The wind died down as they got further west, and Raul brought the plane to twenty-five thousand feet. The flight became smooth. Soon the only sound was that of the engine droning in the darkness. By the light of the instrument panel, Sofia looked at one of the maps Raul kept. She thought about her father and the many flights, often in old Soviet transport planes, that he had made at night over these waters on his trips between Central America, Chile and other South American countries, and Cuba. How she wished that she could have talked with him about his work. Boris always told her that her father would have been proud of her. She hoped Boris was right.

She thought of her first mission. It was shortly after she returned to Havana, when she was eighteen. She was apprehensive, but it went as Boris told her it would. Dressed in a way that would convince anyone that she was a Havana hooker, she approached a Swiss diplomat in the bar of the Hotel Riviera. The Soviets wanted to have leverage over the diplomat, and she was to accompany him to his room, kiss and fondle him, take off his clothes, partially undress herself, and then walk out of the room. The Russians by then would have shot over forty pictures with a hidden camera. Not showing the pictures to the diplomat's wife and superiors would be the price of enlisting his cooperation.

In planning the mission, Sofia asked what she should do if he tried to stop her from leaving.

"You could deliver a karate chop to his throat or stand aside when 'hotel security' storms into the room and then make your exit," Boris said.

In the post-action evaluation, Boris and the other agents congratulated her, although one laughingly told her that if she were to pretend to be a prostitute again, to be credible she should remember the first rule of hooker school. That was to get paid in advance.

There were other honey-trap assignments in Cuba and France. She showed coolness under pressure in a complex weapons sale in Africa, working with the Cuban troops in Angola. It was in Angola where she graduated to killing. Her first victim was a South African mercenary leader working with the Angolan government. She shot him in her hotel room.

As the turbulence died down, Sofia fell asleep. She woke up, stretched and asked Raul where they were. He pointed on the navigation map to a location just northeast of the Cayman Islands. Shortly, he was talking on the plane's radio. She then called Roberto.

Looking out the cockpit window, she could see the lights of the runway as they broke through the cloud cover. All else was dark. Raul landed, and they taxied over bumpy runways until he brought the plane to a stop next to a low building. There was one lightbulb over the door of the building, and she could see Roberto talking with someone in a Cuban military uniform. As she hugged Roberto, Raul brought her bags to his car. She hugged Raul as well, thanking him profusely.

Once they were in his car, heading to Havana, Roberto said to Sofia, "Boris called. He wants you to come to Moscow."

Chapter Thirty-Six
Cuba

I T WAS WELL AFTER midnight when Roberto pulled up to his apartment, a sleeping Sofia next to him. Leaving her in the car under the watchful eyes of the building's attendant, he brought her bags upstairs. The Uzi slung over his shoulder brought no reaction from the attendant who, to a significant degree, was in Roberto's employ. Roberto then came back down for Sofia and half-carried her to the elevator and into his apartment. Laying her on his bed, he gently undressed her, covered her and turned out the lights. The only sounds he heard as he left the room were her breathing and the soft sea breezes coming through the open doors of his balcony.

Sofia slept until early afternoon and then took a long, leisurely shower. Wrapped only in a towel, she walked into the living room of the apartment, where Roberto stood with his back to her, looking out to the ocean. She dropped her towel and walked silently behind him and wrapped her long, tanned arms around him, saying, "Do you have a busy afternoon planned?"

"Not anymore."

She undressed him slowly, kissing each part of his hard, firm body and then gently pulled him to her.

Later that afternoon, they walked, as she loved to do, along the Malecón and through the old neighborhoods near it. As they ate dinner, Roberto said, "You eat as if you haven't eaten for weeks."

"I haven't eaten this food for a long time. It feeds my stomach and my soul; but it is my soul that is most hungry," she replied. "You said that Boris called from Moscow?"

"He had just arrived. It was a short message. As always, Boris called from a public phone."

Sofia laughed. "He won't use a cell phone more than once, no matter how secure we tell him it is. He didn't even have a phone line in his Paris apartment, and he didn't get mail there. How will he survive when there are no longer public phones?"

"Oh, I wouldn't worry about Boris. He will find a way."

She laughed again. "Maybe he will reinvigorate the Chappe telegraph."

"The what?"

"Oh, it was a French invention in the eighteenth century, a series of buildings that had large windmill-like things on top that could be moved to send semaphore signals to a like building several kilometers away. A series of these buildings could send messages over long distances. I saw one in the countryside. Sort of like signal flags on old ships. It didn't work very well, and soon after these structures were built, the telegraph was invented. *Au revoir*, Chappe."

Roberto grunted and was about to return to the conversation about Boris when, he thought to himself that her comment about the French apparatus, whatever it was—he was having trouble picturing it—was as close to humor as he had ever heard Sofia get. She was a remarkable woman. Barely escaping arrest, her business at risk, a dangerous flight and she was bantering. She might be half-Russian, but they left the dark, brooding part out of that half.

"You said that he wanted me to come to Moscow?" Sofia asked.

"That was the message. He will call you the day after tomorrow."

"We need to meet—you, Boris and me. We have some planning to do. Will you come to Moscow with me?"

"Yes, if you want me to. It is August, so I won't freeze. I suppose that I should go to Zurich, as well. I keep sending them money. I like their bank buildings. They are sturdier than the buildings in the Caymans."

"Hah. It is all electronic anyway, and the money doesn't stay in the Caymans long. Let's walk a bit more. We have a busy day tomorrow. We should drive to Pinar del Rio and visit the branch."

"The guys there always like it when you come to visit. A beautiful woman lifts their spirits," Roberto said.

"I am glad you are coming to Russia with me. I know that traveling is not something you like to do."

"With you as my companion, it will be much more pleasant. And I love caviar."

CHAPTER THIRTY-SEVEN

St. Barth

THE SMALL GROUP HUDDLED at the edge of the St. Barth airport, the rain on their yellow police slickers reflecting the glow of their flashlights. The lights of the Pilatus had already faded as it turned and flew west.

One of the St. Barth officers wondered out loud if they could make it in the wind and rain. Sourel, who was an amateur pilot, responded, "His problem was getting enough altitude with the tailwinds as they are and then surviving the gusts of crosswinds as he climbed. It looks like he made it. He is a good pilot, but I doubt if he would want to try that takeoff again."

The rain pouring down his face, Gerard stared silently at the place in the dark sky where he had last seen Sofia's plane, almost as if he was willing its return. He said nothing as he helped Catherine back to Sourel's Land Cruiser. She was holding her shoulder where it had slammed into the door of the police sedan when it slid into Sofia's Golf.

Pierre had been searching the inside of Sofia's car with a flashlight and came over to Gerard and Sourel to show them what he found. Gerard said, "A clip from a sub-machine gun—looks like it's for an Uzi."

"Yes," said Pierre, "twenty-five cartridges at that. She had at least fifty bullets. She was ready to fight."

Sourel said, "I will keep men on her villa and store, but I need to get the three of you back to your hotel. When this hurricane hits, it will make for a busy night for this small police force."

Putting his hand on Sourel's shoulder, Gerard replied, "Yes, and you have your families to take care of as well. Thank you for all you and your men have done. I will try to find out if she gets to Cuba. Tomorrow, we can meet and talk about our next steps."

For Catherine, it was not a good night. She, Gerard and Pierre ate fruit, bread, cheese and pâté provided by the hotel. It was a mostly silent meal, all three deep in their own thoughts. After Pierre left, Catherine and Gerard tried to sleep as the wind and rain battered the villa's storm shutters. Her head hurt from the rough business in Miami, and her right shoulder ached. As she turned on her left shoulder for what seemed like the hundredth time, she decided that she wasn't cut out for police work. Sometime in the night, she fell asleep. When she opened her eyes, there was light outside and a soft breeze blowing through open windows. She could hear the sound of machinery in the distance. Gerard, wearing a bathrobe, was sitting on a chair looking at her.

"What time is it? Has the hurricane passed?" Catherine asked.

"My dear, it is almost ten in the morning. You tossed and turned and then fell into a sleep so deep that I had to listen for your breathing to make certain that you were okay. I have been outside. The sun is shining. There are many branches down. The sounds you hear are the islanders clearing the roads of downed trees. I talked to the hotel security person and to Sourel. The hurricane turned to the south at almost the last minute, so the high, destructive winds missed the island. There was some damage, but it was light compared to what they anticipated. The airport will reopen this afternoon. How do you feel?"

"My shoulder is sore, but I can move it fine. I am ready to flee paradise. Shall we call Nick?"

"After I go and get you some coffee and orange juice, we can get dressed. Pierre will join us, and we will call Nick in Miami."

Sitting on the villa's small terrace in the Caribbean sun, the turquoise bay sparkling in front of them and the deep blue of the ocean beyond, Catherine thought that, except for a downed palm tree, some branches and an overturned sailboat in the bay, you would not know that this island had narrowly escaped a hurricane only a few hours ago.

Nick's voice boomed over the speaker phone, "I am glad the three of you are safe—that hurricane was a narrow miss."

Gerard described Sofia's escape and his assumption that she was now in Cuba. Gerard said that he was going to initiate some indirect approaches to try and confirm her location.

Nick said, "Damn. An Uzi. She sure didn't want to be caught."

"Yes," responded Gerard, "we underestimated her resolve. Where could she escape to on a tiny island in a hurricane? The airplane took us by surprise, and she clearly was prepared to shoot her way through any barricade to get to the plane. However, if there were any lingering doubts about her guilt, they are erased in my mind by her actions of last night."

"So, what's next?"

"I have asked Pierre to remain here for a day and work with the St. Barth chief to search Sofia's house and store. We will send someone from Paris to follow up. We may have to examine the inventory in her store to see if it is also compromised."

"Yeah, I know," Nick said. "Bendel has become very nervous about this. The robberies and the claims on them are bad enough, but he is now worrying about how much other merchandise is out there, fully insured, that is also phony. He wants all this kept quiet."

"An insurance fraud was committed in France because Pickett initiated his claim there," Gerard said. "And there is the small matter of a murder. The Italian authorities may also have something to say about the situation there. I am afraid your Mr. Bendel's desire for secrecy is not likely to be realized."

"I know that. Bendel is trying to figure out what would happen to the high-end jewelry insurance market if there turned out to be a lot of Sofia specials out there."

"I doubt that she will be issuing refunds, so her customers may not want to know the truth, and they still may pay the premiums as if the jewelry was legitimate," Gerard said.

"Yeah. Or they could sue the folks who appraised them. Or their retailers. It could be a mess. And then there is the question of whether or not this stuff is dangerous—radioactivity and all that," Nick said. "What was that?"

"Oh, it is Pierre, chuckling over the idea of the jeweler's glass being supplemented by a Geiger counter."

"I am glad that someone sees something humorous in all this. But good morning, Pierre."

"*Bonjour*, Nick."

"Kate has been uncharacteristically silent this morning. Are you okay?"

"I'm fine, except that my shoulder got banged up in the chase," Catherine said. "Between my head and my shoulder, I don't think I will apply to the police academy. Although I now have my very own slicker that says 'St. Bart Police' on the back. That will be a Manhattan style statement."

"You always seem to get something to wear when you work on this case."

The conversation turned to the meeting Nick and Martinez had the previous day with the FBI. The FBI agent agreed to pursue a warrant to get access to the bank records of Harald Olsen, the Miami jeweler, as well as his customer files. They were hoping to execute the warrant as soon as this afternoon.

Catherine said, "So you will stay in Miami?"

"Yes, at least for another day or so. What about the three of you?"

Catherine said that she might as well go back to New York, and that Pierre was staying in St. Barth. She turned to Gerard, "And you?"

"I am thinking of visiting Cuba, if I can make the proper arrangements. I should be able to get a visa from the French consulate in New York. Then I will return to Paris." Gerard did not notice the downcast look on Catherine's face. He went on, "So Catherine and I will try to fly out today. We can charter a plane to San Juan and get back that way."

"Okay," Nick said. "I will let you know, Gerard, what we find out here in Miami. Kate, see you in New York in a few days. Pierre, enjoy the beach."

CHAPTER THIRTY-EIGHT
New York

CATHERINE AND GERARD FLEW on a chartered plane arranged by Jean-Claude Sourel to San Juan and took the evening American Airlines flight to New York. The car arranged by Catherine's office dropped Catherine off at her apartment and Gerard at the Carlyle Hotel.

The next morning Gerard visited the French consulate and then met Catherine at the Larsen and McTabbitt office where, joined by Adam Bendel, they had lunch while listening to Nick report by conference phone from Miami.

Nick said that it had been a busy afternoon and morning. The scene at Olsen's Palm Beach store had been chaotic. Olsen was out of town on vacation; his manager claimed not to know where. Olsen's lawyer showed up almost immediately and threatened to get a court order blocking the search. The FBI agent in charge was not intimidated, and they got Olsen's customer records. While the FBI didn't share as much with Nick as he had wanted, apparently all of Olsen's customer records were partly coded. The customers were identified by number for all purchases in excess of one hundred thousand dollars. The manager claimed not to have the code. The correspondence files were thin, probably cleaned up by Olsen before he went on his vacation. There were no records or correspondence with Perez's name on them.

"They got Olsen's bank records this morning, and the FBI let me look at the trail of the $60 million which L & M paid Olsen for the robbery claims several months ago. According to the FBI, Olsen immediately made a payment to the Internal Revenue Service covering whatever taxes were due on the claim. He then wired most of the balance to an account he has in the Cayman Islands. The feds," continued Nick, "are getting in touch with the Cayman authorities, but there are bank secrecy laws there, although they will get the information eventually."

"I will bet the money is long gone from the Caymans," allowed Bendel. "Can the FBI find Olsen?"

"Oh, they could find him, but I don't think they will look for him, at least for now."

"Why not?"

"Gerard, you're the police officer—what do you think?"

"Nick is right. Unless there is some kind of violation in connection with the funds transfer to the bank in the Caymans, I don't see what direct criminal activity they can charge him with at this point. However, we have some evidence to tie him to Perez, and there is the matter of how Perez found out about Catherine and where she was staying."

"Isn't he some kind of person of interest?" Bendel persisted. "He did get $60 million of our money."

"He is, of course, of interest to us," said Gerard, "and I will ask the FBI informally if they know where he is. Our Miami police detective friend, Lieutenant Martinez, will, I am sure, tell us when Olsen gets back to Miami, but my priority is Sofia Mostov. She is likely in Cuba, as, I suspect, is the atomic reactor she used to make her jewels. I plan to visit Cuba tomorrow to look around a bit."

"But," said Bendel, who Gerard observed complained a lot and had the disconcerting habit of thinking out loud in a group setting, "we are still out around $300 million, with no immediate prospect of recovering it. If this whole thing leaks, we may get a lot of questions from people who are paying big premiums to insure jewelry. Then there are the theft claims we already have paid, some on behalf of other carriers who have the primary layers of coverage. Some of our colleagues may wonder about those and begin to challenge the big fees we get for our supposed discreet, expert and highly paid investigative team."

Catherine's face flushed slightly, but she said nothing.

The only noise in the room for the next few minutes was the hushed sound of expensive fabric rustling against expensive leather upholstery. Bendel then got up from his chair and said, "I am going to have to do some thinking about the next steps in this mess." He left the room.

Early that evening, Gerard went to Catherine's apartment. As they sat on her bed, she kissed him, undid his trousers and then stood up and undressed, leaving him to do the same as she laid next to him. She then stroked and kissed him on his face, chest and stomach and rolled over on top of him. It was over quickly and almost wordlessly. As he held her and looked at her, she reached down and put her black panties back on.

He said, "But why? I love to look at you when you are naked."

"I know," she said, "but these are pretty, and they are new."

The next night, Catherine, Judy Weiss and their close mutual friend, Peggy Lucisero, were at a corner table in a small Italian restaurant on the Upper East Side. Peggy was an interior designer whose considerable success was the result not only of her superb taste but also of her ability to listen carefully to her clients and ask them the questions that got to the point of what they really had in mind.

They had barely sat down and ordered a bottle of Pinot Grigio when Peggy said, "Okay, Catherine, what is going on with the French guy? You sounded kind of distant over the phone. And I haven't seen a smile yet tonight."

"Yes," said Judy, "St. Barth in a hurricane, bandage on your head, Pilates cancelled because of a bruised shoulder—is this a safe relationship?"

"It is safe for now," Catherine said with a chuckle. "He flew to Cuba this morning."

"Is he coming back to New York after Cuba?"

Catherine pondered Judy's question and replied that Gerard was planning to go back to Paris from Cuba.

"It sounds a bit like a cooling off," said Judy.

"Or maybe too much intensity, too fast," observed Peggy.

"Hey, don't you two have lives? Can't we talk about something else? Besides, we haven't ordered."

"Okay. Order. But we are both concerned about you. So after we order, we talk."

"Judy, you are one direct lady, but okay," Catherine said.

The restaurant, now in its third generation of the same family, was one of those secrets that New Yorkers like to keep to themselves, and it was a favorite of the three of them. The ordering, after consultation with the chef, who walked out of the kitchen to take their order personally, was done quickly.

"An advantage of early dining," said Peggy. "We get to talk to the chef directly."

"And she appreciates it, Peggy, when you speak Italian with her."

"It's fun," said Peggy. "Speaking Italian when discussing food reminds me of my mother. But seriously, Catherine, how did you get so banged up? A week ago you were your perfect, unblemished self."

"The whole investigation with Gerard is part of what happened." Catherine described her experiences in Miami and St. Barth.

"Wow—a lot of action for our Catherine," Judy said. "So, Gerard protected you?"

"Yes. He is very strong and concerned. I feel safe with him. But the case has been so intense, so exciting, and we have worked together so closely. I was up most of the night with the storm and my aching head and shoulder, and I thought a lot about the two of us. I realized that our close collaboration would, if not end, at least slow down. He may never catch her or any of the others. The L & M money is probably gone.

"Maybe it was the reality of physical danger," Catherine continued. "I don't know what those thugs would have done to me, but they weren't taking me to dinner. The attempted arrest, all the guns, the hurricane—it was scary, although the storm ended up missing St. Barth. Adam Bendel is into covering-his-ass mode. Gerard is upset that this woman escaped and his search for her is more, in his mind, now about two murders and his pride as a cop than it is about jewelry theft.

"So, at any rate, I felt a hollow place—a distance between us. Where do we go now? Our relationship is built around solving a case, around romantic places. That can't go on. Can we build something enduring when our lives return to normal? It's sort of like coming down after a high. Last night we made love, and it was almost mechanical, not his fault—mine. I wanted to do it, but I didn't feel intimate."

Catherine's comments were broken up by the arrival of an antipasti plate. Then Peggy said, "You said you didn't feel intimate—or did you not let yourself—?"

"Because," interrupted Judy, "you were not in the moment but back to the old Catherine, thinking ahead and worrying about tomorrow."

"Now, Judy," Peggy gently chided, "there are tears in those beautiful brown eyes. Our friend has been through a lot in a few days. She needs some time for perspective, to see if there is a possibility of a relationship with this Gerard that has a dimension different and deeper than being Mr. and Mrs. Crimefighter."

"You are right, Peggy. I was being too tough." Judy reached across the table to take Catherine's hands in hers. Then the three friends spontaneously stood up and hugged.

Catherine laughed through her tears and said that the other patrons, now all looking at the trio, must think that they stumbled into a group therapy session.

Their main courses arrived, and they excitedly dug into dishes of veal marsala, lasagna stuffed with duck and lobster, and a cannelloni made with pork and veal, accompanied by a bottle of Barbaresco selected by the chef.

"Food like this does take your mind off personal problems," said Catherine.

"It sure does," said Peggy as they sampled each other's dishes and savored the rich flavors.

"This wine is spectacular," said Judy.

"Yes," Peggy observed, " a big, ripe 2006. Taste the spice and blackberry aromas—and even plum."

"We deserve it," said Judy, and they laughed.

Judy observed that Catherine hadn't said much about Gerard. "How does he feel about the two of you?"

Catherine drummed her fork on a plate and looked into the distance for a few moments. "You know, I don't know. He is very reserved—private—but I guess that I have been so focused on how I feel that I haven't drawn him out. I think he is puzzled by what he must see as a change in my attitude. At dinner last night I wasn't very talkative, and we ended up mostly going over the case. He is a wonderful guy—complex, interesting, cultured, but he has lived alone in a structured, self-absorbed way for a long time. Our time in Paris was enchanting to me, and I loved being with him in New York as well. St. Barth was strange—the weather, the escape—I just don't know."

"Perhaps you need to take some initiative so that you do know. Maybe go to Paris when he gets back," offered Judy. "After all, living a structured, self-absorbed life could describe the other person in this relationship as well."

"Yes," said Peggy, "there are two of you involved here. Thoughts can be solitary, but feelings must be shared by the two of you."

"Sounds like an Italian saying," said Catherine.

"It is now," Peggy said.

Chapter Thirty-Nine
Cuba

As Sofia and Roberto sat at breakfast on the terrace of Roberto's apartment two days after her escape from St. Barth, the phone rang. Roberto answered it and handed it to Sofia. "It's Boris."

"Boris, you sound happy. Moscow must be agreeing with you."

"The weather is beautiful, my old friends seem glad to hear from me, and I have found pleasant rooms in the Pyatnitskaya Ulitsa district—I like the old-fashioned feel."

"Boris, I hadn't expected you to live so close to the Kremlin," Sofia said.

"Ah, *plemyanitsa*, I am protected by a river and canal. And tomorrow I fly to London. I heard from Roberto about your departure from St. Barth. Maybe I will fly with Raul after all sometime. What about the store?"

"I took the best pieces with me and sent a shipment here two days ago. The French police will search the store and my house. They will find no records. I did leave them a souvenir in my car, though."

"What?"

"A fully loaded clip from an Uzi."

"The cops went home and hugged their families that night," Boris said.

"I also wired the balance of the funds in St. Barth to Zurich. There is only enough money in my account to pay for operating expenses of the store if the police keep it open. But the employees will be taken care of." After a short silence, Sofia continued, "Okay—and there is some extra money. Last month I took a mortgage out on the villa. I wanted to take advantage of low interest rates and high St. Barth real estate values."

"Sofia, you always think ahead about money.'"

"The more money I have, the more secure I feel. So, you want me to come to Moscow?"

"Yes, we have to consider our options in view of these recent events," Boris said.

"Roberto is willing to come with me."

"Good, I told him that the caviar is excellent, although this government is no better than the others in protecting the fish so that we can have caviar in the future. Now in Moscow, there are many rich people, but they think only of themselves and today. When will you come?"

"In a week or so. We will stay at the Baltschug Kempinski. Please take care of the hotel reservations and get us a room overlooking the river. And, Boris, this time give us pleasant names."

"Call me tomorrow morning on the second of the cell phone numbers you have for me—I haven't used that one. Also tomorrow I will send you some new papers—maybe you will be Mexicans this time."

As Sofia and Roberto sat down again at breakfast, she asked him what he thought the French detective might do.

"He is persistent. He probably thinks you flew here from St. Barth. There are French agents on the island, and if he has contact with their intelligence service, which he probably has, they could tell him that you are here. So he may come to the island."

"But why would he come? He can't question or arrest me here."

"He is curious. He may think that he can talk to you. He is obviously suspicious enough of you to go to St. Barth and try to apprehend you— perhaps only for questioning. We don't know what he knows."

"He has no evidence to connect me to the Pickett and Antonini events, although the French police could easily find out when I was in Paris and in Rome. How can he connect me to the robberies?" Sofia asked.

"What if the police find the stolen jewels and analyze them? There are four inventories out there. Olsen, Perez and Antonini I do not worry about. They are smart. But Pickett, well, we know the police searched his store, his apartment and his house on the French coast. What if they found the stash?"

"We probably should not put any more inventory into the system for a while. Can you find out if this Gerard de Rochenoir comes to Cuba?"

Roberto smiled. "Of course. We will keep an eye on the airport, and you remember Bernardo at the office in Pinar del Rio? His brother, Ernesto, is a driver for the French Embassy. I have already gotten the word out."

Late that afternoon, the phone in Roberto's apartment rang again. It was Francesco Perez. After greeting Roberto, he asked for Sofia.

"It is Perez," Roberto said. "He certainly has no trouble locating you."

"Hello, Francesco," Sofia said into the phone. "To what do I owe the pleasure of this call?"

"Sofia," Perez began in his perfect Spanish, "the thought of your beauty and the sound of your voice are reason enough."

"Thank you, Francesco, you must have gone to a lot of trouble just to hear my voice."

"I was concerned about you. That hurricane and all—so I called you in St. Barth. No answer on your cell phone. A message on the store answering machine in French about a temporary closing—at least, that is what I think it said. Why don't you have those messages in English and Spanish?"

"So you found me here in Havana to lodge a complaint about my store's answering machine?"

"When I couldn't reach you, I did some checking. I found out that you left the island rather quickly. My compliments to your pilot. He is now a local legend on St. Barth. To where would you fly but Cuba? Although you would have been welcome here in Mexico City. As to Roberto's phone number, as the Americans like to say, I have a big rolodex.

"I am concerned about you," Perez continued. "It is not good for business if my partners get arrested. But I also called because I just received some very interesting information. It is important enough that you, and Roberto, if he cares to accompany you, should come immediately to visit me here. I do not want to discuss it over the phone."

Sofia was silent for a moment. Then she replied, "We will come tomorrow morning. What is the airport you suggest we fly into?"

Perez replied and concluded the conversation by saying that he knew the tail number of her plane. He would arrange to have it met when they arrived.

"So, Roberto, what do you think of our invitation?" Sofia asked once she was off the phone.

"This Perez seems to have many sources of information. He knows the tail number of the plane. He found you here. He is a big-time player. We should go, but can we trust him?"

"Unlike that *pinga*, the late Guido Antonini, my instinct is that we can do business with Perez. He is a tough guy—sometimes too impulsive—but he has a broad, quite sophisticated view of the world. Yes, I think we can trust him."

"You are probably right, to a point."

"We survive and prosper, my dear Roberto, by knowing where that point is."

CHAPTER FORTY
Mexico City

Raul set the Pilatus down at a small airport outside of Mexico City before noon, the day after Perez's call to Sofia. Sofia and Roberto were met by two of Perez's men, driving a gun-metal gray Mercedes S550 that clearly had been augmented with armor plating and darkened, thickened windows.

After about an hour's drive, they noticed that they were in a neighborhood of large villas, all behind high walls and gates. The Mercedes pulled into one of the driveways. The gate opened, and Sofia caught a glimpse of two men carrying what looked to her like H & K machine pistols. They stood next to a small gatehouse. The big Mercedes accelerated up the driveway to the front of a large white stucco mansion. Each window in the front was guarded by wooden shutters painted a deep red. Sofia nudged Roberto and pointed to a man standing under a tree near the front door carrying an assault rifle.

The large wooden front door opened, and a woman in a black-and-white maid's uniform greeted them. She ushered them down a central corridor, past closed doors, through a stone archway to a grand veranda with a swimming pool and a sitting area. The veranda was under a second-floor balcony and had several tables surrounded by comfortable-looking chairs, a couch and a large side table.

The second floor, enclosing the veranda on all sides, consisted of open balconies with symmetrical French doors on the interior leading into the second-floor rooms. The swimming pool was lined with colorful tiles, and a rainbow of colors shimmered through the water. A fountain was fashioned from red terra cotta in the form of a naked woman carrying a bundle with one hand on her head. Sofia thought the white walls; the subdued fabrics of the furniture that seemed to complement the pool tiles; and the quiet broken only by the rhythmic sound of splashing water from the fountain all contributed to a sense of calm. A calm achieved at a cost, she observed, as she looked up at the two men in sunglasses watching them from the balcony.

Perez was the only person on the veranda, and he came to greet them as the maid retreated. Tall and dark-complexioned, with thick black hair swept back into a small ponytail, Perez had a thin face, accentuated by high cheek bones and a prominent nose. His eyes were dark and piercing. *He reminds me of a hawk,* thought Sofia.

Perez was dressed in dark-blue linen slacks, a long-sleeved shirt of soft white cotton and black woven slip-ons with socks that perfectly matched the color of his slacks. Unlike other Mexican men Sofia had known, Perez wore no jewelry except for a gold A. Lange and Sohne watch that had elaborate dials to display not only the time, but the day, the date, the month, the power reserve and the phases of the moon. It was a watch, Roberto would later comment, of a man who collects information.

Embracing each of them, Perez asked if they would like something to drink. He pointed to a small bar in a corner of the veranda that also contained an outdoor kitchen. The range and refrigerator had deep blue ceramic facades.

"Thank you for coming such a long way on such short notice. We have prepared a small lunch, but before eating, perhaps you would like to see my garden." Perez took Sofia's arm and guided them to the back of the veranda, where there was an arch-shaped wooden gate built into the wall.

As they approached the gate, a man emerged from beyond the pool, where they had not seen him, and opened the bolt that secured the gate. Sofia could see the outline of an automatic pistol under his shirt as he followed the three of them at a discreet distance into the garden beyond the gate. The garden was surrounded by a high stucco wall and was ablaze with lush and colorful tropical foliage. There was a greenhouse and toolshed on one side and a small arbor with a fountain splashing in a reflecting pool on the opposite side, where chairs were arranged. Another wooden gate led out of the garden, and a man with a short-barreled Uzi sat on a chair next to it, a small radio on his belt.

As they walked through the garden, Perez reeled off the names and origins of the flowers, shrubs and trees they passed. The fragrances of the garden were almost overwhelming to Sofia. She tried to identify some of the plants, such as violet, gardenia and jasmine, but soon gave up and just took in the powerful sensory sensation of color and smell. She stopped at a golden-leafed plant with a white flower consisting of five graceful petals.

Perez said, "Ah, yes. A night-blooming jasmine. Its fragrance is beautiful and strong at night. Over there is the day-blooming variety." He pointed at a plant with small round white flowers. "Not as beautiful or as fragrant as the night-bloomer. An interesting contrast." He looked at Sofia. "This garden is my refuge. I have designed it, and I personally supervise each planting. It is a dangerous world out there." Perez gestured toward the guard by the gate. "This is a place of peace and tranquility. I show it to very few people. Now let us have some lunch."

When they returned to the veranda, there were three places set at a round table and a buffet of salads; a white fish cooked with black beans; lobster; fresh tortillas; chicken enchiladas with green salsa; and *tacos al carbon*. As they chose their lunches and sat down, the maid appeared with champagne and white wine.

"We have arranged lunch for your pilot and a place for him to rest," Perez said. "You are both welcome to stay the night as my guests or return to Havana later. But let me tell you why I asked you to come here.

"First, I have found our business relationship very satisfactory and profitable. I like stability and reliability in my partners. Here in Mexico, we have a saying that an honest politician is one who, when he is bought, stays bought. Roberto, I respect the effective way you apply this principle in Cuba. My business, as you know, is to use the fungibility of money to, shall we say, diversify investments on behalf of my colleagues. This work requires long-term relationships. I think of the two of you and your colleagues as long-term partners.

"Second, Sofia, I know about your background, and I have much respect for the organization that you were part of and still maintain close relationships with. That kind of network can be helpful to me in my work. At the same time, I can be of help to you. Your business plan using your jewels and distribution network was brilliant. It has been profitable for each of us. But, as always, the risk of this business is the weak link. And the jeweler, Pickett, was our weak link."

During these comments, Sofia said nothing but looked directly at Perez. When he mentioned Pickett, Perez noticed a set in her jaw and said quickly, "This is not a criticism. I engaged him as well. You recognized the problem, and I agree with how I believe you handled the situation." As Sofia started to respond, Perez held up his hand and said, "You don't have to say anything. All I am saying is that I respect direct action. But the Pickett problem set in motion a French police investigation and a parallel insurance company investigation, as you know.

"While you became a direct target of the investigation, my name was brought in as well. I always want to know more than those on the other side. I am protected by my paranoia, so I wanted to know what the investigators had found out about you and me. I focused on the woman investigator, Catherine York. My attempt to get her to a place where we could determine what she knew did not go well. She was accompanied by two French detectives and another man, and they were alert and tough. So three of my men were jailed in Miami, and we just got them out. They won't say anything of value to the police, but they won't be of use to me either for a while."

Perez stopped to take a bite of lobster and a sip of champagne. The songs of tropical birds were the only sound as they ate. Sofia wondered where Perez was going with his comments. Then he resumed, "However, Catherine York's unusual degree of protection and the fact that she accompanied the French cops to St. Barth on the mission to apprehend you increased my curiosity about her. Her company, Larsen and McTabbitt, is an old, high-level insurance company. Ironically, I think they have some of the coverage on this property and my art collection. They have a Paris office. We have contacts in Paris. We found out that she had been in Paris a few weeks ago and that she met with a Dutch gemologist. All this occurred after Pickett's house in Brittany was searched by the police, who apparently left for Paris in a hurry. Exactly the behavior one would expect if they had found something in Pickett's house.

"We have business partners in Amsterdam." Sensitive to the silence of his two guests, Perez said, "I am getting to the point now. We have helped them in St. Martin, Curacao, Bonaire and Aruba, as well as in New York. I asked them for help with this gemologist, and I sent two of my colleagues from Madrid to Amsterdam.

"They identified the gemologist, a Van Bilt, and yesterday morning in Amsterdam, my colleagues and some of our Dutch partners interviewed him. He was not initially cooperative, but that changed quickly. He said that he had examined, at French police headquarters, many jewels that the police had recently recovered. A number of them were in wrappings with the name of Pickett's store on them. Van Bilt concluded that the jewels were brilliantly executed frauds and reported his findings to the police. This Catherine York woman, as well as the same French detective, Gerard de Rochenoir, who was in Miami and St. Barth, were present during Van Bilt's examination."

Perez stopped to let his comments sink in.

Roberto asked, "Where is Van Bilt now?"

"He is permanently out of business," Perez said.

"Good."

Sofia said nothing, and she seemed to be enjoying her lunch. Roberto watched Sofia and Perez from behind his sunglasses. Then she said, "Francesco, I congratulate you both on your deductive skills and on your affinity for direct action. The handling of the Dutchman has some of the characteristics of my former employer."

"I am not surprised," Perez said. "My colleagues from Madrid once worked for that organization."

"Ah, yes. We trained well. For what end I do not know, except that we are apparently quite marketable. Roberto had a suspicion"—she reached over and put her hand over his—"that the French police had concluded that some of the stolen jewels were not genuine."

"Yes," commented Roberto, "I thought it strange that in the absence of such a conclusion, the police would show up in such force at Sofia's St. Barth villa rather than merely invite her into their offices for questioning."

"Sofia has the instincts of a survivor," Perez said. "She didn't wait to find out how much they knew. But you two may be out of the jewelry business for a while. What will you do next?"

The conversation stopped as Sofia and Roberto contemplated Perez's question.

Roberto spoke first. "We have plenty of money. We can bide our time and sell stones at wholesale later. Sofia is safe in many places. Cuba, Russia, South America, perhaps here, and she has many names."

"As I said to you at the beginning, you are important to me as colleagues. And your position, Roberto, in Cuba, as well as Sofia's associations, are of value to me. Perhaps I can be of help to you?"

"Thank you, Francesco," said Sofia. "You obviously have something in mind."

"Oh, nothing specific. But you may not know that I am a graduate of Stanford Business School."

The two of them looked at him quizzically. Perez took another sip of champagne and gestured with the glass, almost spilling some over the edge. "Yes, I have a diploma and two T-shirts to prove it. After I graduated and went to work for banks in New York and Mexico City, they sent me alumni magazines and asked me for contributions. Then I went into my current business and soon after, a Mexico City prosecutor, who died shortly thereafter in a car accident, had the poor taste to mention my name in a newspaper interview and—*poof*—no more correspondence from Stanford. Too bad for them. Maybe I would have given them a building."

Roberto laughed and said, "Perhaps a chemistry lab."

Perez said with mock earnestness, "Perhaps you are right. A building would not have been a good idea. But I did learn things there. One of the oldest lessons that American business schools teach is about the American railroads. They all eventually went bankrupt, and the lesson is that if the railroads had thought of themselves broadly as being in the transportation industry rather than narrowly as being the railroad business, they would have entered other transportation businesses and survived. When the professor lectured about that in my first year, I raised my hand and said that the airlines are all going bankrupt as well, so maybe the problem was not the railroad business but that transportation isn't a good business."

"Okay," said Roberto, enjoying Perez's expansiveness, "I will bite. What was your professor's response?"

"He said that he was having trouble understanding my question—my accent and all that—and that I should see him after class."

"And?"

"He wasn't there after class. I guess he thought I was a dumb Mexican who wasn't worth his time." Perez's voice trailed off as he made that comment, and he cupped his chin with his hand.

After a silence, Roberto asked, "So, what does your business school education tell us about our business?"

"I think it tells you that you are not in the jewelry business."

"What do you mean?" asked Sofia, suddenly alert.

"Your jewelry business was just a way to clean money. It was a means to an end. There are enormous amounts of cash flowing through businesses like the ones I represent all over the world. The challenge is not generating cash but keeping it from being identified by governments who can use it to track down people they want to put in prison.

"Now, with these terrorists getting in the act, cleaning money is even harder because money transfers are monitored more closely," Perez continued. "My colleagues can generate much cash; I can eventually invest it in clean businesses, where their profits are protected, but the bottleneck is in between. Your jewelry business was one way to get through that narrow opening. You figured out how to do it. Come up with some other approaches. I will work with you as a partner—I need some new challenges. Maybe Stanford will put me back on its mailing list."

Before they boarded the Pilatus for the trip back to Havana, Roberto listened to a message on his cell phone. It was a call from Bernardo, one of their employees in Cuba. "The visitor has arrived."

CHAPTER FORTY-ONE
Cuba

GERARD FLEW TO HAVANA from New York, changing planes in Jamaica. At the suggestion of the French consulate in New York, he went through the special visitors' line at the Havana airport. He quickly concluded, though, that he would have been smarter to enter as a regular tourist. There would have been fewer people in sunglasses watching him as he went through the formalities.

Gerard exited customs and surveyed the shabby arrivals hall of the Havana airport. In the crowd of greeters, he saw a short Cuban man in a blue cap wearing a wrinkled white shirt and khaki pants and holding a sign with Gerard's name on it. He thought to himself that, if there had been anyone in Havana who didn't know he was in town, that person was now fully informed. The man in the blue cap introduced himself as Ernesto, took his bag and led him to the French Embassy Toyota parked nearby.

Later that afternoon, one of the intelligence agents assigned to the French Embassy met Gerard in the lobby of Havana's Hotel Seville, and they walked along the Prado promenade, eventually ending up near the El Floridita bar. The agent was about fifty years old and wore the light-colored slacks and white linen shirt that was the ubiquitous uniform of Cuban men. He had a two-day growth of beard. Gerard wore a cream-colored linen suit that he had originally intended to wear in St. Barth. His pink cotton shirt was unbuttoned at the neck. The agent's name was Olivier, and on their stroll, Gerard asked him about the location of the atomic reactor the Soviets had worked on in Cuba.

"Inspector de Rochenoir, we have a small operation here," Olivier said. "Mostly we watch political developments. Sometimes we talk to the Americans, sometimes we don't. As to the supposed reactors, the Americans thought there were two, one in the west in the area called Pinar del Rio, and one toward the east near a town called Esmeralda. Both of them were adjacent to small military bases operated by Soviet intelligence. The reactors were never completed, and they are not a French affair. We are careful not to appear too curious. We want good relations with this government and with their allies to the south."

Gerard decided to ignore the veiled warning. He responded by saying that he understood the Americans had concluded that the facility in the west was once nearly operational.

Olivier shrugged. "Even if that is true, the Americans were and still are paranoid about the Cubans and the Russians. Why would it be of interest to anyone now? The Cubans surely are not operating an atomic reactor; they don't have the resources or the motivation. As to the Russians, the only ones remaining on the island from the old days are a few rather pathetic types who never returned to Russia after the USSR pulled out. Some have Cuban wives or girlfriends—the Cuban women are beautiful—and some even have families here. The other Russians are tourists who are loud, rich and often drunk. They also lust after Cuban women—there is a lot of prostitution here."

Olivier led them into El Floridita, a dark, somewhat shabby room with a large bar at one end and tables scattered about. On the wall behind the bar there were several photographs of Ernest Hemingway and, at the end, a bust of the writer.

"It looks like it hasn't changed much since Hemingway drank daiquiris and mojitos here," Gerard said.

"It probably hasn't. But like most businesses here, the government runs it. Keeping it the way it was is good for the tourist business, and they don't have the money to fix it up anyway. It is a tourist bus stop, but right now it is quiet. Just don't eat here."

They sat at a table near the door. There were only a few other customers. Olivier, sitting where he could see the door, said to Gerard, "So what brings you to Cuba? And why are the French National Police interested in an old atomic reactor on this poor island?"

"I am investigating a crime. We believe that one of the people involved is a Cuban who has been living on St. Barth and is now here."

"You haven't answered my question about the reactor, but who is this person?"

"A woman named Sofia Mostov. Do you know her?"

Olivier stirred his mojito. "I have been here ten years, and I still don't like rum much."

"If you don't like this posting, why don't you request a transfer?"

His lips pursed, Olivier replied, "Where would I go? This island seems to be my destiny. I know too many of its secrets. Your Sofia Mostov is one of them. She is only part Cuban—her mother. Her father was a Soviet agent. He was supposedly killed on a mission when she was young. Then her mother died. She left the island. Came back maybe seven or eight years later. Was working with the Soviets. Left again. Turned up in Angola. My predecessors lost track of her for a while, then she started coming back here on and off. Has a boyfriend. We didn't pay any attention to her until we got a request to check on her a few weeks ago. Probably instigated by you."

He stopped, waiting for a reaction from Gerard. Gerard said nothing. Olivier then said, "Her boyfriend is very well-connected here. Has a lot of money."

"What does he do?"

"The less I know about him, the better. He has nothing to do with our interests. In Cuba, if you ask too many of the wrong questions, your sources of information dry up. If my sources don't talk to me, I am ineffective. If I am ineffective, maybe they send me to a place where there isn't any rum at all and the women are not so beautiful. Worst of all, it might be cold. So, I don't know her friend, except that he is a businessman in a place where there aren't supposed to be businessmen."

"Do you know if Sofia Mostov is on the island?"

"I could find out, but what are you going to do—arrest her?" Olivier asked.

Gerard smiled. "No, but I might want to talk with her. On another subject, would it be difficult for me to do a little touring of the island—go to the Pinar del Rio area, for instance?"

Looking away from Gerard, Olivier said, "It is not a part of Cuba visitors go to often. If you go there alone with no Spanish, you will get lost. If you go with an embassy driver, you might as well put an announcement in *La Granma*, since they all report to my Cuban counterparts. I am sure your presence is now known to the government. I haven't seen anyone come in here who I recognize, but you will probably have someone watching you soon."

"I think they watched me from the minute I got off the plane."

"Perhaps. I don't have to warn you about the phone in your room or the room itself. Also, I don't know if you are interested, but if a woman strikes up a conversation with you that looks like it might lead to some fun … "

Gerard raised his hands, palms facing Olivier. "Don't worry, I will be careful. So will you be my tourist guide?"

"Our orders are to cooperate with you. You are obviously a big shot. I will pick you up at your hotel tomorrow morning. Don't discuss this trip with anyone. Maybe they won't bother to follow us. I suppose you have maps."

Gerard tapped the breast pocket of his jacket.

The next morning, Olivier, dressed exactly as he had been the previous day, met Gerard at his hotel. They walked several blocks to an old blue Peugeot sedan parked on a side street. "I have found someone who can fix these. We have a few on the island. It reminds me of my father's car in Lyon."

They drove mostly in silence west out of Havana on the *autopista*. Olivier maneuvered the old Peugeot, which Gerard noticed had new Michelin tires and an excellent radio, around the usual jumble of Cuban traffic. They reached the town of Pinar del Rio, and Gerard pulled out an aerial map of the area, marked with GPS coordinates. Olivier looked at it and said, "I didn't know the French police had such detailed photographs of remote sections of Cuba."

"We don't. I got this from your people in Paris. You are not the only person who trades in favors." Then Gerard pulled a small GPS unit out of his travel bag, and they drove through a sparsely populated area. There were tobacco fields and houses by the side of the road where old men sat on ramshackle porches, some smoking cigars. A group of children played with scrawny dogs. And, always, dust flew up from the unpaved road. Then they saw a cluster of buildings, perhaps seventy-five yards from them. Gerard motioned to Olivier to pull over to the side of the road and got out of the car to study the buildings through his binoculars. The two of them watched as a vehicle approached them from the buildings, and Gerard put his binoculars back in the travel bag.

A late model Japanese SUV stopped next to the Peugeot, and two Cubans jumped out, wearing fatigue pants and dark glasses, with pistols strapped to their waists. One was also carrying an AKA-74U. The other had a large snarling dog on a leather leash.

The Cuban with the machine gun said, "What are you doing here?"

Olivier responded that they were tourists.

The Cuban looked carefully at both Frenchmen and then looked inside the car. "Where are your cameras?"

Olivier responded that they didn't have any cameras with them.

"Let me see inside that bag," said the Cuban and pointed his machine gun at Gerard, who handed him his bag. After looking through the bag, the Cuban dropped it on the road and, gesturing with his gun, said that this road was closed just beyond, and they had to turn around.

Olivier said that no one in town had told them of a closed road.

The man doing the talking raised his gun slightly and said to Olivier, "That is because I just closed it. It is not safe for you here. I advise you to turn around."

Gerard saw another vehicle pulling out of the cluster of buildings.

"Okay," said Olivier. "Thank you for the road information." Gerard and Olivier got back in the Peugeot, which Olivier turned back toward Pinar del Rio. "So," said Olivier, "find out anything?"

"Quite a bit," Gerard said. "There is activity going on at the old base, and the people there don't want anyone to get close. The aerial photographs show a building that is likely a reactor, which I could see behind the large building. I think that it is probably a working reactor because it is obviously well-guarded. An abandoned reactor, even if we had found one, would have only told us about the past. Something is going on there now. I suppose that trying to find out who owns or operates this place would be difficult."

"I could try, but the inquiry would reach a dead end at some obscure government office. It could be what you think it is, whatever that is, or it could be some Cuban intelligence base—after all, that's what the Soviets used it for. It sure as hell is not a place to stop in for a cool drink and a chat. That dog looked big enough to tip over my beloved Peugeot."

Several hours later, as Gerard stood at the front desk of his hotel to pick up his key, there was a message. The message, typed and in French, said:

> *"Please call me at the following number so that we can arrange to meet for a drink. You never completed purchasing a bracelet. Your friend must be disappointed."* SM

After reading it, Gerard stood quietly for a few minutes. He then noticed that his cell phone showed a voicemail. Listening to it, he heard Pierre's voice; the message had been sent a few hours before, when Gerard was in western Cuba, out of signal range. The message was short. "Whatever time you hear this, call me—office or home."

It was late in the evening in Paris, but Gerard called Pierre at his apartment.

"*Bonsoir*, Pierre, you are up late."

"I was at the office late tonight trying to catch up on paperwork after St. Barth when the phone rang. It was our liaison in Amsterdam. This morning the police found Dr. Van Bilt dead in a field outside of Amsterdam."

"How did he die?" Gerard asked.

"The medical examiner is not finished yet. But get this—two of the fingernails on his right hand were gone, and they don't think he died of natural causes."

After a long silence, Gerard asked, "We don't know if this is connected to our case?"

"No. He was apparently called yesterday and asked to come to a meeting. He left his office, and no one saw him after that."

"We have to assume it is about our matter and that they tortured him to find out what he knew. These are bad—very bad—people."

"Yes," Pierre said. "If his death is connected to the case, he probably talked, and they know what we know about the jewels. I have already arranged for security for Frankel, although they probably have what they need now."

"I will call Nick. They should provide protection for Catherine. They may come after her again. I have reservations to fly back to Paris. I will call you when my plans are definite."

"How is Cuba?"

"Perhaps getting interesting. Sofia Mostov left a note for me at the hotel. She wants to meet me for a drink. And I have already been threatened with a machine gun."

"Sounds like a pleasant trip. Don't drink anything with her. She was KGB. They like to poison people. Stay in touch. I am going to sleep. I will call the Dutch police in the morning."

Gerard went up to his room and called the number on Sofia's note.

Sofia answered the phone in Spanish and switched to French when Gerard identified himself. "So, Inspector de Rochenoir, welcome to my island."

"Thank you, Madame Mostov," responded Gerard.

"You must be thirsty after your drive in the country. There is a bar next to the hotel with the yellow facade, just off the Plaza Vieja. I will meet you there in an hour and a half."

"I will be there." The line was then disconnected.

Then Gerard called Nick Reschio and left him a voice message about Van Bilt's death and his concern about Catherine's safety.

An hour and a half later, Sofia and Gerard were seated opposite each other in a small bar. She had chosen the location for their meeting, and as Gerard walked in from the bright Havana sunshine, it took a moment for his eyes to adjust to the dim light inside. He saw her sitting in a corner, wearing a light yellow dress. Sofia Mostov was hard not to notice as he looked at her and took in the surroundings. There were three men drinking at the bar, and Sofia had positioned herself so Gerard's back would be to the door. Gerard preferred to always sit where he could see the door, but he concluded that this was her show. If they wanted to kill him in Cuba, they had plenty of chances and didn't need to do it here. It went through his mind that he could have asked Olivier to watch his back; it would have been interesting to hear his response.

After a moment, Gerard walked to Sofia's table. She was drinking a rum and tonic. She looked up at him, smiled and motioned him to the other chair at the table.

She said in French, "Thank you for joining me. Would you like something to drink?"

"Okay, perhaps a coffee."

She motioned to the waiter and ordered a coffee. Then she turned and looked at Gerard. "Were you surprised to hear from me?"

"Let's say it was an unexpected pleasure. We never had the chance to talk when I was last in St. Barth."

"No, I decided to leave before the hurricane struck," Sofia said. "As you know, fortunately it missed the island. But what brings you to Havana?"

"Oh, I was in the region, so I decided to come and visit. I have heard it is a beautiful island."

"It is. But there are much more scenic places than Pinar del Rio. It is mostly an agricultural area."

"You guard your agriculture carefully."

She smiled and said, "Perhaps we want to protect against genetically modified crops."

"Yes. Most people prefer the genuine items—whether it is wheat or diamonds. As to diamonds, your studs are beautiful. The color is so intense—it complements your dress."

"Thank you. Being in the business, I have many choices of jewelry."

"It must be convenient for you," Gerard said. "But I understand that your shop in St. Barth is closed."

"I plan to reopen soon. My managers are excellent. However, we don't need to talk about my St. Barth store. I sent you a note because I thought it would be much easier for you if I arranged a meeting rather than have you waste valuable police time trying to find me. The longer you are here—well, Havana can be a dangerous place—many of the cars are old, the streets are crowded, there are a lot of accidents involving pedestrians. And the food doesn't agree with everyone."

Gerard tasted his coffee. He thought it was bitter, but he thought to himself, *That is the style of Cuban coffee—don't become paranoid.* "I had always heard that the Cubans were hospitable people. So far, I would have to conclude that such a reputation may be an exaggeration. But I do have some questions for you. I have a complicated case on my hands. A murder in Paris, a massive insurance fraud, a murder in Italy and, now, perhaps one in Amsterdam."

"Your case does sound complicated—and certainly dangerous. You must have other cases. Perhaps you should leave this one alone and spend your time on the others that pose less risk to you."

"I don't recall asking you for advice as to how I spend my time."

"Since your case is no concern of mine, I merely thought I would be helpful to you," Sofia said. "There is nothing for you here in Cuba, so why spend time here? A police officer of your status must be quite busy."

"Three murders, jewelry thefts and insurance fraud are important."

"I have heard about Pickett and Antonini. Who is the third murder victim?"

"You can prove that you have been in Cuba for the past several days?"

She responded with a sharp tone, "I don't have to prove anything to you, but as a matter of fact, I have been in Cuba since I left St. Barth to avoid the hurricane."

Gerard continued in a calm voice, "Yesterday, a Dutch gemologist named Van Bilt was found tortured and murdered in Amsterdam."

"So?"

"He was consulting on my case."

"I don't recognize his name. At least, he wasn't one of my customers. It is of no concern to me. But I am still curious as to why you are pursuing this case so vigorously. Is it the murders? The jewelry thefts? The supposed insurance fraud? Or do you just enjoy the chase?"

"The chase is certainly an added element. I like to get my man—or woman." Gerard looked straight at Sofia, who smiled slightly. "And, this may come as a surprise to you, but we police officers actually like to solve crimes and apprehend criminals. We think it has a deterrent effect."

"Only if you catch the criminal," Sofia said.

"Since we are talking about motivations, let's assume mine are the love of the chase and a certain—shall we say, idealism—about confronting crime in the interests of social order. What motivates you?"

"You French need a fully rationalized explanation for everything. What motivates me is simple—money and independence."

"Ah, sometimes one has to give up one to get the other, but as interesting as this conversation is, I would like to come back to the case."

"I suppose you would," Sofia said. "I would disagree with you a bit, however. For me, money is the source of independence."

Sofia then signaled the waiter for another rum and tonic and asked Gerard if he would like something to eat. "This bar has authentic Cuban food."

When Gerard declined, Sofia said, "You seem to be all business. I was hoping we could have dinner and get to know each other better. I would still like to sell you a bracelet. Ah, yes—jewels—that reminds me, how is Catherine York, the investment banker, or is it insurance investigator?"

"As far as I know she is well."

"If you see her, tell her I am still waiting for her telephone call."

There was a lull in the conversation as Sofia reached for her drink. Gerard watched her, his arms folded. The yellow dress was French, certainly not Cuban, and expensive, with a low-cut neckline. Sofia wore a turquoise necklace, and Gerard could smell a whiff of her perfume. She had well-muscled arms and shoulders. She was a beautiful woman. Her green eyes sparkled as she laughed. *There was no sign of the coldness one might expect from a killer,* he thought, *except that she always looks straight at me. She would probably seduce me, take pictures and remove me from the case. Easier than killing me. But if she is the murderer, she obviously has no compunction about eliminating people who somehow get in her way. But why Pickett?*

Gerard leaned forward and looked directly at her. "Why did you kill Valerie Pickett?"

She looked back at him. He thought she set her jaw ever so slightly before she replied, "Pickett was a good customer. I am a businesswoman, and it is not good for business if your customers die."

"Apparently it is not healthy to be one of your customers."

"You are referring not only to Pickett, but also to Guido. A tragedy; he was such a gentleman."

"You were in Paris when Pickett was killed and in Italy when Antonini was killed."

"You are investigating crimes in Italy as well as in France?" Sofia asked. "A very busy detective. I go to Paris often. There are—what, a dozen murders a day in Paris? Am I a suspect in each one that occurs when I am in Paris?"

"You could take yourself off the list of suspects in connection with the Pickett murder by telling me about your whereabouts, what you did and who you saw from 4:00 PM on July 24 through the next morning."

"Since there is no reason for me to be on your list, there is no reason for me to respond to your questions. As to Antonini, I was in Rome on business last month. I don't even know the date he was killed.

"But you are not drinking your coffee," Sofia said, changing the subject. "I suppose you are worried about poison. The only risk to you from strong Cuban coffee is indigestion. If I had wanted you dead, you would have had an accident in Pinar del Rio, while you were snooping around with that drunk of an intelligence agent. Although, come to think of it, there is a much greater chance of being hit by a car in Havana than out there—more cars in Havana."

She took another sip of her drink and said, "I didn't ask you to this meeting for verbal sparring. Since you came all the way to Havana from New York, I decided that it was only polite to meet with you, and to suggest that, since you and your insurance investigator friend must each have other matters to work on, perhaps it would be best for the health of both of you to focus on such matters and to leave this alone. As the Americans would say, your continued investigation can only lead to dead ends. Enjoy tomorrow in our beautiful city as well as your flight back to Paris tomorrow night."

Gerard tipped his head to the side, and Sofia said, "Yes, I know about your airline reservation for tomorrow." She was silent for a moment and then said, "I am getting bored with the jewelry business. I am considering a new career. Perhaps we will meet again, Inspector de Rochenoir. Now, I must leave. The coffee is on me."

And with that Sofia Mostov got up from the table and left the bar.

Gerard sat there for a few minutes and contemplated his coffee. He then walked toward his hotel, sat on a park bench and called Nick Reschio.

"Gerard, are you still in Cuba?" Nick asked. "I got your message. So those bastards knocked off our gemology expert?"

"We don't know who did it, but the assumption we must make is that it is connected with our case. The body showed signs of torture."

"Dammit. Now what?"

"If Van Bilt divulged the results of his analysis, which we must assume he did, they know what we know about the jewelry. They may go quiet for a while, or they may continue their violence. It is hard to predict what these people will do. I just talked with Sofia Mostov. She is very dangerous, and I am concerned about Catherine's safety."

"You met with the Dragon Lady? What did she say?"

"Oh, nothing of substance," Gerard said. "She is somewhat indirect, but I believe she threatened to have me killed."

"That's all?"

"Yes."

"You are the master of understatement. After I got your message, I called Kate. She is in Wisconsin for a few days visiting her folks. The family went camping somewhere, but she is expected back to their house tonight, and she is scheduled to return to New York tomorrow. I will alert her and have our security people primed to keep an eye on her. What about you?"

"I will return to Paris tomorrow night. I will keep you informed. Anything new on Olsen?"

"No, he has not come back to Miami," Nick said. "The three guys who tried to grab Kate are out on bail, but the judge pulled their passports and ordered them not to leave the Miami area. They aren't saying a thing."

"I'm not surprised," Gerard said. "I will talk to you from Paris."

"Okay, be careful."

As Gerard walked into the lobby of his hotel, Olivier sidled up to him and said in his conspiratorial way of talking, "So, you found Sofia Mostov?"

"Actually, she found me. Were you my protection?"

"Inspector, in Havana everyone is on his own these days. Your only protection is getting on a plane and going back to Paris."

"Ah, another blow to Cuba's image as a hospitable place. I have a reservation tomorrow night to fly to Paris. There is nothing more that I can do here. A little sightseeing, and I am gone."

211

"Maybe I will see you tomorrow. Enjoy the evening. Be careful."

Gerard had dinner at his hotel, took a stroll and enjoyed a fresh H. Upmann Torpedo cigar. His thoughts kept returning to Catherine York.

The next morning he called his office and, after lengthy reports summarizing the status of his other cases, he had the call transferred to Pierre in Amsterdam.

"How secure is this line?" asked Pierre.

"I think it is okay," Gerard said. "I am using my special phone. Why?"

"I have spent most of the day with the Dutch police. They are good; I have never worked with them before. I smell a Cuban connection. Van Bilt had no enemies that anyone knows of. Led a quiet life in Amsterdam. Appraisals, second opinions, did some work for the diamond cutters here. The background check turned up nothing suspicious. A family guy, wife, no children. Comfortable but not rich. No recent change in his financial condition or lifestyle. Yet he gets plucked off the street after he gets off a tram—at least, that's what they think—and disappears. Then he turns up in a field with a painful manicure. And even though he was found in a field, the medical examiner thinks he was drowned first."

"How?" Gerard asked.

"Probably in a bucket of water. There are bruises on the back of his head and neck consistent with someone forcibly holding his head down."

"Brutal."

"Yeah."

"And probably unnecessary. You spent time with Van Bilt. He wasn't the type to hold out long if someone wanted information from him and was roughing him up to get it. But fingernails and water torture are usually reserved for professionals who are trained to resist."

"Maybe they wanted to send a warning," Pierre said.

"Perhaps, or maybe they only know one way to do it and don't give a damn about anything else."

"Sounds like the drug guys."

"It does, but where does Sofia fit in?" Gerard said. "I spent some time with her. I will fill you in when I get back. Murder, yes. But brutal torture—I don't think so. And she probably was in Cuba when the Van Bilt thing went down. Oh, one more thing—has anyone attempted to break into Van Bilt's office and get his files?"

"No—nothing that was mentioned to me."

"They probably got everything they needed from him personally."

Gerard then asked about the search of Sofia Mostov's villa and store. Pierre said that she apparently had cleaned out a lot of files. "We will know more when the team from Paris arrives tomorrow, but it doesn't look like she is planning to go back to the island any time soon. When are you coming back to Paris?"

"I was coming back tonight, but I am going to stop in New York first," Gerard said. "I will call you tomorrow."

"Okay, be careful while you are still in Havana."

"Everyone is telling me to be careful. I am eating only crackers, drinking bottled French water and looking four times before I step off a curb."

Gerard then remembered that Nick had told him that Catherine was returning to New York from Wisconsin today, and he called her at the office. She was at a meeting, and he was transferred to her voicemail. He left the message that he was flying to New York, would arrive late in the evening, and would like to see her tomorrow. He tried her cell phone but also had to leave a message. He wondered whether the modern technology allayed or increased his frustration at not being able to talk to her directly. The trip to New York through Jamaica seemed long to him as he went over in his mind many times what he would say to Catherine.

CHAPTER FORTY-TWO
New York

CATHERINE HAD GOTTEN BOTH of Gerard's voicemails when she returned to New York from Wisconsin. She was surprised. In their last conversation, he had said that he was returning to Paris after Cuba. She wondered why he was coming to New York. Her emotions were, she concluded, a jumble of apprehension, excitement and curiosity.

Catherine called Judy Weiss and, after inquiring about Judy and describing her time in Wisconsin with her family, she mentioned that Gerard was coming to New York that evening and wanted to see her.

"Well, my dear," Judy said, "you waited a while to drop that one on me."

"Judy, it is no big deal. He probably just wants to tell me about what went on in Cuba and talk about the case."

"Oh, really? The last time I checked, there was phone service between Paris and New York. How do you feel about seeing him again?"

"I am not sure how I feel," Catherine said. "I am excited, but I am prepared for the relationship to end. As I have told you, there isn't much left for us to do together on the insurance fraud, and the case is really all we have together."

"Oh, I can hear right over the phone the sound of the protective barriers going up. And I got the impression there was a lot more going on between you two than solving a crime."

"I suppose you are right about the barriers, but—I don't know—I just don't want to get hurt again. And I am struggling with how much I would miss him if it is over."

Hearing the catch in Catherine's voice, Judy said, "My advice: Take it one moment at a time. Don't anticipate. You are a wonderful woman. Although he is a man, and they are hardwired to be slow to get it, he may have just figured it out. Just stay in touch—no radio silence, please."

They talked for a few more minutes. Then Catherine sat and stared at the phone. Judy knew her pretty well, she acknowledged. She tried hard not to think about the next day.

———

Gerard had told Catherine that he was staying at the Mark Hotel in New York, only a block from her apartment, but when he checked in at eleven in the evening, there was no message from her. The lack of a message disappointed him more than he wanted to acknowledge, and as he rode up to his room on the elevator, he had to say to himself, *Gerard de Rochenoir, you are a sixty-year-old man of the world. Stop feeling like an adolescent.* As he unpacked, he decided that, in this case, talking to himself wasn't doing much good.

The next morning, he waited until nine to call Catherine at the office. She wasn't in yet, and he left his number at the hotel. At nine thirty, she called him back, ending what he decided was one of the longest half-hours that he could remember. The conversation was brief, and they agreed to meet at her office in two hours.

Catherine was sitting behind her desk when Gerard was ushered into her office. Gerard quickly took in the feeling of her space as she rose and walked toward him. The white walls and colorful contemporary art reminded him of her apartment. Her desk was an elegant rosewood piece resting on two stainless steel trestles. There was a sitting area with a low glass table surrounded by three chairs, which he recognized as Herman Miller designs, covered with expensive brown leather. Behind her was a large window overlooking Park Avenue.

They greeted each other with a hug that Catherine later remembered as affectionate but restrained. She asked him to sit down at the table, and she joined him. They looked at each other, but neither of them spoke. Then Gerard complimented her on how lovely she looked and noted that she had some color in her face. She thanked him for the compliment, observed that the Wisconsin weather was perfect for a camping trip and asked him about Cuba.

He looked at her, and he felt a tremor in his hands as he turned to face her directly and took her hands between his. She did not resist, but looked at him quizzically.

"I will tell you about my time in Cuba, but that is not why I came to New York." She felt slightly more tension in his hands as he said, his eyes closing for a moment as if he was summoning his thoughts from a place deep within him, "I have thought a lot about you over the past days—*et, la vérité.*" Gerard smiled and said, "You have me thinking in French—I cannot get you out of my thoughts in any language." There was another silence. "I want you to be in my life, and I want to be in your life. I want us to have a life together. Put simply, *simplement et directement. Je t'aime.* There I am doing it again! I love you.

If someone had walked into Catherine's office at that moment, they might have thought that she had a piece of modernist sculpture at her table. Two people, seated, the man holding the woman's two hands between his, the two of them absolutely motionless, looking into each other's eyes.

Then Catherine gently withdrew her hands from Gerard's and stood up. Gerard still sat, feeling his heart beating so loudly he thought for sure that Catherine could hear it. She walked a few steps around the table, pulled him up, put her arms around him and kissed him. Time seemed to stop for both of them as they embraced, their bodies seemingly joined to each other. They kissed again.

Catherine looked up at him and said, "My first impulse is to say that I don't know what to say. Except that I do know what I want to say. When I got your message that you were coming to New York, what went through my mind was that either you wanted to talk about the case or you were going to tell me that it was over between us. But my deepest hope was that you would want to"—she stepped away and raised her hands in a gesture of looking for the right thing to say—"continue to be with me. I couldn't allow myself to believe that you were in love with me, because"—again she gestured with her hands—"because I was so afraid of letting my guard down and being hurt."

Gerard put his arms around her again, and she said, "You see, I love you, too." And then Catherine started to cry. Gerard took out his breast-pocket handkerchief and wiped her tears. She looked up at him again and said with a smile through her tears, "Gerard, are you crying, too?"

Dabbing his eyes, he said, "If we are going to share a life together, I suppose we can share a handkerchief." They both laughed.

After another long hug, Gerard said, "We have much to talk about."

"Yes," Catherine replied, "but not in my office. I will cook you dinner tonight."

CHAPTER FORTY-THREE
New York

GERARD ARRIVED AT CATHERINE'S apartment a half-hour early, and she was in her bathrobe as she opened the door. "Mr. Policeman, you are early. I just got out of the shower."

"I know, but I couldn't wait to see you," he said as he handed her a bouquet of flowers.

"Why don't you take off that nice cashmere jacket? I wouldn't want it to get wrinkled." As he laid his jacket on a chair, she said with a smile and a tilt of her head, "Are you going to stop with your jacket?"

Gerard embraced her and reached down to untie her robe, opening it up and holding her naked body against his. She undressed him as he tried to take his shoes and socks off, and they stumbled laughingly into her bedroom, leaving a trail of his clothes on the way. As they lay on the bed, he kissed the nape of her neck and her breast. "You smell like lilacs," he said.

"My new soap. It's French."

"And your bathrobe is cashmere, is it not?"

"Yes, it is. You would know. It is very soft."

He helped her out of the bathrobe and then gently stroked her body with the robe, starting with her shoulders and side and finishing with her stomach, thighs and between her legs. He then repeated touching her with his hands. Then he kissed her on her forehead, her eyes and her lips, his mouth and tongue following the curves of her body. As she lay back with her eyes closed, Catherine reached down and took his head between her hands and gently moved him up and over on his back and began to kiss his body and caress him with her hands.

She then pulled him onto her and gently put him into her. Their bodies moved together in a crescendo rising to an intense moment. Then they were quiet, his arms under her shoulders, hers around his waist. As he began to move out of her, she said, "Where are you going? I have waited a long time for this moment."

After a while, he got out of bed and came back with a package, which he gave to her. She unwrapped it, opened the felt box inside and gasped. "Gerard," she said, "it is breathtaking."

"May I put it around your neck? Your beautiful body requires a piece this beautiful." He then slipped the necklace of rubies, each one surrounded by diamonds, around her neck, and kissed her breasts again.

"I see by the name of the box that you decided to shop somewhere other than Sofia Mostov," Catherine said.

"Yes, I was concerned that we not have trouble with your employer when you insure it." They both laughed.

She kissed him and said, "Thank you, Gerard. Not only do you have exquisite taste, but you move quickly."

"I have wondered if I would ever feel as I do now, whether this day would ever come for me. Now each day of our future together is precious to me."

Gerard and Catherine dozed in each other's arms. Waking up, they concluded that the lamb chops and asparagus Catherine had planned for dinner was not what they wanted, and they sat at her kitchen table and ate pâté, drank red wine and talked. They decided that the two of them would travel to Wisconsin so that Gerard could meet Catherine's family. Following that trip, they would go to the south of France to visit Gerard's sister and nephews. Catherine observed that she now knew why she had been working so hard for the past few years. "I probably have more vacation coming than anyone else in the whole company," she said.

Gerard described his experiences in Cuba to her. He said that he would call Pierre the next morning to get an update on the case and that they would brief Nick tomorrow at the office. They continued to talk about their future until they, both tired, went to sleep. Somewhere in the night, Gerard woke up and felt her warm body next to his and listened to her soft breathing. He began to stroke her thighs, and they made love again.

CHAPTER FORTY-FOUR
New York

THE NEXT AFTERNOON, GERARD, Catherine and Nick assembled again in the same Larsen and McTabbitt conference room where they had met twice before. Nick began by saying to Gerard, "I understand that Kate is going to use up some of her vacation time to travel with you." Gerard smiled and nodded. "I am very happy for the two of you, and so is Amy. I called her. She has always liked Kate, and you got an *A* plus from her for the Le Bernadin dinner. When the timing is right, Amy and I would like to throw a little party for the two of you."

"You are very gracious, Nick," Gerard said. "Thank you. I look forward to the party and getting to know you and Amy better. Now, allow me to bring you and Catherine up-to-date on some developments in the case that I learned about from Pierre this morning."

Gerard said the French police had found a bank account in France owned by Valerie Pickett with substantial funds. Pickett apparently didn't keep everything in Switzerland and, while it would take some time to sort things out, the authorities, Gerard said, were confident that there would be a recovery of a substantial part of the insurance payment.

"That is good news," said Nick. "My boss, Adam Bendel, will be pleased. He will probably reduce his daily calls to me for updates on the case from three to maybe two."

"The news on money from Italy is not so good," said Gerard. "Guido Antonini's insurance proceeds are in his accounts in Switzerland, and there are a number of people hovering around claiming that he owes them money. Vultures around the corpse," mused Gerard. "But we made an interesting discovery. Actually, the Italian police get credit. You remember that Sofia said she was borrowing her Rome manager's car to go to the Pompeii museum in Naples?"

"Yes," Nick said.

"Well, the museum is closed for renovation. And the police have *autostrada* surveillance pictures of the manager's car south of Naples on the afternoon of Antonini's murder."

Gerard went on to report that the Miami police and the FBI had tracked down Harald Olsen, the Miami jeweler, in Canada and had asked the Canadian police to pick him up. "They have issued warrants relating both to a suspected insurance fraud and as a person of interest in the attempted kidnapping of Catherine," Gerard said. "The FBI also thinks that they may be able to recover some of the insurance proceeds paid to Olsen as part of a deal they would make with him. But," Gerard added, "the Perez connection may mean that he won't cooperate."

"Sounds like a candidate for the witness protection program," offered Nick.

Catherine then asked Gerard about Sofia. He replied that Interpol had issued international warrants for her arrest on suspicion of the murders of Pickett and Antonini, as well as insurance fraud. He said that he had just learned that she was planning to fly from Havana to Moscow.

"I don't think we will get any help from the Cuban police. Both the Italians and we will pressure the Russians to arrest her and turn her over to us. The FBI will weigh in as well, but I am not optimistic that anything will come of these requests. She hinted to me in Havana that she was looking at other businesses. She is clearly out of the jewelry business—for a while, at least. She wouldn't risk selling her fake stuff in Russia, since the people who could afford to buy it would be unpleasant about being cheated."

"So what happens to her?" asked Nick.

Gerard replied that he didn't think she would be happy spending the rest of her life confined to Russia and Cuba. "Besides," he added, "she has to weigh the possibility that either the Russians or the Cubans might turn her over to us or the Italians at some point as part of a change in the attitudes in those countries. She is well-connected, but not indispensable, and I am sure she knows it.

"I am very patient," Gerard continued. "We will monitor her movements as best we can, and sooner or later, probably somewhere in Europe, we will find her and arrest her. Not only do I intend to find her as a matter of professional pride, but"—he walked over and put his arms around Catherine—"there is someone who will always remind me to do justice."

Made in the USA
Lexington, KY
24 May 2010